GIRL:BROKEN

S. WILLIAMS

Copyright © 2021 S. Williams

The right of S. Williams to be identified as the Author of the Work has been asserted by him in accordance with the Copyright, Designs and Patents Act 1988.

First published in 2021 by Bloodhound Books.

Apart from any use permitted under UK copyright law, this publication may only be reproduced, stored, or transmitted, in any form, or by any means, with prior permission in writing of the publisher or, in the case of reprographic production, in accordance with the terms of licences issued by the Copyright Licensing Agency.

All characters in this publication are fictitious and any resemblance to real persons, living or dead, is purely coincidental.

www.bloodhoundbooks.com

Print ISBN 978-1-914614-37-8

ALSO BY S. WILLIAMS

Only You

*For Josephine
Forever*

People will never stop dying and being destroyed.
 — *Proverbs 27:20*
 International Children's Bible (ICB)

JULY
RAIN

The rain is coming straight down like it's from a tap. A million taps. There's no wind to feel, no distraction to be had; just the steady downpour. Constant and unstoppable. As if someone's punched a hole in the sky. I watch Daisy ahead of me. Sometimes I can see her, and sometimes not. The city is busy tonight, with people scraping across its dark surface. That's why I can't see her. Because of other people.

Hiding her.

Daisy's got her head down. It's her default position these days. Looking at her feet. Watching them as they move one in front of the other. Over and over, like she's constantly falling, then constantly catching herself. Every few seconds she raises her gaze and does a quick scout of her surroundings then lowers it again.

I match my pace to hers. Mirror it. Slide completely in sync with her. It's the best way to get to know someone. To be them. Do exactly what they do. Get inside their head.

That way you can know what they think. See what they see. This is how I know what's going on. When to time my move.

Daisy kind of stutters in her walking, and I do the same. We're step-counting. It's a way to not be complacent with your surroundings. Count to one hundred steps then change stride. Make a break. Stops things being constant. Stops you forgetting where you are. What the dangers are.

It's a good method.

Keeps you safe and in the moment.

Helps you stay in control.

Except I've seen something she hasn't.

Poor Daisy. She's been doing so well too. Since I started watching her. Following her. She's hardly put a foot wrong.

Different cities. Same dance.

Walk.

Look up.

Look down.

Walk.

Repeat.

This city centre.

The rain. The neon lights with their siren call. *The Big Issue* seller. The mad Jesus man shouting his lunacy. The suits and the skirts and the gangs and the goons. Buses and cars sharking through the roads, their headlights parcelling up the gloom. The buskers and the beggars and the hawkers selling terrible jewellery. The dirt and the litter and the cracked paving.

She sees everything, but only registers what she's interacting with.

What's interacting with her.

CBT. Cognitive Behavioural Therapy. What a joke. Like sticking a plaster on an amputation.

She sees everything but misses the only thing that matters. The thing that's going to switch her.

I don't though.

I'm in her footsteps, seeing what she sees.

Girl:Broken

And what she doesn't see.

That's why I'm here.

I watch as she stops.

Not step-counting.

Not anything.

There.

Her lizard brain has sensed the danger. The primal part of her head that has kept the species safe since the beginning of time.

She half turns, then starts to walk again, then stops. People bump into her, mutter under their breath, or look away like she's a mistake they made.

It's amazing to watch. It's like she's out of signal. Like she's a phone and someone's switched off her data feed.

But it's the exact opposite.

Daisy puts her hand over her wrist and shakes her head slightly.

Then she falls to the ground. Just straight down to the wet concrete, like she's taken an elevator.

And screams.

Bingo.

Like the rain, the commuters are unstoppable. They stare but no one helps. No one wants to touch the mad girl. They go round her like she's a rock that has just been dropped. Commuter memory that means don't stop. Don't make eye contact. Deny reality. Like madness is contagious.

Which gives me time to move in.

Control the situation.

What a shame for Daisy.

She's been trying to live her life but it's not working.

Because, like I said, I know something she doesn't.

She's got no chance. Never had.

I reach her and pick her up. Quieten her. Hold her so she's

not a spectacle any more. Help her to pull herself back together.
　　The crowd settles down.
　　Moves on.
　　Nothing to see here.
　　Nothing to see at all.

PART I

DAISY

1

31ST OCTOBER

Grize Cottage
North Yorkshire Moors, Nr Lealholm

Joseph looked out of his window across the flat expanse of the Yorkshire Moor. It was late afternoon and the weather was closing in as the light fled away over the heather. The clouds, low and fast above the rough moorland, were taking no prisoners; their dark shadows racing over the grey-green of the thick scrub. There were no other dwellings nearby to break up the weather, or to spoil Joseph's view of the brutal beauty of the bleak countryside. The daylight had dimmed so low he had switched on his reading lamp, causing a ghost-reflection of himself to stare hollow-eyed back from the window as he looked out. He placed his focus between his reflection and the moor, letting his mind drift, sifting through his thoughts.

Behind him the phone trilled, pulling his thoughts back into the room. The noise it made was old-fashioned. It was a nineteen eighties corded device in cream-coloured plastic that sat incongruously on his wooden desk. The sound it produced was more a purr than a ring; discreet and muted. He picked up the bone-shaped receiver and leant against the desk.

'Professor Skinner,' Joseph said into the mouthpiece. His voice was courteous and professional; a neutral RP accent with a very soft northern flattening of the vowels; a voice that commanded attention from his students, but allowed warmth and empathy to bubble gently under its surface. It had taken him a lifetime to develop it.

'Professor? It's Thomas Hayes from admin at Leeds University.' The low fidelity of the phone's vintage earpiece made the caller's voice sound cold and metallic.

'Mr Hayes, hello! How are you?'

'Fine, thanks. Sorry to call you so late in the afternoon but I wonder if you received my email regarding Doctor Rowe?'

'Apologies, Thomas, my internet is down at the moment.' Joseph paused for a beat, then smiled. 'Actually, it's down half the bloody time out here, to be honest. Was there something urgent I can help you with? To do with Cass Rowe, you said?' Joseph turned and looked out over the moor. 'Is she all right?'

Doctor Rowe was an expert in theoretical psychology, and a colleague of Joseph's, although he hadn't seen her in many months.

'Yes, she's fine,' said Thomas, reassuring. 'Thing is, though, she is booked in to give an early morning lecture here on Friday, and has just got in touch to say she can't make it...'

Exactly what the Head of Admin thought of that seeped out in Thomas' tones: irritation and slight annoyance.

'...which frankly puts me in a bit of a bind. I had dropped you a line to see if you might be able to help?'

'How so?'

Joseph watched out of the window as a Merlin hawk swooped down onto the ground, then flew up again. It was too far away for him to see what it had caught; possibly an adder or a vole.

'Well, when Doctor Rowe broke the news, she mentioned that you might be able to stand in? That there was some crossover on the syllabus and perhaps...?'

The administrator left the sentence hanging, the hope and slight panic poorly hidden in his voice.

Joseph reached across for his diary. He would normally just check his phone, but his partner had stolen it.

'It's a bit short notice, Thomas,' he said, opening up the faux-leather book. He ran his hand through his hair, noticeably thinner as he neared his sixties. Not that he was counting. Often. Much.

'You're telling me! This has been in the schedule for months! You know how hard it is to timetable these things. And now that everything is monetised, there is a certain expectation. I know sometimes these things are unavoidable, but...'

Judging by Thomas' tone, Joseph had a fair idea about his thoughts on the unavoidability of the matter.

'Quite. Friday, did you say? This Friday?'

'I know, I know.' The tone of the administrator's voice reminded Joseph of sad food: resigned and bitter. Like motorway service station soup. 'Too little notice? It really was a shot in the dar–'

'As it happens, I *am* free that day.' The only thing that was written in his diary was:

Haircut: present from Mark. Noon.

'Or at least I am until lunchtime. Did you say it was an early-morning lecture?'

'Yes, pre-breakfast. You're free?' The relief in Thomas' voice was almost physical. 'That's wonderful! Doctor Rowe said she caught your lecture in Nottingham, and that it would complement the cultural psychology option of the course. Can I ping across the details?'

'No internet,' reminded Joseph. 'Ping it across, by all means – I'm sure it will be back up in a while – but just in case you had better give me all the details now. I'll write them down as we speak. You are aware of my lecture fee?' Joseph reached into the inside pocket of his jacket and removed a pen.

'Of course, I have it in front of me. It really is fantastic of you to step in like this. Let me give you the relevant information.'

Joseph wrote down the time and place the administrator related to him, along with the access code and web address to upload his lecture and notes, which would allow the students to prepare.

'Okay, Thomas. When I'm back online I'll confirm by email and send in my invoice, so don't worry, panic over, you can pen me in for 7.30am on the third.'

The administrator's voice almost crawled out of the phone.

'That's just completely saved my life, professor. Thank you.'

'No problem. I'm sure Doctor Rowe would do the same for me. See you on Friday.'

Mr Hayes thanked him once again, and then hung up. Joseph gently placed the handset back into the cradle and walked back to the window, gazing thoughtfully out. The hawk was nowhere to be seen, and the sky looked bruised and swollen; like it was swallowing the daylight but had nowhere to store it. Visibility was rapidly diminishing, as it did on the moors. Many times, when Joseph had first moved here, he had nearly been caught out by the swiftness of the night. With less light outside, his reflection in the windowpane was more pronounced, along with the vague outline of his desk and the sofa against the far wall. There was a quiet knock, and in the ghost-room-reflection, he saw the door next to the sofa open. He turned and smiled at his partner.

'That was Leeds University. It looks like I'm going to be giving a lecture on Friday.' He looked at his watch. 'They tried to reach me electronically, but I explained about the connection out here.'

'That it's fucking rubbish?'

'Quite,' said Joseph. 'So I'll need to go into Whitby and dial on to the web. Do some research and pick up some information that's being sent. File my lecture.'

'And we can get some Woof?'

Joseph smiled wider.

'Woof?'

'Woof,' the partner confirmed. 'So you can prove it exists.'

'Absolutely.'

2

AUGUST

Inspector Slane watched the Leeds city centre feeds on her laptop, the screen split into individual camera shots.

She'd culled them from all over. Outside the shopping arcade. Inside the train terminus. Up and down all the main streets and any of the small mewses and squares that have public CCTV. The bus station. The images varied in quality. Some were time-triggered, giving a strange, stuttered existence to the people being digitally captured. Some were smooth and almost 4K. Slane suspected they were the ones owned by private companies; corporations paid to monitor the city centres all over the north.

Ever since the red flags went up she'd put Clearview into action; the controversial computer algorithm that analysed the thousands of faces in crowds to find the single one. Often used to spot terrorists or criminals, and increasingly used to spot drug dealers and those juveniles that made up the county lines.

And used by Slane to find one young woman.

First in Cardiff. Then in Leicester. And finally here, in Leeds. Daisy.

Except Slane had got more than she'd bargained for.

Once the flares went up – the red flags that told her someone was investigating something that really shouldn't be known about – it became urgent for her to find the woman. To keep tabs on her. To keep her safe. The searches that had been done on the net had been from a Leeds internet hub, possibly a stealth data-café, and had set alarms going deep in the branch. Alarms so deep there were only a handful of officers who even knew they existed. Even understood what they signified.

Slane watched Daisy, alive and well on a Leeds pavement two weeks earlier, screaming and kicking at ghosts like she was being dragged to hell.

Slane blinked, then looked down at the girl's file, and corrected herself.

Like she was being dragged to hell *again*.

The inspector watched the scene play out. Then she leaned forward and pressed a button, restarting the feed. She watched it through again.

Then again. Not only looking at Daisy, but at everyone else. Trying to see what had caused the woman to collapse.

Some movement in the corner of one of the playbacks caught her eye.

'Well, well,' she said softly, staring.

She knew she'd find Daisy eventually. It was inevitable. If the young woman was alive then it was impossible to hide forever, no matter how far under the radar you were. And once the flares went up it was just a matter of time.

And Slane had found her.

But that wasn't all she'd found.

Because there was more than one person on the screen she recognised.

Slane watched as the girl fell to the ground, screaming in

silence; none of the feeds were wired for sound. Watched as the crowd surged by, hiding her from view. Watched as, when the crowd cleared, she was gone.

They both were.

Slane smiled humourlessly and reached for her phone.

3
23RD OCTOBER

Jay finished texting and slid the phone into the pocket of her cargos, zipping it safe. She wouldn't ever put it in a handbag. Too easy to steal. And if you stole a phone, especially her phone, then you stole a person's whole identity these days.

Not that she owned a handbag. Or a clutch bag. Or shoes with pointy heels. Or hair products.

They wouldn't go with the tattoos.

Or the dreads.

Mind you, she thought, *neither had the police force.*

'Why have you made your body look like a war zone. Why can't you make it easier for yourself and just fit in.'

That's what her mother had said to Jay, in her soft Yorkshire accent, like dew in the heather. After the incident. After the suspension. After she had been furloughed from the force.

Thinking about her mother, Jay shrugged subconsciously.

'You can talk,' she whispered, looking at the warm light washing from the lamp on her desk. For a second, an image of her mother, walking out of Holloway, slashed in front of her eyes. Jay had been three the first time she remembered her mother being prosecuted, along with all the other protestors. It wasn't the last.

Jay sighed at the memory. She was sitting in the library, on Commercial Street, hiding from the rain. It was privately owned, over two hundred years old and was harder to get into than Hogwarts. Everything about it was everything she loved. From the smell of the books to the polished brass and wood. From the subdued lighting to the quietness and respect of the other members. If ever she had a spare moment in the city, she came here. It centred her. Helped her to get perspective.

She scrunched her toes on the hard floor, feeling the wood through her thick socks. She smiled and checked the time on the large clock on the wall.

Five past ten.

Nearly time to meet Daisy.

Jay stopped smiling and thought about the situation she had got herself in. Perspective was something she was sorely missing.

Because Jay was fucked.

Double fucked. Triple fucked.

Also, she was becoming emotionally attached to Daisy and that just wasn't acceptable. Not in a million years.

Not because the woman was so damaged, although God knew that alone would make it unethical. Daisy was so messed up it was amazing she could function at all. Hence all the therapy sessions. Hence all the meds.

But because she was work.

Daisy thought Jay was her friend, and she *was* her friend, even though she *was* work. Not when Jay had started, of course, but as they had got to know each other. Jay felt it deep down. Like they were cut from the same cloth. But Jay was also lying to her. Pretending to be something she wasn't.

Like she was with her mother.

Like she was with her ex-colleagues.

Like, she felt with increasing certainty, she was with herself.

She wished she'd never taken the assignment. Never let herself get dragged into this dark subterfuge she found herself in, with no easy route on how to get herself out.

Jay blinked.

The clock on the wall now showed ten past ten.

Time to go.

She pushed her chair back and put her engineer boots on, lacing them tight. Standing, she shrugged into her jacket.

She walked out onto the street and made her way down toward the station, criss-crossing through all the little alleys and snickets that made up the centre of the city. As she passed The Angel pub a street boy asked her for some money. He couldn't have been more than seventeen. Reaching into her cargos for change she saw the tremor in his hand. She found a few pounds and dropped them into his paw. She wondered if he would get to keep them or have to pass them over to a handler. Even begging was being commercialised these days.

She stopped off at Bean There, Dunk That and picked up a couple of coffees to go.

By the time she got to the apartment block, she was soaked through. She stood outside the converted mill and reached into her pocket, pulling out her keys attached by a silver chain to her belt. She sorted through them until she found the correct one. Flicking the rain from her hair, she slotted the key into the lock and turned it. Pushing the door open she stepped into the vestibule. Inside, on the wall, were numbered pigeonholes, giving a reminder to the building's industrial past. These days they were used for post and were fitted with little locked doors. Jay selected another key from her chain and unlocked her mail. Gave a cold smile when it came up empty.

Nothing from her mother.

Nothing from her ex-employers.

Nothing from her *new* employers, who had set her up here in Daisy's block. But then she would have been amazed if there was. Her new employers were not ones to leave a paper trail. It was all in the name, really. Undercover. Clandestine. Secret.

Maybe the text she had sent in the library would change all that.

Because Jay couldn't take it anymore.

Couldn't lie to Daisy.

She pressed her hand against the biometric pad that allowed entrance to the lobby of the flat complex and looked at the camera. The system read her and the red light above the door turned green. There was a click as the electromagnets were disengaged and the door was released. Jay pushed it open and walked through. The reception area was all about retaining the feel of an industrial past. Brick walls that had been treated with some sort of sealant. Wooden floors that shone with polish. Leather sofas scattered like they had been dropped from Dorothy's tornado. A metal cage lift that looked like it belonged in a Hitchcock film. By the time she began climbing the brass-railed stairs to the first floor, the entrance door had already closed and locked itself.

4

AUGUST

Beata hurried through the wet streets, her ankles already soaked where the morning traffic had splashed her. She hunched her shoulders and kept moving, pushing against the wind, her thin mouth set in a scowl. Beata hated Leeds, with its roads like rivers and its distressingly cheery people. Like they enjoyed the horrible weather that seemed to batter the city no matter what the season. Even in the summer, it seemed to suck away warmth into the grim stone of the buildings.

But however much she hated Leeds, she hated her boyfriend and his friends more. All they did was hang around the flat all day, smoking and drinking and watching porn whilst she worked three cleaning shifts to pay for it all. Her boyfriend said there was no work for him here now, but after summer he would have no trouble. That the building trade would pick up and he would be the one bringing in the money. If the government didn't throw them out.

Beata turned off The Headrow and walked up Briggate, past one of the hipster hairdressers that seemed to have cropped up all over the city like salon-confetti. Beata glanced in through the window. Blurred by rain on the glass she could see razors and shaving foam and all the accoutrements to shape a painfully on-trend beard.

Beata's boyfriend didn't have a beard; just the stubble of a don't-get-up-till-noon, beer-for-breakfast, live-off-your-girlfriend, waste of space.

Don't worry, I'll be working soon, he said. Beata smiled humourlessly as she turned into Harrison Street, by the Japanese Karaoke place. Beata didn't believe him. She'd been here eight months, acquired herself good work with the agency, moved into her own flat and had even managed to fit in a college release course. Another year and she would have been able to put a deposit down to buy a flat, rent it out, and move up the slippery English property ladder. If she was allowed to stay. If the bloody Brexit didn't throw her out.

But then her boyfriend had shown up. He'd lost his job, he said. Back home. He'd been kicked out of his flat, he said. He needed to move in with her, he said.

And now all her money went on him. She'd dropped out of college and taken on an extra shift just to make ends meet. And when she got home he expected her to cook for him and his friends. Or worse. Recently she had got the feeling that her boyfriend had ideas about her that were definitely not to her liking. She'd seen the way he looked at her, joked about her with his mates.

Maybe we should give up on the building and go into another trade, he had said the previous night, leering at her. His friends had burst out laughing and elbowed each other, like they were sharing a joke. It made Beata feel sick.

Then later, after his friends had gone home and he had come to bed, he had woken her up and taken her. Hard. After he had finished he had left the bed to continue drinking. As he walked out she had heard him call her something under his breath.

Kurwa.
Whore.
That was enough for her. She was going to end it.

She hurried down the road to her second job. She had already been up since half past four cleaning offices, and now she was late. The roads were almost empty. Only others like her, cleaners and night workers. Uber cars taking the odd reveller home. Beata moved to the curb as a young jogger, in the hoodie and tracksuit uniform that seemed obligatory, ran past her, oblivious. She felt sore where her boyfriend had been rough, and as she walked carefully on the road she started making plans on how she could get rid of him.

When she'd first come here she'd stayed away from the Polish community. She didn't want to get sucked into the same sort of life she'd left behind. She did not think her boyfriend would come to England. If she was being honest she didn't even think of him as her boyfriend, until he turned up and moved in and turned her life to shit. As soon as he got his feet under the table he had started transforming her flat into Zabkowska, the town she had left behind in Poland. Every time she came home there seemed to be another suspect character in her kitchen, eating her food. Half the texts she got were demands to bring more beer. More vodka. Like her boyfriend was a Polish stereotype joke.

The problem was he was in her flat. If she were simply to walk away she'd lose her deposit. She needed to think of a way of getting him out or getting her money back.

She slipped out of Harrison Street and walked left. The rain had reduced to just a drizzle, the kind that seemed to magically appear under the clothes without any obvious means as to how it got there. Leeds-rain. Beata pulled her scarf tighter around her neck, heading towards the new offices on Trafalgar Street.

And anyhow, he'd find her. Everyone seemed to be in

everybody else's business in this town. Everyone knew everybody else. The whole city seemed to act like a village. Maybe it was because it was surrounded by wild countryside. The community seemed to cover the place like a web.

Beata took her Juul vape out of her bag and slipped into the Grand Arcade. Once inside she stared out of the glass doors, thinking about her life. Across the road, she could see a homeless person asleep in a doorway. The light bleeding from the street lamp, mixed with the first blushes of dawn, made him seem disconnected. More like a painting than a real person. Or maybe it was because she was looking at him through the misted glass of the arcade. Beata gave a hard smile and sucked on her vape device. At least she assumed it was a he. It could just as easily be a she. There seemed to be so many homeless recently. You'd think, if you didn't have a home or a job, you'd go and live in a city that got more sun. Less rain.

Suddenly she brightened. Maybe she should just leave. Just forget the deposit and go to a new town. London, or Bristol. Maybe even France. Somewhere she wasn't known. She was a good worker. She would always be able to earn a living. Just stay away from any Polish agencies. She took a last drag then put her Juul away in her bag. Maybe she could get a new bank account, without her boyfriend finding out. She grabbed the handle and left the warmth of the arcade.

Outside the air was bitter. She looked over at the sleeping figure in the doorway. She could just make out a tin can next to him. Beata smiled sadly. What sort of desperation, or optimism, do you have to have to put a begging cup out in the middle of the night while you were sleeping? Beata blinked and made a decision. Maybe her luck would change if she helped someone else's. Checking the non-existent traffic, she crossed the street, digging into her pocket for some pound coins. At this time in the morning, the street was empty. It was just her and the boy in the sleeping bag. Or girl. As Beata got nearer she could see a dark stain spread from the sleeping bag onto the street. She wrinkled her nose. The boy had pissed himself. Beata understood. Understood drinking yourself unconscious to blot out the reality you find yourself in. She pulled out her hand and dropped in the few coins she had. As they hit the metal of the tin they made a sad little sound, like a beaten-up wind chime.

Beata straightened, then frowned. Now she was nearer she should be able to smell the urine. The puddle was quite large and, in the LED lighting, dark and shiny.

But all she could smell was copper.

'Hello? Mister?'

Beata looked up and down the street, feeling the muscles in her stomach and groin twist. She was alone. The copper smell was high and sharp, like old pennies that had been scraped clean with emery cloth. Beata had smelt it before, in the hospital where she cleaned at the weekend. It was the smell of blood. She looked down at the dark patch she had thought was piss. It looked like an oil slick.

'Mister? Miss? Are you all right?'

Beata squatted down. The person was huddled in the doorway, with the sleeping bag pulled over their head. They were turned away from her, on their side, as if in sleep they did not want to face the life that had happened to them. Beata reached forward and gently shook the person's shoulder.

'Mister? Can I help you? Have you hurt yourself?'

It wouldn't surprise her. People pissing blood because their liver had packed in. Slitting their wrists because they just can't take the madness and the loneliness. So drunk they collapse on their own bottle, lacerating themselves but falling unconscious anyway. It happened. It happened all the time. As she pulled on the shoulder the sleeping form turned towards her. Beata stood quickly, then realised it must have been her shaking that caused the body to move. That it must have been balanced on its side so that any movement would have caused him to roll toward her.

Because this man wasn't moving by himself. Not anytime soon. Not ever.

Beata felt a bubble of scream fill her mouth.

Bizarrely, she could hear a song playing, tinny and somehow at the wrong speed. Slowing down and speeding up, like it kept running out of power.

The person was old. Maybe sixty. Maybe younger, because life on the street made the features appear older like they were trying to accelerate out of life. His mouth was clamped shut and unsmiling, but that didn't matter because someone had carved another one across his throat, and this one was grinning.

Bizarrely, the dead man was wearing earbuds. That was where the song was coming from. Tinny and insistent, like tiny voices inside the dead body's head, trying to get out.

She recognised the song, and the incongruity of it made the whole scene even more nightmarish.

Culture Club's 'Do you Really Want to Hurt me?'

Like a question that had already been answered.

Beata stared at the body, listening to the song bleeding from his ears. Watched the life dripping from his throat, and then screamed.

By the time the police arrived she'd thrown up on the pavement, her breakfast mixing with the dead man's blood.

5
23RD OCTOBER

Daisy woke up strange and wrong.

Strange wasn't the problem. Daisy often woke up strange.

Strange thoughts in her head, remnants of dreams like ripped sheets on a washing line after a storm.

Strange cuts on her body, physical marks of a dream that wanted to fight its way out of her, as if she'd trapped it in her sleep. That was why she kept her nails short. Biting them to the nib.

So 'strange' wasn't the issue. She understood strange; had factored it into her routine. Processed it over the years.

This was different.

She stayed on her mattress, eyes closed, letting the room tick around her as she tried to get a sense of the wrongness. There was a slight bitterness in her mouth like she had eaten a lemon in her dreams. She licked her lips, focusing in.

'No,' she said quietly. The taste wasn't it. Something else.

Daisy's mattress lay on the floor of her room, with no frame beneath it as support.

No frame, no legs.

No legs, no gap. No space between the bottom of her mattress and the floor. Nothing to hide under. Nothing to grab her feet as she stood. Pull her into the darkness.

It was the same with cupboards.

She didn't have cupboards; just shelves. Places she could see into. Cupboards have doors; things that hide and conceal. Shut away and keep secret.

The only door in Daisy's flat was the front door, which she kept locked whether she was in or out. Locked and bolted.

Double-locked. Triple-locked.

The locksmith who'd fitted them said that she was the safest woman in Leeds.

She'd sat in the room as he worked, not making eye contact, concentrating on his work.

After he'd left she'd got in a second locksmith.

She knew about locksmiths. They always kept spare keys. In case the client lost a set. Two separate locksmiths was safer.

Best to double up. Double down.

And then the bolts for luck.

She had a hook by the side of the door where she kept the keys. Like a jailer's hook. She needed them by the door in case she had to get out quickly. Because you never knew. Never knew when you needed to run.

Daisy opened her eyes. They were startling to look at. The irises two different colours: blue and brown. Complete heterochromia. Her sense of wrongness increased. She stayed still, laying on the mattress in her boxers and T-shirt. She kept the heat of the flat high, so she didn't need a duvet. She listened. She could hear the old couple in the flat above her, moving with their old-people movements. Slow and somehow heavy with the weight of their lives. Outside was the white noise of the city; traffic and builders and the aural detritus of living in a human anthill. Her windows weren't double glazed. It was one of the reasons she'd chosen the flat. It was converted badly from its original industrial use with too little money spent on it then and since. These were old-school windows. Windows you could open and climb out of in an emergency. Escape.

They had bolts on too.

She could hear a mobile from another part of the building, and the sound of a toddler starting World War Whatever with its mother.

Daisy winced subconsciously.

She counted down from ten, holding her breath and fixing her gaze to the ceiling. When she got to zero she breathed out through her nose, like the therapists had taught her, rolled off the mattress, and stood. Her floor was made up of the original wide strips of rough pine, installed when the building was a mill. The old wood was saturated with oil and grease. It had been sanded and coated but was still an industrial map of heavy machinery and child labour. No amount of sanding was going to eradicate that. Daisy walked to the wall and pressed her hand against it. Steadying herself. Trying to find the cause of her disorientation.

She knew what it was already, somewhere in the car crash of her subconscious. All the therapies had taught her that. She just needed to let her mind left-turn itself. Let her see the pattern.

Daisy moved away from the wall and walked out of the bedroom and into the hall. She walked down the narrow corridor and stood in front of the flat entrance. When she'd moved in she'd had the flimsy wooden door replaced. What was the point of having good locks on a shit door? One good kick and the hinges would have popped right off. She'd had it removed and replaced with solid oak. She'd wanted a metal one, like in the Manchester war zone estates, but the building manager wouldn't let her.

She checked the locks. Checked the bolts. Checked her keys

hanging on the hook by the side. Keys for her flat and for the lobby downstairs. Keys for Jay's flat, in case of emergencies.

Daisy placed her hand on the door. Turned the handle to double make sure.

Locked. Safe.

Satisfied, Daisy slowly swivelled around. In front of her she could see the doorway to her bedroom on the left, and the doorway to her bathroom on the right. At the end of the hall was an opening into the kitchen/living space.

Three rooms and a hallway. Bigger than she needed for what she owned, but any smaller and the shakes got too much. The ringing of the phone was drilling into her. Ghost-fish were beginning to swim across her vision; a sure indication of the pain to come. She walked down the hallway, her bare feet whispering on the pine.

Then she stopped. The phone ceased its ring at almost the same time. The sense of wrongness had increased. Ramped up.

Daisy moved to the edge of the hall, stepping sideways, and placed her back against the wall. From this angle, she could see into her bedroom. The room she thought of as her sleep-room. Where she closed the world down.

Her dead-room.

Empty.

On the wall was her whiteboard. A place for her to write her thoughts so they wouldn't split open her head. Or to fill in the spaces if she had forgotten something. It was blank; there was no message to herself from the previous night.

The phone started ringing again, causing the ghost-fish to swim faster, slicing pain across her vision. She carefully moved her head, scanning the hermetic world of her flat, listening to it ticking around her. After a beat, when she was sure there was nobody in there with her, she continued walking down the hall.

Through the doorless doorway at the end, she could see her

kitchen. The cooker she never used and the open-fronted cupboards with the plates and cups that she never touched. She had no idea how many people had eaten off of them before she moved in, and wasn't going to add to it, buying disposable plastic cups instead.

She walked through the doorway.

As well as the cooker there was a small tabletop fridge, a microwave and a mini dishwasher. The kitchen was annexed off by an L-shaped worktop-cum-breakfast bar, and the rest of the room was living space.

There was a low table and a record player on the floor near the corner, the records neatly resting against the wall, and a long oblong mirror with a sheet over it.

No TV. No computer.

The phone was on the table. Daisy stared at it. She could see the screen flashing in time with the ring. Could feel the noise as pulses in her brain. The dorsal insular. The cluster of matter in her head where darkness coalesced.

Daisy felt a sense of relief. Not because of the pain, but because she had found the cause of her tension. The thing that had made her wake up wrong.

It was the phone.

She stared at the device, its screen lighting up with each burst.

It stopped ringing.

In the silence, Daisy walked to the table and sat down cross-legged in front of it. She stared at the mobile, waiting. She blinked when the phone rang again. Flashing.

She read the words pulsing on its screen.

Daisy. Daisy. Daisy.

She looked toward the locked front door.

Double-locked.

Triple-locked.

Bolted.

The phone stopped ringing.

Daisy stared at it. The thing that was off-kilter. That meant everything was quite fundamentally wrong.

Daisy looked at the phone and wondered how it had got there.

Not just on the table, but in the flat.

Because Daisy did not own a phone. Not a landline and not a mobile.

Daisy had never seen the phone before.

Her face spasmed slightly when it rang again, flashing her name.

6

3RD NOVEMBER

We are now approaching Leeds Central Station, where this train will terminate. Please make sure you have all your belongings with you, and on behalf of the on-train staff, I hope you have enjoyed your trip with Northern Rail, and have a pleasant continuing journey. All alight at Leeds Central, as this train will terminate here.

'I think you mean the journey will terminate, not the train,' muttered Joseph absently, staring out at the driving rain that lashed at the platform as it swung into view. There was a general flurry of activity as the commuters grabbed the building blocks of their working day – coats, laptops, consciousness – and began to make their way to the exit. Joseph remained seated, waiting until the carriage was almost empty. He had caught an early train to give himself time to become centred before the commencement of his talk. He did not like to rush into a lecture, even one arranged at such short notice.

When the walkway was clear, and the doorway deserted of frantic commuters, Joseph stood. Retrieving his briefcase from the overhead storage shelf, he made his way up the aisle and off the train. Despite the early hour, just past six, the station was busy. Office workers getting an early jump on the day. Office cleaners, tired and washed out, heading to their next job. Construction workers wearing clothing with more pockets than could possibly ever be needed, talking on their phones whilst slurping down coffee from corrugated cardboard cups. And here and there, Joseph noticed, street panhandlers: homeless men and women begging money for tea. For food. For drugs or alcohol.

Joseph watched as the river of people went around them as if they weren't even there, merely rocks in the commuter stream. Joseph inserted his ticket into the slot by the automatic gates and quickly left the station. Outside, the day was still dark, street lamps still glowing, lighting up individual drops of rain as they ripped at the buildings, driven by a bitter Leeds wind.

'Right,' he said.

Pulling his overcoat tight around himself, Joseph hurried along the road towards the Corn Exchange, and the indoor market. As he slipped inside he was immediately assaulted by the cacophony of commerce; wooden shutters being removed from stall-fronts, metal security blinds being wound up, produce of all kinds being arranged and displayed, ready for the day. Market store-holders greeting each other and exchanging banter as they put the finishing touches to their businesses before the public began to flow through en masse. Joseph looked around, searching for a café bench to sit at and relax before heading off to the university. Deciding to follow his nose, he ambled along the stone aisles, then sat down on the stool at the Moroccan coffee stand. Joseph took off his coat, which was steaming slightly as the rain began to evaporate in the heat of the market, and placed it over the back of his chair. He glanced around, and then raised a finger at the man behind the counter. The man – Joseph guessed the owner – wore a traditional

Girl:Broken

djellaba with a fez. He smiled in response to Joseph, showing an impressive array of gold teeth.

'What can I get you, mate?' He indicated the handwritten board suspended from the roof of the stall. Joseph smiled at him. The man's outfit might have been traditional Moroccan, but his accent was pure Leeds.

Joseph looked around the stall. 'What do I smell?'

'Khoudenjal, finest in the city, my friend.'

'I'm sure. Then one khoudenjal, please.'

'With the trimmings?' The stall owner pointed to a selection of cakes and exotic pastries.

'You bet.' Joseph pulled his wallet out of his jacket pocket, extracted a ten-pound note, and placed it onto the little silver plate on the counter, covering it with the holding stone, a beautifully painted smooth round piece of sandstone.

While his tea was being prepared, Joseph unsnapped the clasp on his briefcase and pulled out the notes on his lecture. Although he knew the material well, the short notice, and the bespoking he had done to some of the examples he was going to give, warranted a read-through.

Joseph spent the next few minutes power-briefing himself. When he had finished and looked up, the spicy tea and delicate sweets had been laid out in front of him. The tenner had disappeared. Joseph returned his notes to the briefcase and tried one of the pastries. It was delicious. He sipped the equally delicious tea and watched the world of semi-legitimate commerce happen around him. Across from the food stall was an electronics kiosk, declaring that it could unlock *fones while u w8!* Joseph didn't doubt it. It might as well say *u steal m, we'll wyp m!* Joseph noted the name of the stall and continued with his exotic breakfast.

After ten minutes the alarm went off on his watch, indicating that he had thirty minutes before his lecture. He stood and pulled on his coat. The stall owner ambled over, reaching into the change bag around his waist.

Joseph waved a hand. 'No need for change. That was the best khoudenjal I've ever had!'

The man smiled widely, treating Joseph to the glare of dazzling dental bling.

'For real, bruv! You have a wicked day, yeah?'

Joseph assured him he would, then picked up his briefcase and left the market.

Five minutes later he arrived at the nondescript building that contained the lecture hall.

Joseph took a deep breath, then stepped inside out of the rain.

7
AUGUST

Jay knocked on the door, waited until she heard the shout, then entered.

The woman sitting behind the desk looked to be in her late fifties, with dirty-blonde crew cut hair flecked with grey and a smile that was ripped straight off Kaa, the snake from *Jungle Book*. Jay had never seen her before.

'Ah, Ms Starling! So glad you could make it. Please, take a seat... I won't keep you a moment.'

The woman's smile turned off and she started jotting down notes in a folder in front of her.

'Ma'am,' said Jay, noting the badge on the woman's jacket, removing her hat and sitting down stiffly. She knew she was about to be fired, but she was fucked if she was going to give this woman the satisfaction of seeing her hurt. The fact that she hadn't called her 'officer' or 'constable' might mean that she'd been fired already, and this was simply the news coming in late. Which is probably why they'd sent this outsider, rather than her own senior commander. Inside, Jay fumed. One little hit of a superior officer and it had come to this. And after all the shit she'd taken!

All right, it might have been more than a little hit, but he had asked for it. Calling her what he had. It was just a shame no one had been around to witness it. Just the silent CCTV, with the man facing away from it so you couldn't even see his lips move.

The woman in front of her continued making notes in a folder. The noise of her pen scratching across the paper set Jay's nerves on edge, causing her to clench her fists under the desk. Finally, the woman looked up.

'You broke his jaw in two places, Ms Starling. Very impressive.'

'Not really, ma'am, I was trying to remove his head.'

Jay saw no point in contrition. They'd fired her anyway. Plus it wasn't her style. Never had been. Not at school, when she ever went. Not at home. Not even in the academy.

She blamed her mother.

'Why?'

'Why what, ma'am?'

'Why were you trying to remove his head?' The inspector glanced down. 'It seems like a perfectly nice head to me.'

Jay blinked. That was not what she had expected. 'He said some offensive things to me, ma'am.'

'And this was your way of reporting it? By smashing him in the face with your elbow?'

Jay stared straight ahead. 'If I'd used my fist I'd have probably broken my fingers, ma'am.'

The inspector burst out laughing.

Jay's eyes slid to her, confused.

'Oh, I'd have loved to have been there.' The inspector chuckled. 'From all accounts, the officer you hit was a raging homophobe and racist. You probably did the force a favour.'

Jay gaped at her.

'I'll still have to suspend you, of course. There were no

witnesses. He said you had it in for him because he turned down a sexual advance you made. He said you were trying for...' she glanced down at her folder, '... a promotion fuck.'

'What? The wanker!'

'His word against yours. And he's the only one with a broken jaw.'

'That's so unfair!' Jay seethed. 'The fucking dinosaur called me a–' she bit down before she could get into any more trouble. The inspector tutted sympathetically.

'You do seem to have had some trouble fitting in, Jay.' Her eyes flicked down at her notes again. 'Despite good scores in your training you have never really seemed to have settled, have you?' The inspector glanced at her hair. 'Never really been a team player.'

Jay felt the old anger rising again. 'I fit in fine.'

The inspector's smile broadened again. 'We both know that's not true, Jay! And I'm not talking about your cultural background or sexuality. None of those things should have a negative dimension in today's force. I'm talking about your heritage. The baggage you've brought with you.'

Jay stared at her.

'Ma'am?' she said eventually, an eyebrow raised. She felt that there was a bomb ticking in her head, and wondered if there was a custodial sentence for hitting an inspector.

'I understand your mother actually did some time in prison?'

Jay felt her fists tighten again. 'I'm not sure of the relevance–'

'And as a consequence you spent a portion of your youth being somewhat...' the inspector paused as if trying to think of the most delicate way of putting it, '...wild?'

'I was never arrested.'

'No, but you were forced to attend some time in therapy sessions I understand. Anger management and such.'

'How do you...? That's confidential.' Jay was fairly certain that wasn't in her employment file. The lawyer who'd got her the deal at the time said there would be no record on the PNC.

'I promise I won't tell.' The inspector smiled kindly. When Jay didn't say anything the woman nodded sharply. 'That all seems to be in order.'

The inspector closed the file. 'Jay Starling, I am formally suspending you of all duties pending an inquiry into your actions pertaining to the assault carried out on Detective Charmers.'

Jay felt a cold weight. She knew it had been coming, but to hear it out loud felt like a hammer hitting the final nail into her coffin. That was the end of her police career. She placed her hat back on and stared straight ahead, determined not to cry.

'Yes, ma'am.'

'Good. And now that's out of the way I'd like to offer you a job.'

Jay stared at her. The woman nodded back expectantly. 'Sorry?'

'Your past makes you almost uniquely qualified.'

Jay swallowed, causing her ears to pop. She was sure she must have misheard. 'I don't understand. I thought you said I was suspended.'

'From normal police duties, yes. This is different. In a way what you did to Charmers is perfect. It's the ideal camouflage. I'm offering you the opportunity to go undercover, Starling. To work with us at F-branch. All very secret, I'm afraid. You won't be able to tell anyone. Not your co-workers. Not your mother. No one. As far as anybody will know you will be fully suspended, but you will be working for me. You'll also have to sign a non-disclosure contract.'

The woman stood and offered Jay her hand.

'And you'll need to stop calling me "ma'am". My name is Inspector Slane.'

Jay didn't know what to say, so instead, she shook the inspector's hand.

8

AUGUST

The training Jay was given wasn't hard; it was really just like being at school.

What *had* been hard was not being able to tell her colleagues. Getting the formal suspension. But Slane had said it was necessary.

'It's the way we work, I'm afraid. Nobody must know that you're being employed by F-branch. We have to occasionally investigate the police force itself, so anonymity is paramount. The only contacts you'll have with us are myself, Grant and Collins. Your Head of Command knows, of course, but he and I go back a long way. When this is over he'll be able to debrief his team and you can go back to your old role.'

'Cool.'

Jay was relieved that her altercation with Charmers would be downgraded. That she would be able to return. She thought about what Slane had said. 'What do you mean, investigate the police force? Like if there is an official complaint or something?'

Slane had shaken her head. 'No. More systemic than that. Why do you think I believed you when you told me what DI Charmers had called you, rather than take his side? We look beyond any individual complaint and seek the root. Which is why our work is so dirty.'

'How do you mean?'

'Put it this way. If you want to catch a racist in the act you need to infiltrate a racist network.'

Later Jay had looked up F-branch. She was right. The organisation had infiltrated all sorts. The government. Police forces. The IRA. Militant environmental movements.

'I wonder if you ever came across my mother?' she had muttered as she searched.

∽

'So what's this Daisy done?' Jay asked on her first day.

'Nothing yet, as far as we know,' said Slane. 'She has only just come back on our radar. When she was younger she was part of an organisation. No longer active, but nevertheless someone we were very keen to track down.'

'What kind of organisation? Like a terrorist cell or something?'

'No, nothing like that. It would be called a cult, back in the day. It no longer exists, but we are still keen to gather as much information about it as we can. The controlling members are all dead, but we have been given information that an aspect of it might still be active. If that is the case then they may wish to get in contact with Daisy.'

'What, and re-recruit her?'

'Perhaps.'

Jay frowned. Slane seemed to be being deliberately vague, but then perhaps she had to be. F-branch was a very secretive part of the police force. As far as Jay had been able to research, it wasn't even supposed to be active anymore. When she had mentioned this to Grant he'd grinned at her, tapping his nose.

'Exactly. But nothing ever stops. Not really.'

'You needn't worry about that side of the operation,' Slane had said. 'All you need to do is befriend Daisy. Keep tabs on her. Make sure she doesn't run or get taken. Find out what she knows. We've arranged a simple backstory for you. Close to your own so you don't get caught out. Anger issues. Problems with establishment. That sort of thing.'

Jay had grinned at them.

'Fucking doddle.'

9

SEPTEMBER

Daisy kept finding her gaze sliding to the new woman in the group. She didn't seem the same as the rest of them.

More concrete somehow. Like the stuff she was made of was more substantial.

Or maybe that was the anger.

You could see it behind her eyes. Like little fires burning, ready to be stoked by whatever fuel supplied them. Whatever the woman was kicking against.

Daisy had seen it before. Not in this group, but in others. Other cities. Women who felt the only way to cope was to not bend. Beat up the world to suit their shape, rather than trying to find a way of fitting in.

Hiding.

Daisy hadn't been in Leeds long, and this was one of the first groups she had managed to find. It was difficult. She couldn't go to any of the regular programmes that were run by the NHS, or one of the charities. There would be too much chance of her being noticed. Too much of an opportunity for her to be spotted. Too many questions.

Same with the meds. She couldn't get them from a doctor;

she had to obtain them from the grey economy. The network of socially excluded people who couldn't, or wouldn't, engage with the official medical community. Or any official community.

She had to live on the fringes. In the shadows. Off the radar of anyone who might be looking for her.

Daisy realised she was paranoid. That no one was looking for her. She understood that anyone who might have once had an interest in her was dead, but that didn't matter. Because even though they were dead, long gone and buried, there were always others.

That was the thing about monsters. Even if you thought they were in your past they never were. There was always more. Under the bed. In the closet. Waiting behind a smile with a rope and sack. A van and a plan.

Whispering inside your head, telling you to shut down. Stop fighting. Close the door forever.

But the thing was, Daisy was a fighter too.

Not like this new girl, with her couldn't-give-a-toss-hair and her run-away boots. With her combat trousers like she was ready for war. But deep inside, where she had to live to cope with the world. Where she kept her little boxes of secrets, all locked away so they couldn't come out and eat her.

That was why she came to the sessions. Why she tried so many different ones. Slowly, year by year, she hoped she could open the box and let the monsters out. Let them out, catch them, and throw them away forever.

Daisy smiled.

The new woman, she suspected, would let them out, then kick them to death.

She gave a shy glance over and was shocked to see that the woman was staring straight back. Daisy felt panic rise inside her. She couldn't cope with people looking directly at her. Found it almost impossible to maintain eye contact. She always thought that whoever was looking could see into her. See the mess she was.

'Hi.'

The woman with the hair was standing in front of her, smiling.

'My name's Jay; I think we live in the same block. Do you fancy coming for a coffee?'

10

23RD OCTOBER

The rain-in-shadows bled down the grey walls of Daisy's living room. Down Daisy's face and body, as she sat against the wall and stared at the phone, vibrating like an insect on top of the low table.

The noise was harsh in the still room. Each ring cycle triggered the flashing of her name. Daisy. Daisy. Daisy. Like it was hitting her. Sonically slapping her around the face to get her attention. Well it had her attention.

Someone had been in her flat. Impossibly, someone had been in her flat and messed with her space. Daisy's eyes flicked off the phone, toward the door hidden at the end of the hall by the kitchen wall. The locked and bolted door with the keys hung up at the side on the hook like they always were. Always there because she always locked the door. Double-locked it.

Daisy tried to remember what had happened the previous night. Tried to picture it in her mind. What she had done after leaving Jay.

She couldn't. The ringing of the phone infected her thinking. Sliced up her memory. She just had disjointed images. Stutters of time that didn't make sense.

Walking down Boar Lane, away from the train station, step-counting, she'd tried to hide from the rain. Looking through the window of Waterstones, her reflection had ghosted back at her. Sitting at the bus station, letting bits of herself glide away to all the other places on the destination board: York, Huddersfield, Manchester. Emptying herself out so she could survive another day.

Daisy frowned.

She couldn't remember going home. Letting herself in. Locking the door.

Taking her meds.

Daisy's vision blurred. She could feel her heartbeat speeding up as the black hole of the previous night presented itself to her, adding to the wrongness. Multiplying it. Increasing it to the power of fear.

She felt paralysed. Invaded. Someone had been in her flat whilst she was asleep. Got in somehow and left a phone for her.

And she hadn't woken up.

Daisy's eyes widened.

With an explosion of movement she checked her body. She felt her breasts under her T-shirt, trying to sense if they were bruised. If they had been groped or squeezed. Felt her groin through her boxers for tenderness. Ran her tongue across her lips and the roof of her mouth, checking for the telltale dryness of the after-effects of drugs.

Rohypnol. Molly. Scoop.

The rape drugs.

Daisy found nothing, but that didn't mean nothing had happened. No bruising did not mean no rape. If she had been unconscious the rape could have been slow. Gentle. Lubricated, even. Daisy forced herself to breathe in through her nose. Out through her mouth. The phone stopped ringing.

Maybe that was what had happened? She'd been drugged

and brought back here. Maybe that was the rapist on the phone. Maybe he knew something about her. Knew how to press the buttons for absolute fear.

Because rape wasn't about sex. Not really. Not ever. It was about power. Power over someone else. Power over your own existence. Daisy knew all about it. Daisy felt her skin spasming as another thought slid into her brain.

Maybe there were pictures on the phone.

Daisy rarely used the internet. Didn't own a smartphone or a computer. But she'd heard the stories. At the group sessions and from Jay.

File sharing. Dark places where sickos posted their human trophies. Places on the internet where bad people could meet and discuss and display their conquests. In one of the control sessions Daisy had attended they'd been shown a heavily redacted clip from a site called 'Sleeping Beauty'. The spiel at the head of the site had said all the right things. That the images were of consenting adults. That the site was dedicated to specialist role-play. That you had to be a member to enter. All the right things. But when it came down to it, it was still images of unconscious women being abused by predators in masks. Daisy had fainted during the session.

The phone rang. Daisy watched it. After an agony, the phone stopped ringing.

She tried to piece together the previous night, but she couldn't. In fact, there were more and more times lately. Times when the day seemed to have gaps like there were jigsaw pieces missing in her narrative. She'd find herself in the park with no idea how she got there. Or at the internet café where a whole hour seemed to have gone by, with her daydreaming the time away.

It had gotten so bad that she had decided to change her meds.

Daisy sucked in a shaky breath, knelt down and began to move forward on her knees. She inched across the wooden floor, sliding one leg at a time to make the least noise, as if the phone was alive and she could somehow sneak up on it. When she was a foot away she stopped. The phone looked expensive. Looked new. It was housed in silver metal and didn't appear to be scuffed or scratched, despite not being in a case. Its glass face was black and frightening. Like a mirror that sucked in rather than reflected.

Daisy blinked as the phone rang again. It seemed to move slightly with each ring, and Daisy guessed it was vibrating. Underneath her flashing name was an image of an arrow, slowly moving across the screen from left to right, with 'swipe to answer' written underneath it. Daisy blinked again, tightening everything inside her, then picked up the phone.

Daisy swiped, following the direction of the arrow.

The phone stopped ringing and a box with a smiley face emoji replaced her name. Above it were two words written in a cheery blue font.

Open me.

Underneath were two flashing arrows pointing at the box.

Tap to open and view. That was the meaning.

Holding her breath, Daisy tapped.

There was a pause as the smiley face box disappeared, then an image filled the scene. Daisy felt her breath leaving her body, like she'd been punctured. Felt her eyes widening as she took in what was being displayed.

Not an image of her sleeping.

Not of her flat, or her being raped.

Just a picture. A hand-drawn mermaid, sitting on a rock. And written underneath:

The hook.

Daisy stared at the screen, her eyes scanning and rescanning, trying to input the data into her brain. She shook her head, tiny movements of disbelief.

The mermaid wasn't a picture, she realised. Or at least not from a book. The edges were blurred, and the detail too vague.

It was a tattoo. It was a tattoo of a mermaid on somebody's skin. The image was too cropped to see where on the body the tattoo was, but Daisy didn't need to know. It didn't matter where it was.

Daisy let the phone drop onto the floor like it was on fire, unable to hold it. She stood, ran to the bathroom, and threw up in the sink.

11

3RD NOVEMBER

'This one was taken two years ago in Uganda. The girl who shot it is dead now, probably due to taking this photograph, or ones like it.'

Behind Professor Joseph Skinner another image dropped. The thirty or so students that made up the audience for his pre-breakfast lecture received it on their phones at the same time it appeared on the screen. Not only did they receive the photo, they got the whole lecture in text format, complete with notes, references, suggested links and reading.

Why not? reflected Joseph. *They'd paid for it*. Would be paying for it for the first ten years of their professional lives, probably. Skimmed off their salary like the juice from a black-economy loan shark. It made Joseph feel slightly dirty. But like everyone else, he had a job to do. And he needed to give them value for money. Needed to give them *bank*, as his son would say.

That's why they were here, sitting in a windowless theatre in the middle of the city with their generic energy drinks and their Narnia phones. Money.

And all before breakfast. In his student days he'd still be in bed, whereas, Joseph thought sadly, these kidults probably couldn't even afford to sleep. Ten thousand pounds per year fees plus living costs will burn a hole decades deep into a pocket. The professor looked out at the small gathering, the students at the periphery slightly blurred due to his bifocals. The students in front of him were crystal clear and looked like middle-aged children. He guessed that there was no room for experimentation in their life; that they were already getting a run-up on corporate life, sartorially speaking. He supposed they felt they had to. That the competition was so fierce that the office profiling had to start way back in school. Possibly before. Maybe at conception.

Hence the neat haircuts and smart clothes, instead of dreads and ex-army cargos.

Hence the Red Bull and smartphones, instead of Coca Cola and roll-ups.

Hence the full attendance of a pre-breakfast lecture.

Joseph looked past the students to the back of the room. A man and woman sat quietly watching him. The man was squat, had a fade-cut and was wearing a suit that was clearly tailored. The woman, on the other hand, seemed to have fallen into her clothes by mistake. Both were accelerating fast out of middle age and looked about as natural as sharks in the lecture setting. Joseph stared at them a beat, squinting in mild confusion.

Then dropped another image.

'This one's from South Sudan. Another girl. It's interesting to note that nearly half the so-called child soldiers in the world are female. Although not all fight, of course. Many are taken and used for domestic purposes. Camp maintenance. Or sex. Often they are sexually branded.'

As the image changed behind him, one child replaced with another, Joseph studied his group for reactions.

'Typically it is not a single child who is taken, but the whole community. Sometimes it is from the school, like the Chibok children in Nigeria, taken by the Boko Haram in 2014; or perhaps an entire village is razed, and all the adults are killed. Sometimes they are even sold or encouraged to go by their families, under the belief that they are giving their children a better life. Many end up here, trafficked into sex or servitude.'

In front of him, the students were attentive, highlighting relevant text on their phones or tablets. Not even laptops anymore. Everything straight onto the cloud. Joseph wondered what they saw as their career path. Oxfam, maybe, or Amnesty. Some NGO for sure. A girl near the front raised a hand. It is the first interaction Joseph had witnessed. He'd done this lecture many times, and could guess what the young neatly dressed woman was going to ask. Which was why the next photo had been carefully cued up.

'Yes?'

'I'm wondering, sir, if most of the child soldiers are from Africa? As far as I can tell from your lecture, in almost all of the case studies you've given us, the children are either from one of the sub-Saharan countries or the conflicts in South Asia.'

Joseph smiled. 'There is one from South America in there too, I think you'll find, but I take your point. The wars of the Congo, and Afghanistan. Iraq and Sierra Leone. Children as young as thirteen were sent to Guantanamo Bay. All these children are what we would call children of poverty. In fact the first US soldier to be killed in the so-called war against terrorism was shot by a fourteen-year-old boy.' The carefully cued image dropped behind him and there was a visible tensing from the students. It was not an image they were expecting.

'It's interesting, isn't it? We see a black child, part of Kony's Lord's Resistance Army, maybe, and it's shocking, and awful, but not surprising. We've seen it before, become numbed by it. Smiling and holding rifles not designed for their size. Or posting a YouTube statement wearing a suicide belt. And after a while we learn to accept the stereotype. Rationalise it, even. See the soldier more than the child.' Joseph turned and looked at the image, projected large and 4K clear on the wall. A boy, possibly no more than fifteen, smiling into the camera, holding his rifle high. At his feet was another child, dead. Half of his head is missing. Both the boys are white European.

'Over two hundred and fifty thousand children fought for Britain in the First World War. In total, from all parties, almost a million. They were rounded up and boot-conscripted with no regard for the statutory minimum fighting age.'

Another image dropped. The tension increased.

'In the Second World War the German army had an entire regiment made up of children. The Hitlerjugend, or Hitler Youth. The entrance age was thirteen, where boys were expected to be shaped into soldiers and girls were prepared for motherhood.'

The image showed a row of smiling, blond-haired children, their uniforms gleaming in the sun.

'But we don't have to go all the way back to the world wars of the twentieth century. This was taken thirty years ago.'

On the screen was a suburban house. Something about the framing was wrong. The colours seemed too bright. The photo was taken from some distance, through a telescopic lens. It was replaced with an enhanced image of the same photo, concentrating on a downstairs window. There was a tightening in the room. Through the window could be seen three blindfolded girls, maybe eleven years old. They were kneeling on the floor. Standing over them was a man.

'The cults. The shot you're looking at was clipped moments before the house was raided. It was one of a few properties this particular cult had peppered around Britain. A network of like-minded pederasts creating their own food supply. This particular shot is quite unusual. Each house usually had only one girl. Due to the suicidal nature of the cult, we never knew why, but possibly to take away the chance of alliance. And if you think it doesn't happen today just check out Operation Doublet in Rochdale.'

The image changed, replacing the kneeling girls with a rural setting. A boy and girl, grinning and firing machine guns at the corpse of a deer, or possibly an antelope. Both the children were white. Marble white, as if the photograph was capturing their first exposure to sunlight.

'And this is what happens when indoctrination goes unchecked. We think that they are probably brother and sister. We put them at around twelve or thirteen. The girl is pregnant, by the way.'

More tightening. More tensing. This was not what the students had been expecting. Not easy for them to process.

'Where was this taken?' asked a boy near the back of the group, just in front of the man and woman in the opposing suits.

'Arkansas; with a long-range camera. It is what is sometimes called a survivalist commune, or Prepper site, hidden away in a private forest in the foothills. As far as we can determine, there are over one hundred children living there.'

Joseph ran his fingers through his hair, feeling the weight of his lecture on the room.

'I hope you have found this informative. You will find all the relevant information on your devices. If you do not have one with you, a link to the lecture will have been sent via email to your university inbox. All the cases we've looked at today are indexed in your notes. If you wish to research them any further, Professor Google will be available to you at your leisure.'

There was a smattering of applause and Joseph bowed his head. Once the applause had died down all the students stood and began packing away their notebooks and phones, and tossing their empty cans in the bins.

Joseph packed his satchel and walked down the aisle to the back of the room. The man and the woman stood and walked towards him. Now he was closer he could see that the woman was in her mid-fifties, her jacket and matching trousers a dark blue, with a pair of sturdy brogues. Her hair was dirty-bleached and choppy. The man looked older, maybe sixty. His features were hard and unreadable. They stopped in front of Joseph, blocking his path.

'A very interesting lecture, professor,' said the woman. Beside her, the man reached into his jacket. 'Did you do much work in the field yourself?'

'A fair bit,' said Joseph, eyeing them suspiciously. 'It's not the kind of research you can do third-party. I'm sorry, but are you with Admin? I've emailed my invoice over–'

'No, we're not with Admin,' interrupted the man. Joseph now saw that the object he had removed from his jacket was some form of identification. 'My name is Collins, and this is Inspector Slane. We are working in conjunction with a task force attached to West Yorkshire Police.' He handed Joseph his ID. Joseph looked at it. The government stamp was quite impressive. Joseph handed it back.

'I wonder if we might ask you some questions?' said the woman, Slane.

Joseph smiled nervously. 'About the lecture? I didn't realise the police were so academic.'

The two officers didn't smile back.

'Actually, it is related, circuitously, to your academic work, professor,' Slane said. 'I wonder if you would mind coming with us to the incident room. There is something, we believe, that you may be able to help us with.'

'Well, I'm afraid I've got a hair appointment at twelve, but if you'd care to ring me I'm sure my secretary could set up–'

'It won't take too much of your time, sir.' Inspector Slane

smiled. Joseph noticed she had slightly yellow teeth. Smoker's teeth. 'It has nothing to do with you personally. More that we would like an insight from you. In your professional capacity.'

Joseph knew he was being buttered up, but it still felt nice. He pushed his chest out slightly and looked at his watch. 'I suppose I have a few moments. It is far, the station? Or perhaps we could get a coffee here?'

'Incident room,' said Collins. His voice was rough and wet, like he'd swallowed an autumn garden fire. 'No, not far.'

'Thank you, professor,' said Slane, retreating a few steps and opening the door. There were only himself and the police officers in the lecture room. 'It really is good of you to give up your time.'

'Joseph, please,' he said, putting on his overcoat.

Slane nodded and walked through the door. Joseph followed, with Collins bringing up the rear. Slane walked with authority through the corridors and out of the university building.

Outside, the rain seemed to be in a hurry to leave the sky and hit the ground. So much so that it was bouncing right back up like it had forgotten something. Joseph put his briefcase over his head in an attempt at shelter.

Seconds later, an unmarked police car pulled smartly up next to them. Joseph felt Collins' firm grip on his arm as he was bundled into the back of the car. Collins got in next to him and Slane walked around and climbed in the front passenger seat. As soon as his door was shut the vehicle pulled smoothly away and accelerated into the stream of traffic.

12

23RD OCTOBER

The ringing of the phone ripped through Daisy like lightning, and she thought she might throw up again.

'Daisy! Open up, It's me! I've got coffee!' The voice was muted by the thick wooden door, but instantly recognisable. Daisy felt relief wash over her.

Jay.

She realised that the sound wasn't the phone, with its picture like a bullet from the past, but her doorbell. She raised her head and looked at her reflection. There were flecks of vomit around her mouth and the white of her blue eye was scarlet with a burst blood vessel.

The doorbell rang again, this time for longer, with little urgent stutterings. Daisy turned the cold tap on and washed the sick from the sink. Splashed the icy water on her face with her hands. She didn't dry her skin with a towel. She didn't own any towels. Towels could be weaponised. Taking in a shaky breath she left the bathroom and stood in the hall. Her tee and boxers were wet from the sink. She stood still, unsure of what to do. She hadn't known Jay long but she trusted her. Or at least she trusted her as much as she trusted anybody, which was close to zero.

But that was okay because she trusted everybody else less than zero.

The picture of the mermaid kept on staggering across her view.

What the hell had happened the previous night? How did the phone get into her flat? And how did the picture of the tattoo get onto the phone? How could anyone know?

Because nobody knew about the tattoos. Not anymore. Not for a long time.

Daisy jumped as the doorbell sliced into the silence. This time it was accompanied by an urgent knocking.

'Daisy! Open up. It's me! I've got coffee!'

Daisy made a decision.

She ran to the door, her bare feet slapping on the wood, and grabbed the keys off the hook. Fumbling, she turned the keys in the lock, slid the bolts back and flung open the door.

'But you took so bloody long to open the door that I've drunk the coffee.' Jay stood on the landing, a smile on her face and her arms wide, a corrugated cardboard cup in each hand. The smile quickly slipped as she took in Daisy's appearance. The soiled T-shirt and sodden boxers. The bloodshot eye. The smell of fear and the jumpy micro-movements of her tensed body.

'Jesus, Daisy, what the fuck happened to you?'

Daisy stepped forward and grabbed Jay's waistcoat. Pulled her into the flat. Jay stared at her, concerned. From across the landing Daisy caught sight of her nosey neighbour, peering suspiciously out of his flat, before she slammed the door closed.

'What's going on? I was joking about the coffee. Has something happened?' Jay stretched out her hand but didn't touch Daisy. Just offered her the coffee. She knew better than to touch Daisy.

'Has someone done something?' Jay searched Daisy's face, as if trying to work it out. Daisy wasn't looking at her. She was still holding her keys in her hand, her knuckles white. Jay looked down the hall, checking the flat, then gently pressed the cup against the back of Daisy's hand. After a moment the heat from the liquid registered, and Daisy looked at her.

'Daisy, tell me what's wrong,' she said gently.

Daisy's gaze finally settled and she took the offered coffee. Jay looked back, eyebrows raised in a question, then wrinkled her nose. 'Have you been sick?'

Her eyes slid to Daisy's shirt, normally so pristine; took in the vomit. 'Jesus, Daisy, have you OD'd?' Jay pulled her phone out of her cargo pants. 'I'm calling for an ambulance!'

'No!'

Daisy reached over and placed her hand over Jay's wrist, stopping her before she had even swiped the device awake.

'No, I'm okay. I haven't OD'd.' Daisy couldn't remember what she had done the previous night, but she was certain she hadn't taken a bucket of drugs. Her body didn't feel that way. Didn't have the sensation of separation that heavy medication brought. The acidic smell of lemons flashed across her mind, but she shook it away. If she'd OD'd it would be more than lemons she'd be smelling. It would be the olfactory equivalent of concrete.

'What is it then? What's wrong?' Jay searched her eyes, careful not just to focus only on the blue one, but to allow her gaze to flicker between the two, passive and inclusive rather than aggressive and dominant.

'I need to show you something. Make sure it's not just in my head.'

'What is it?' Jay said again. She was beginning to feel stupid, repeating the same sentence over and over. Daisy grabbed her arm and pulled her forward. When they walked into the living room she merely pointed. Jay followed her gesture, staring at the mobile sat on the low table.

'But you don't have a phone, do you?' she said, brow creased. 'Why is there–'

'Someone's been in. Someone's been in without me knowing.'

Jay looked down at Daisy's hand, still clutching her own like a lifeline. 'But how? You always lock the...'

'I don't know,' said Daisy, her voice beginning to rise. 'But they have.'

'Okay,' Jay said softly. The flat was ticking with the sound of Leeds-rain hitting the windows. Moving with the grey shadow-rain seeping down the walls.

'It woke me up. Wouldn't stop ringing until I answered it.'

'It's not ringing now. Whose is it?' Jay started to walk forward, but Daisy pulled her back.

'I answered it, but it wasn't a call. It was a picture thing. Whatever you call them.'

'A photo file?'

Daisy looked at her.

Jay saw the confusion on her face. And fear. Fear beginning to come through strong.

Daisy shook her head slowly.

'It's not mine. Someone put it there when I was asleep. It made me wake up wrong.' Daisy let go of Jay's arm and turned to look at the phone. 'Not mine,' she repeated like she needed to convince herself. Jay stayed looking at her for a moment, then walked forward and picked up the device. She pushed the power button on the side and swiped the screen. There was a moment of image static and then the phone showed the last thing that had been viewed on it.

'Is that...' Jay squinted. 'Is that a child's drawing? A girl on a swing?'

'It's a mermaid,' said Daisy quietly. 'It's a tattoo of a mermaid.'

'Right!' Jay nodded. 'It's not very good, is it? And what's this line coming out of her back?'

Jay turned the phone sideways, trying to get a better look.

'It's a fishing line,' said Daisy, staring at the shadow-rain trailing down her wall. 'The hook is in her back, and she's being reeled in.'

'*The hook*,' Jay read. 'I get it.' Then she looked up at Daisy. 'Actually, I don't have a fucking scooby. What's this all about?'

'I told you. I woke up to it ringing. When I answered, *that* was on it.'

'But it means something to you? I know you said you've never seen it before but it means something to you, yeah?'

Jay watched with dismay as tears formed in Daisy's eyes. Form, be born, then slowly slide down her face. Jay wanted to run to her. Hold her. Protect her.

But she didn't.

Because she was work.

Shit, thought Jay.

She stood, putting the phone back on the table.

'Okay, Daisy, what the fuck's going on?'

13

3RD NOVEMBER

'It's been a while since I've been in the back of a police car,' said Joseph, as they slipped through the traffic. The rain had eased off somewhat, but the driver was still having to use the wipers. Joseph studied him in the rear-view mirror, oversized so that the passenger in the front seat could use it as well, as was common in an unmarked police car. He noted the broken nose and the scarred tissue around the dead-stare eyes. The leather jacket and Swarovski-crystal earring. Joseph thought he looked more like a gangster than a policeman, with his boxer's face and street clothes. The driver never glanced at him, just stayed focused on the road.

'When?' Collins asked, turning in his seat and looking at him.

'I beg your pardon?' The bulk of Collins made Joseph feel a little crowded. Collins had the kind of squat, solid musculature one would normally associate with a brick.

'When?' repeated Collins. 'When were you last in a police car?'

'Oh, I see!' said Joseph. 'About ten years ago.'

'What was it involving, if you don't mind me asking?' said

Slane, turning in her own seat and looking back at him. Her gaze was clear and penetrating. Joseph suspected she made a good detective; decisive and direct.

'Oh, it wasn't anything criminal,' said Joseph quickly. 'Similar to this, really, I imagine. I was helping the police on an immigration matter.'

Slane smiled at him. 'I see. That doesn't sound like it would be part of your specialism, professor.'

'Yes, well, there were, um, complications. There were trafficked children involved. I'd really rather not discuss it if that's all right?'

'No problem, Joseph, I was just interested. Is it all right if I call you Joseph?'

He nodded.

'Good,' she said, then: 'Ah, here we are! I told you it wasn't far.'

Joseph looked out of the window. The car had stopped in what appeared to be an abandoned industrial estate. Everywhere was grey concrete and steel shutters. Glass-ripped carpet on the roof perimeters and fire-scarred breeze blocks.

'Bloody hell, where have you taken me to, Beirut?'

'It's up for redevelopment,' said Collins. 'Therefore cheap rent. You know how under-resourced the public sector is? With a police presence here the owners lease it to us for nothing. They know that no one's going to come and do any damage while we have a base on the estate.' Slane got out of the car and walked round to let Joseph out. There were no door handles on the inside of the vehicle.

The car had stopped in front of a two-storey building. The upper windows were blocked with sheets of riveted metal, with barbed wire and glass shards on the flat roof perimeter. The lower windows were protected by rusting metal bars and the door to the building was barred by a padlocked roller shutter.

'Where's Fielding?' Collins eyed the locked door, his wet-dry voice sounding annoyed. The driver slipped past him and walked up to the shutter and undid the padlock.

'She's gone to check on Lawrence, sir,' he said, heaving the door upward. The scrape and screech of the cog system set Joseph's teeth on edge. 'He hasn't radioed in for a while so she's making sure everything is kosher.' The driver's accent was hard Nottingham; all dead vowels and backstreet consonants. Joseph watched him as he disappeared into the mouth of the building.

'You know, I'm really not sure if I do have time...'

'Don't worry.' Slane smiled and took Joseph's elbow. 'I know it looks grim but it really isn't what it seems.' She steered him towards the doorway. Joseph reluctantly allowed himself to be guided. 'The investigation is quite delicate and so this environment suits us perfectly.'

'Yes, but what is the investigation?'

Collins entered the building and Slane stood aside, allowing Joseph to walk in front of her.

'I really would rather tell you inside, Joseph,' said Slane. 'It won't take too much of your time. You don't have to be at your hair appointment until noon, is that correct?'

Joseph nodded. As he walked into the hall he was momentarily unable to see as his eyes adjusted to the ambient dim. When his vision cleared he was not reassured. The corridor he found himself in was unlit and the floor covered in debris. A rusting bike frame was staggered against the cracked wall, and old magazines lay rotting on the concrete floor. The whole area smelt of urine from a shut-down liver.

'Don't worry,' Slane repeated quietly behind him. He could hear the laughter in it; not mocking, exactly, but amused. 'It's all part of the disguise. First door on the left.'

Joseph saw Collins walk through a doorway and disappear from view. Breathing shallowly so as not to gag on the acidic reek of urine, Joseph followed, carefully stepping over an old spray paint canister. When he had passed through into the next room he stopped and gazed around him, until he felt Slane's gentle push on his back.

'Told you,' she said.

Joseph found himself in a large rectangular room, clean and well lit, with a Smart Board against the far wall, and trestle tables against two others with laptops and desktop computers. There was a vintage filing cabinet on his left, against the wall in which the doorway was situated, and a coffee machine to his right.

'Coffee, sir?' said the driver. Joseph nodded absently and walked to the centre of the room, gazing around. The driver tapped a couple of buttons and the machine spat out a plastic cup. A few seconds later a dark liquid dribbled into it. Slane shut the door and walked to the drinks machine.

'It's not Caffè Nero, I'm afraid, but it's hot and wet and guaranteed to make your heart race,' she said, picking up the drink and bringing it over to Joseph.

Joseph took the offered cup. 'This is amazing. I would never have believed this was here.'

Slane smiled. 'As we said, it's cheap and discreet and off the radar, press-wise.'

'Why would you need to be off the radar?'

'Can I take your coat, sir?' The driver held out his hand. Joseph shrugged himself out of it and handed the garment over. The driver nodded smartly, took the coat and draped it over a chair. Joseph had needed to put down his briefcase to get out of the coat, and Collins picked it up and took it to the trestle table. Then he snapped the case's clasps and opened the lid.

'Hey!' said Joseph. 'That's my property! You can't–' He looked down. Slane's hand was on his arm.

'It's all right, Joseph,' she said, soothingly. 'It's just a precaution. This is a sensitive area. There can't be a security breach. It's for your own protection. Make sure there are no bugs or tech there that shouldn't be, okay?'

Joseph watched as Collins searched through his case, and flicked through his diary and lecture notes.

'Who's Mark?' he said, pointing at the diary entry.

'My son...' Joseph said reluctantly. 'But aren't you required to ask my permission? Get my consent or whatever?'

Slane smiled at him again. 'Do you mind? It really is for your own safety.'

'I suppose not.'

'Thank you. Grant?' Slane looked at the driver who, Joseph saw, was searching his overcoat. He turned to look at her, shaking his head and holding up Joseph's mobile phone.

'Clean,' he said. Slane nodded. Grant brought the mobile over and handed it to her. She looked at it a moment, then stared at Joseph, raising her eyebrows inquiringly.

'Where did you get this, the Ark?'

'I'm not too keen on technology,' Joseph said defensively, holding out his hand. 'It makes phone calls, takes photos and receives texts. That's all I need.'

'I'm amazed it even does that,' said Slane, looking at it a moment longer, then handing it to him. 'I wonder if you'd mind me patting you down? I know it might seem over the top but...' she shrugged apologetically.

Joseph sighed heavily and made a point of checking his watch. 'If you must.'

'Thank you. Sorry,' said Slane, then expertly searched him. He could feel her fingers as she felt his pockets, his body. He felt mildly violated.

After a moment she looked over at Collins and nodded. 'All good,' she said.

'Of course it is,' said Joseph. 'I only came to give a lecture.'

'I'm sorry, Professor Skinner,' said Collins. 'But due to the delicacy of the case this task force is set up for, I'm afraid we have to be extra careful. If the press got wind of it...'

'And what exactly is this task force set up for? Because I'm not sure how I can be of–'

'Cults and mind control,' said Collins, cutting Joseph off. 'Immersive Charisma Syndrome. The relationships formed within closed and coercive social groups. That's your area of expertise. Correct?'

Joseph paused, reassessing, then nodded. 'Some of them, yes. What has that got to do with...' he stopped, seeing what was posted on the Smart Board. He took a step towards it. Near the top of the screen was displayed the image of a faded photograph containing a red-brick house. The photograph was old, the skin of it cracked and brittle looking. The house was detached, set back from a country lane. It had an unloved feel about it. Uncared for. There were rusty railings around a narrow strip of grass at the front, and the entire structure seemed to have been cut into a wooded bank, creating an alley leading around the sides to the back. In the faded colours of the picture, the windows looked grimy: unwashed and dusty. There was a thin trail of dark smoke moving up into a grey sky from the chimney.

Next to it was the scan of another photograph, of the same house. Also cracked, the colours equally faded. In this one, though, the house was not only in disrepair, it was in pieces. Blown apart or demolished. Still recognisable as a house, but only just. The railings were all twisted. Only the left side of the building and a portion of the front remained intact; like an unfinished jigsaw. Smoke was obscuring the debris. Joseph scanned the rest of the board. Next to the image of the ruined house was a picture of a man. Joseph walked a little closer. It was a headshot, face-on. Like a passport photo. The man, perhaps thirty, looked earnestly out at the camera. Underneath was a printed name.

Walter Cummings.

Joseph blinked. Next to the picture was another photograph, this time of a girl. Joseph guessed she was pre-teen, maybe ten or eleven. This also had a name printed beneath it.

Daisy.

Joseph stared at the two faces intently, then at what was printed at the top of the board.

Joseph felt like a splinter of ice had been pressed into his spine.

'Why have you got this here?' he said. 'This is old news.'

'Not anymore. This is why, Joseph,' said Slane. 'This is why we are being extra careful. Under the radar.'

Typed under the photographs was:

The Fishermen cult house. Surrey. 1995

'The picture of the three girls. In your lecture.' Collins came and stood next to Joseph, looking up at the board. 'They were survivors of The Fishermen, weren't they?'

Joseph nodded, not able to take his eyes off the images. 'Yes, but not from this house. There were a few scattered across the country.' He looked at the board a moment longer, then turned and addressed Slane, eyes narrowed. 'But how do you know? About the house in the lecture? It wasn't mentioned by name.'

'It was listed in the notes,' said Slane, now standing by him, looking at the board. 'In the index you posted online for the students. In the appendage. You uploaded them two days ago. As soon as it was in the cloud it triggered a red flag. Anything to do with The Fishermen registers with us.'

'Of course,' said Joseph, nodding to himself. 'All source photographs are indexed and referenced. But I still don't see how that can have anything to do with you. That cult died out decades ago. All the members committed suicide. The last of them blew themselves up in that house.' He pointed at the board.

'Absolutely.' Slane picked up a tablet from one of the trestle tables, glanced at it, then handed it to the professor. Eyebrows raised, he took it.

'What am I looking at?' he asked.

'Two months ago a homeless man was found murdered. His throat had been cut so deeply that it was amazing his head was still attached. The woman who found him said that a song was still playing on his media player.'

'I'm sorry, but I'm not sure what–'

'As far as the police are aware it was nothing more than a brutal murder, possibly drug-related. Possibly some sick form of vigilante. Clean up the streets. That sort of thing.'

'Right...' said Joseph, his face still showing confusion. 'I thought *you* were the police.'

'As far as the normal police are concerned.' Slane smiled. 'Look at his wrist, professor.'

Joseph looked down at the screen. There was a thin slice of exposed skin between where the victim's coat had ridden up and his fingerless glove. Joseph squinted, then used his hand to expand the image on the screen. He stared at the enlarged area of skin, shaking his head.

'That's not possible,' he said. 'They all died. Everybody died.'

On the dead man's wrist was a tattoo of a mermaid.

'Apparently not. Walter, it seems, escaped.'

Joseph looked up at her. She nodded, pointing to the picture of the man on the Smart Board. Joseph realised that it was the same person. Younger. Not ravished by years of living on the streets. But the same person.

'Or at least he did until he was found on the streets of Leeds with his throat cut.'

'But it's not possible,' repeated Joseph.

'I'm afraid it is, professor. Walter survived. Which means others might have too. Which means that The Fishermen might still be active.'

'What was the song?' said Joseph.

'I'm sorry?'

'On the media player. What was the song he was listening to? When he was murdered.'

Slane smiled as if she knew she had found her man.

'Culture Club. "Do you Really Want to Hurt Me"?'

14

23RD OCTOBER

'I mean you never, like *never*, keep the door unlocked. It's a bloody fortress in here! If you don't let someone in, they're not in, right? End of story.'

Daisy nodded. Her heterochromia made Jay feel that Daisy could look right inside her head. Know what she was thinking. Jay smiled grimly to herself. She hoped not.

'And you didn't? I mean I've never known you to let anyone in. Except me, of course.'

'I can't remember.'

Jay could sense the frustration and fear coming off Daisy like radiation.

'I remember I had a session, and bits of walking home.' Daisy's hands moved as she talked, a physical narrative to colour-in her recollection. 'I remember it was raining.'

Jay nodded agreement.

'It was proper Leeds-rain. It was bouncing.'

Daisy creased her face in concentration.

'I was step-counting. Breaking the journey into pieces. Varying the lengths.'

Jay understood. It was something they'd been taught in one

of the grey classes: a survival session where the object of the therapy was not to heal but to manage. To give mechanisms to help function in life. To do more than just hide away in a box. One of the therapies was to own the journey. To break it down and take control of it. Make certain buildings important, familiar. Know exact distances. Map the journey in real-time by step-counting. Anything to keep the fear at bay. Be a moment in time and a point in space. Take control. Own the quantum.

Personally, Jay liked to give the quantum a good kicking. She thought most of the therapy meetings she'd visited with Daisy were bollocks.

Jay silently chided herself. But then what did she know? She was just a lying cow who was fucking over someone who thought of her as a friend. Her gut spasmed with shame and guilt.

'And then the next thing I remember was waking up wrong, on my bed, by the ringing coming from...' Daisy pointed at the phone.

'So somebody *could* have mugged you. Which would explain why you can't remember. Used your keys to get into the flat. Maybe drugged you, although that doesn't explain how the door could be locked but the person leave you the keys.'

'Maybe they made a spare set? While I was–' she fluttered her hand, 'out of it.'

Jay nodded. She didn't mention about the bolts. Because there was no way someone could have left and rammed them home. The flat must have been bolted from the inside. Jay had heard them sliding back when Daisy let her in.

Which didn't really leave many options.

'Maybe. But it still doesn't make any sense. Why drug you? Why break in and leave you a phone with an image of a mermaid on it? Then sod off, locking the door behind them?'

She paused, then looked at the woman. 'Daisy,' she began softly.

'It wasn't me!'

If Jay was shocked by the vehemence of her denial she didn't show it. Jay had been around Daisy long enough to know she was fucked-up. Beyond fucked-up. But she also knew things Daisy didn't.

Like she wasn't paranoid. People really were watching her.

Jay was watching her.

Jay felt another twist in her stomach. There was no way she could keep this up.

'Daisy, I–'

'Look, would you wait for me, outside? I need to clean up, and I'd feel safer if I knew you were watching the door.'

'Do you want me to stay in here? I don't mind.'

Daisy glanced at her bathroom, with no door.

'No, outside would be good. I'm really sorry, but–'

'No need to apologise.'

Jay came and stood in front of Daisy. Gently placed a feather of hand on her arm.

'I'll only be outside, take your time…'

Jay tried a smile, but Daisy didn't smile back.

'Just outside,' Jay repeated gently, and turned, walking back to the door.

Daisy watched her leave, holding her breath. Once the door had closed she let it out in a slow release, like she'd been taught.

She couldn't tell Jay about the mermaid. About The Fishermen. About her past. She simply couldn't. She'd only just started remembering herself. Neither could she tell her about all the blackouts; the blank gaps in her memory. Because if she did she'd have to confront it. And not only the now, but the then. The everything.

And there was no way she was going to do that.

She took a shaky breath and walked toward the bathroom.

The phone rang.

'Shit!' Daisy halted and turned; stared at the phone.

Daisy. Daisy. Daisy. The flashing was the same as before, except the font was now red.

Red for danger, she thought haphazardly. Red for blood. She looked through the doorway into the hall, hoping to see Jay, but the front door was closed. She wondered if she should go and get her.

Instead, she ran to the table, grabbed the phone, and swiped to answer.

'Hello?' she whispered. 'Who are you? What do you want?'

For a moment there was silence, just the crack of dead air.

Daisy frowned.

And then it began. Like it had all those years ago.

The song. The song that meant the darkness was coming.

'Do you really want to hurt me?'

With a scream Daisy threw the phone against the wall, smashing it into silence.

15

3RD NOVEMBER

Joseph stared at the picture. 'This doesn't make sense. They all died. Every single one was documented as deceased. I've read all the files on them. There were no survivors except their victims. The children.' Joseph tapped his finger on the table in front of him for emphasis. 'None.'

Collins nodded at Grant. 'Pull up the history and put it on the board, please.' Grant nodded back and picked up his tablet and tapped and swiped. Joseph continued to stare at the Smart Board, taking in the detail of the house in the picture. Then he studied the photograph of Walter and the girl.

'Was he one of The Fishermen from Surrey? The family that perished in the bomb?' He peered at the name. 'Walter Cummings.' Crease lines tramlined his forehead as he searched his memory, trying to place the name.

After several moments he shook his head. 'Are you sure this is right? I don't have–'

'Don't worry about the name for now,' interrupted Collins. 'He was a member of The Fishermen. Cummings was the head of the family at the Surrey house. The house mother died in the explosion.'

Joseph was startled by the harshness of Collins' tone; as if he had been challenged. He looked at the detective, but the man had already turned away.

'Are you ready, Grant?' Collins said to the driver.

'Sure.'

Joseph saw that he too had a tablet and was transferring something to the Smart Board.

'Over here, Joseph,' said Slane.

Joseph turned and saw that Slane had set out four foldaway wooden chairs in the middle of the room, facing the Smart Board. 'Grant is going to run the heritage media we have pertaining to the case. It will give you the scaffolding to understand the reason we need your help.' She sat down and looked at him expectantly. After a beat, he walked over and joined her. Collins and Grant did likewise.

'Heritage media?' said Joseph, his tone slightly mocking as he sat down. 'Do you just mean old footage?'

Slane smiled. Joseph saw that behind the professionalism she was tired.

'Yes, but it doesn't have quite the same ring, does it? Yes please, Grant.'

Before Joseph could say anything else, Grant swiped his pad. Blurred silent images appeared on the Smart Board.

'Very hi-tech,' he muttered, but then fell silent as the images came into focus. It was footage of the house in the photograph, filmed from a moving vehicle, part of which was in the shot. Joseph guessed it was from a camcorder, with a magnetic tape. The colours were washed out and grainy, the image unsteady, leading Joseph to believe that whoever was doing the filming was also doing the driving.

'Damson Cottage,' Slane explained. 'An abandoned four-bedroomed property in the Surrey countryside that was squatted, from nineteen ninety until nineteen ninety-five, by a family cell of The Fishermen; as far as we know the last national cult in Britain to-date, Al Qaeda and QAnon notwithstanding.'

Slane paused to allow the film to play for a moment, then continued. 'This was taken in the late summer of their first year.' The film continued, staying focused on the house as the car was driven slowly down the road. Joseph thought it must have been shot by someone used to working undercover. There was no slow-down as the cottage was passed; just a constant speed from the opening shot as the house came into view, to the end-frame as the property became obscured by a bend in the lane. 'In the five years they were in residence, we believe the family tortured nine children, aged between eight and thirteen.'

Joseph could feel the air deaden around him, like the past was stealing it. The drive-by was replaced by another film, this time of a walled garden. It was still summer: the heat of the day practically leaping out of the frame. The grass was straw-coloured and there was a large inflatable pool set up, the type with rigid sides, like a miniature swimming pool. A hosepipe snaked from out of shot and into the pool. In the foreground was a man in swimming boxers and a sodden T-shirt, presumably from having been in the pool. Joseph immediately recognised him as the man in the photograph. Joseph glanced across at the name beneath the photographs.

'Walter.' The name came out as a whisper.

'Walter Cummings.' Slane nodded. 'Not one of the founder members of The Fishermen, but once recruited, one of the most active. Head-father of the family at Damson Cottage. This footage was found in the wreckage after the explosion.'

'The suicide-pact,' said Joseph. Nobody answered him.

Walter was gurning at the camera, giving a thumbs up. It seemed, thus far, like a million other home movies from the period. Then he turned slightly away from the camera and shouted something.

'How come there's no sound?' Joseph asked.

'The Fishermen never recorded audio,' said Collins.

'That's right.' Joseph nodded, remembering. 'They believed they owned all the voices of their victims.'

Presumably responding to the shout, a child climbed out of the pool. Because of the raised edge of the structure, Joseph had not realised she was there. She must have been right up against the near side.

Hiding, Joseph thought.

The child could not have been older than ten. She was wearing a bikini. Joseph could see a scar on her shoulder and a tattoo on her hip when she turned. Although the camera was too far away he knew what it was. His mouth felt dry.

It was a mermaid.

'The families used to brand the children, to show which house they were made in. That's what The Fishermen called what they did. The making. Like a cake.' Slane's voice was empty, professional. No inflection of emotion. On the screen Walter Cummings put his arm around the girl, his finger stroking her chest just below her neck. To Joseph it looked like the girl was trying not to cry. Cummings looked down at the girl and her face seemed to blur for a moment, before rearranging itself into a smile more heartbreaking than anything Joseph had ever seen.

'Once they were made they used to tattoo them. To show that they had made the change.'

'The mermaid,' said Joseph quietly. 'To show they were more than human.'

'Exactly. They also used to brand them.'

'What's the name of the girl? She's not the one in the photograph.'

'Her Fishermen name was Gemma. After the family blew

themselves up she made it all the way to twenty before she killed herself.'

The camera stayed on Gemma's face for a moment, then blacked out.

'Which quite effectively rules her out,' said Collins.

Joseph stayed looking at the screen, the image of the child still playing on the retina of his mind's eye, then he came to and looked at the police officer.

'Rules her out of what?'

'The murder of Walter Cummings. No loss whatsoever to the world but an absolute nightmare for us, seeing as he was meant to be dead already.' Collins stared at the professor as if he personally was responsible. 'Blown up and catalogued and cremated.'

Before Joseph could answer, his mobile phone rang, car-crashing into the tense silence.

'Excuse me, I'm so sorry but it might be my son, Mark. Do you mind?' Joseph raised his eyebrows and reached into his pocket, pulling out his phone. Without waiting for an answer he pressed the green button to accept the call and placed the device against his ear.

'Good morning. Professor Skinner speaking; may I help you? Ah, Hilda, how are you?' Joseph listened and nodded. When he saw the quizzical look on Slane's face he put his hand over the mouthpiece. 'Sorry, it's my secretary, I won't be a minute.'

Slane nodded and walked away, pulling out her own phone and tapping in a number. Collins went to stand in front of the Smart Board. Joseph removed his hand and placed it in his pocket. 'Very well, thank you. The students seemed to enjoy it at any rate. Actually, rather excitingly, I've been picked up by the police!' Joseph smiled at Slane, who was staring at him. 'No, nothing like that; they just want my opinion on something. In a professional capacity.' He paused while the person on the other

Girl:Broken

end of the phone spoke. Joseph raised a finger. 'Yes. I understand, and you're right. He is.'

Joseph mouthed 'client' and shrugged apologetically. Then: 'Hang on, I'll ask.' He pulled the phone away from his ear and said, 'Excuse me, but which one of you is in charge? Is it you, Inspector Slane?' He looked inquiringly at her.

'It's me,' said Collins. Joseph turned to him and smiled. 'Ah, of course. All it is, Mr Collins, is,' Joseph paused. 'It is Mr Collins, isn't it? There was no title on the identification you showed me. Just David Collins.' Joseph looked over at Slane. 'Sorry, yours didn't even have a first name.'

Slane smiled and Collins scowled.

'Just Mr,' he said.

'Good. What it is, Mr Collins, is that Hilda is wondering where to send the bill to.'

'I'm sorry?' Collins looked incredulous.

'The bill. For my time. It is usually a flat daily rate, but if it looks like it might be something pertaining to my work perhaps we could sort something out?' Joseph smiled at him expectantly. Collins looked like he was attempting to crush his own teeth.

'You need to end the phone call, professor; we can sort out your fee later. Right now you are helping with a live enquiry.'

'Oh, yes of course. Apologies.' Joseph turned away slightly. 'I'll keep a track of my hours. Hopefully no more than five. What? Yes, I won't forget. Noon. It's written in my diary. Okay. You have to go now, Hilda, I'm busy. I'll see you later.' Joseph finished the phone call and looked at his device. 'Sorry about that. If Hilda doesn't check up on me she thinks I'd forget my own head. By the way,' he held up his phone, 'I don't suppose anyone has got a charger, have they? The battery is almost empty.'

'For that? I'd have thought it would have run on steam.' Slane put her own phone away and looked at his mobile. She grimaced sympathetically. 'No, sorry, and I doubt you'd find one to fit that these days.'

Joseph tutted. 'I left mine at home. The charger. I wasn't expecting…' He gestured at the room. 'Never mind.' He turned back to the board; to the picture of Damson Cottage and the two photographs. He leaned forward. 'And it is definitely him? The man who was murdered?'

Joseph didn't really need to ask. The resemblance was obvious, now he knew.

'Without a shadow of a doubt,' said Slane, wiping her hand through her hair. 'Grant, can you cue up Walter's sheet? Thanks.'

Joseph shrugged. 'So, what, he escaped from the bomb? Faked his death somehow. I'm sure this sort of thing happens. Explosions are messy. You just have to assume whoever is supposed to be in there is in there. Then he kept his head down. Moved around. As long as he kept below the radar then you'd never know. Homeless. Living in squats. You can see how it could happen.'

'Sure,' said Slane. 'It could be done. Half the people on the streets are hiding from some past or other. And you're right, Joseph, he was living on the street. From the state of him, had been for some time. Or in a flophouse. And yes, he could have escaped the blast. God knows the police at that time were not always the most thorough at crossing all the Ts. If it looks like it all fits then why make trouble? But we believe there is much more to it than that. Grant?'

On the Smart Board, an image popped up.

'Jesus!' said Joseph. The image was of Cummings slumped in a doorway. His eyes were open and staring blindly, and a large gash had been cut into his throat. 'That's horrible!'

'Yes it is,' said Slane. 'This was taken shortly after he had been found by an office cleaner.'

'Is there really any need for me to see this?'

'Apologies. Can you see what has been placed over his head?'

Joseph took a deep breath and leaned forward. 'Earphones?'

'Yes. Standard fare. It was what they were attached to that was so interesting.'

Joseph saw that the wire from the headphones trailed down to a pocket in his filthy coat. The picture was replaced by another.

'They were attached to this.'

The new image showed Cummings, still dead, staring, and covered in his own blood, but now the device that had been in his pocket had been removed and placed on the ground, in the concrete doorway by the body. Next to it was a ruler for size identification and a police identity tag. Joseph squinted.

'What is that?'

'That is a Sony Walkman circa 1994. You can tell by the top loading.' The screen went blank again.

Joseph shook his head. 'I'm not sure I follow. What has this got to d–'

A new image appeared, silencing him. It was Cummings, but young again. He was in the living room of a building, presumably Damson Cottage. There was a fire behind him, with flames bouncing shadows onto the walls. Cummings was on his knees and smiling. There was a paper banner over the hearth, saying 'Happy Birthday'. The person he was smiling at was out of shot. He had one hand hidden behind his back and with the other he was beckoning the unseen person forward. A young girl stepped into the shot.

'We only knew this girl by her number.' Slane was speaking in her professional voice again. Neutral and flat, pure information with no inflection. From behind his back, Cummings brought a box wrapped in shiny paper. A present. The girl smiled with delight and began ripping the paper off.

'They all had numbers of course, as well as a house name – one given by The Fishermen – but we never found out her birth name. This is her fourth birthday. We believe that the person filming is Heather Tayler; the house mother.'

The girl unwrapped the present and took it out of its box. It was a Sony Walkman. She laughed with delight and the man slipped the headphones over her ears. He then pressed a button on the Walkman; Joseph guessed it was the play button because the girl immediately looked amazed. She put her hands to the headphones, pressing them more tightly against her ears. The man smiled and gently turned her around, so she was sideways on to the camera.

Joseph's brow furrowed. 'What's going on?'

'All the houses had one. We think it was one of their methods. Although it's not the original machine – that was found in the debris after the explosion – it is exactly the same make and model. Inside was a tape of the Culture Club song, "Do You Really Want To Hurt Me?"'

Joseph nodded.

'And as that was the only tape we found, we're guessing it was the only one they ever gave.' The man got up and walked to the fire. As he leant down Joseph noticed that there was what looked like a poker protruding from it. The man, Cummings, removed it. Joseph now saw that it wasn't a poker.

'No,' whispered Joseph.

'The same song that was playing to the corpse of Walter Cummings.'

The thing that Cummings had removed from the fire was not a poker. It was a branding iron. He held it high and walked back to the girl. She was oblivious, still with her hands clutched to her ears. Cummings lifted the back of her T-shirt and firmly pressed the red-hot end of the firebrand into her flesh.

'No!' Joseph's voice was a horrified whisper.

'The same one that was playing on a phone found in a woman's flat in Leeds.'

The effect on the child was immediate. The little girl's hands flew out sideways and she screamed. Even with no audio, Joseph could hear her scream.

'A phone that incidentally also had a picture of Walter's tattoo on it.'

'Turn it off,' Joseph said.

The man, Cummings, pulled the burning metal off the girl's flesh and tossed it toward the fireplace. Then he took the girl's hands and pressed them over her ears, grinding the headphones against her skull.

'We believe that Cummings was the one who branded them all. Went round all The Fishermen houses. Which means that the person who killed him knew what went on in Damson Cottage, and all the other cottages. The cottages where everyone was blown up and no one survived.'

'I don't care,' said Joseph, bile flooding his mouth and, thankfully, tears blurring his eyes. 'Turn it off. I don't want to see anymore.'

16

23RD OCTOBER

'Here you go, ladies. Please: enjoy!' The impressively lined face of the vendor beamed at them, bowing slightly. Jay and Daisy were handed glass cups of steaming mint tea, served from a large metal teapot that had probably sat on the hotplate in the tiny food station since the beginning of time. They thanked him, crossed the narrow passage of Crown Street, and sat on the side steps of the Corn Exchange. The tea was from Caravanserai; an African traveller's café, and free for anyone who wanted or needed one. Daisy stared at the elephant statue that sat above the café, giving the building a surreal feel. From the window of a small seating area above the culinary activity, the sounds of someone playing a djembe drifted into the morning.

Daisy sipped her tea.

'What do you think it's called?' she said, pulling a mint leaf out of her mouth and rolling it gently between her fingers.

'What do I think *what's* called?' said Jay, finishing off rolling a cigarette and placing it in her mouth. From out of her waistcoat pocket she pulled a brass Zippo lighter and fired it up. The smoke she blew out into the air appeared blue in the sunlight.

'The big silver urn. The pot he poured the tea out of. It's got to have some special name, don't you think? Some kind of ceremonial translation. Like the vessel-that-eases-travellers'-woes, or something.'

Jay stared at her, incredulous. 'Fuck knows. Anyhow that's not important right now, is it, Daisy? What with everything else that's going on.'

Daisy flinched at the anger in her voice, and Jay immediately felt guilty. When she'd finally gone back into the flat to check if Daisy was all right she'd found her fully dressed and showered, just sitting on the floor of the living room. Not doing anything. Just... staring. Like she was empty. Frankly, it had scared the hell out of her.

'Sorry. I didn't mean to sound angry; I'm just worried for you. The phone's useless by the way.'

At the mention of the phone, Daisy's body stiffened. 'I'm sorry. I didn't mean to break it.'

'Good. So we're both sorry. Look, you've had a shock. Somebody's invaded your space and fucked you up. I get it. But with the phone T-boned against the wall – good throw, by the way – there's no chance of skimming any data off it.'

Daisy looked at her, lost. Jay wanted to reach over and hug her, but she didn't. She felt like if she did that she'd infect her. Infect her with her lies and deceit. And Daisy didn't deserve that. She'd clearly already been through so much. Inspector Slane hadn't given Jay the details, but what she had let slip was enough for her to know the woman must be broken, and no amount of half-baked therapy sessions were going to fix it.

'Phones are like libraries,' she explained. 'All the information is there if you know the indexing. If the phone was intact there would have been a chance I could have traced where the picture came from. Who sent it.'

'From your contacts in the police.'

Jay grimaced. 'Yes. Even though I'm suspended, some of them still talk to me.'

'Why *did* you get suspended? You never told me.'

Jay took a moment to answer. She knew she was on dangerous ground. When they'd first met she'd told Daisy that she'd been put on probation, but given no real detail. She'd hinted that there were things in her past that she had been unable to process. Things she hadn't been able to share through the official channels. She'd needed an 'in' with the woman, and that had seemed to do the trick. Gave them a basis to make a bond.

She pushed smoke out of her nose. 'Breaking my superior officer's jaw had been a bit of a problem.'

'Why? What did he do?' Daisy stared at her, a look of amazement on her face.

Jay sighed. 'He called me a prick-tease, but that wasn't why I hit him. He was just the final straw on a very weak back. I told you I used to get stick when I was young, yeah?'

Daisy nodded.

'For hardly ever being at school because my mum was a new-age activist. For my skin, because no one could stick a label on it. For my sexuality, because it never fitted into one of their boxes. And finally for my anger, because kicking against the system was all that made sense to me.'

'And then you joined the system,' said Daisy shyly. 'You joined the police force.'

'Yeah, well, we've all got to rebel at some point. It was either that or become an accountant. Anyhow, when my boss came onto me, I told him I was gay. Then when he found out I'd dated guys in the past he took it personally and insulted me. When I hit him I was really hitting the world. When I tried to explain, they grounded me. Wanted me to see a psychiatrist.'

Daisy nodded. 'But the therapy was still their therapy. Still part of their system.'

'Bingo.' Jay flicked the butt of her cigarette. They both watched it spin, finally bouncing off the stone step below.

'It wasn't just that,' said Daisy softly, after a few moments. 'There was something else.'

For a moment Jay panicked, thinking Daisy was calling out her story. That maybe she'd seen through her. In a way it would be a relief. 'What?' she said quietly.

'When you were gone. Waiting outside.'

Jay realised she was talking about earlier. 'What else?'

Daisy just shook her head. 'I'm starting to remember. Little bits of my past. That picture... the tattoo.'

Jay held her breath. She watched as the pale girl bit her lip. She could tell Daisy was suffering, in turmoil as to how much to confide. Jay felt sick inside. On one level it was exactly why she was here. Not just to protect her and make sure she didn't run again, but to find out how much she knew. How much she remembered about her past. Slane said she had suffered severe trauma as a child and had locked her memories of it away. As Jay watched she could practically see scraps of them breaking through. It was like watching a ship sink.

'What about it?'

Daisy bit her lip.

'I've seen it before.'

Jay stared at her, wide-eyed. 'Where?'

'Here.'

Daisy lifted the hem of her T-shirt an inch. Jay felt the breath leave her as she saw the tattoo, old and blurred, of the mermaid.

'I can remember them doing it, sort of. Like a dream. I was young. It meant that I belonged to them.'

'Jesus, Daisy,' whispered Jay. 'Why didn't you tell me before?'

'I didn't remember then. It was only seeing it on the phone

that brought it back. It was like it was shut off in a room in my skull.'

Jay watched helplessly as Daisy rubbed the tattoo. Like she was trying to rub it away.

'Hey.' Jay kept her voice soft. 'Don't worry. After the session today we'll get the locks changed.'

Daisy looked at her gratefully. There was a chime from Jay's waistcoat. She'd converted her Moto smartwatch into a pocket watch, fitting it into a frame she'd bought online and attaching it to a chain. It wasn't particularly practical but she thought it was cool as fuck. It was paired with her phone, with its own LTE connection. She took out the device and swiped it awake.

'Great,' she said, squinting at the notification. 'It's from my ex-boss; I've got an evaluation this afternoon.' She looked up and smiled. 'Maybe you can use your special method to dismantle my phone as well?'

Daisy smiled back.

'Come on,' said Jay. 'Let's go for a walk by the canal. I need to clear my head if I'm going to be around so many cock-merchants later.'

The multi-mapped face of the vendor beamed at them. 'Can I take these back, ladies? You're finished, yes?' He had a tray with empty glasses on it, and the silver tea urn. 'Or would you like a refill, maybe? Perhaps you are ready to order?'

Jay shook her head regretfully, placing the glasses on the tray. 'No time today. Maybe tomorrow, okay?'

He nodded amiably and went to collect the glasses off the customer down the way.

'Excuse me!' said Daisy. The man turned and raised his eyebrows. 'Could you tell me? What is the name of the teapot you use? My friend and I were wondering.'

The man looked confused.

'The name?'

'Yes,' said Daisy. 'What do you call it?'

The man thought for a moment, then smiled kindly at her. 'Teapot,' he said, then turned back to his task. Daisy stared at his back for a moment, then looked at Jay.

'Don't,' Daisy said, but it was too late. Jay was already pissing herself.

They stood.

'I'll catch you up in a minute,' said Jay. 'I'd better just reply to my super. Let him know I got this message.'

Daisy nodded and walked away.

Jay got out her phone and typed a quick message. The watch was great for reading texts but no good for typing them.

daisy found a phone in her flat. door bolted. she must have put it there herself.

relevance?

had picture of a mermaid on it. a tattoo.

There was a long pause, before:

be careful. there's been a murder. might be related.

???

come in for briefing 2morrow

Jay put the phone away and looked at Daisy.

Who are you? she thought.

Daisy saw her looking and smiled.

Jay reached deep down inside and grabbed a smile for her face. 'Right, let's go.'

17

3RD NOVEMBER

'Before we go any further, Joseph, I'm afraid we're going to have to ask you to sign a confidentiality document. Really we should have done so straight away but thought you had to see what was at stake to be convinced.'

Joseph looked at Slane, not really seeing her. Images of what he had just viewed in the footage stayed playing in his head, refusing to fade. The casual way Cummings had burned the child. Branded her. The smiling image of him as he hooked his arm around the girl with the tattoo. What also chilled him, as much as the violence and violation, was the way the video hadn't shuddered when the red-hot iron had touched her skin, and what that must mean. The camera had remained rock steady, like the person shooting it was not shocked by the action. Was not fazed by what occurred. Or perhaps, Joseph thought bleakly, they knew it was coming. Perhaps they had filmed it happening before. Perhaps many times. Slane had said that Cummings did all the branding for the various Fishermen houses. Maybe his housewife did all the filming.

'I'm sorry?' he said, focusing back on the present. Slane was holding out a clipboard with some kind of document attached to it.

'I know it was horrible, Joseph. The Fishermen, as you are probably aware, were almost unique in their depravity. Fred and Rose West and Charles Manson rolled into one. They had six houses scattered throughout England. Each of the houses had a "Fishing Family"; usually a man and a woman, who abducted children, and brought them up as their own.'

'Each household would brainwash the children,' continued Collins.

Joseph turned and looked at him. Collins was sitting on the trestle table, his gaze static. Looking, it seemed, at nothing.

'They would abuse the children physically and mentally. Rape and mutilate them. Anything to break them down so they could build them again in their own image.'

'Mould them into copies of themselves,' said Slane.

Joseph turned back to her. He rubbed his eyes. They felt gritty like they'd been contaminated. 'Truly awful,' he said. 'I've read all the reports, of course, and seen the extant footage.' He paused and looked at them thoughtfully. 'Although I've never seen that. Where did you get it from?'

'There were certain surviving tapes that were classified,' said Slane. 'Considered too inflammatory to reside in the public domain.'

'Of course. I understand. That was truly shocking. But I'm still not sure how I can help you. My area of expertise, as you pointed out, is the study of the cult itself, and the effect it has on its members. You have no cult here, except historically. If Cummings was murdered by someone who knew who he was, then it is surely just a police matter?'

'That might not be correct,' said Collins.

'What? What might not be correct?'

'That the cult is historical.'

'I beg your pardon?' Joseph was momentarily flustered. 'Of *course* it's historical. The whole cult imploded, then quite literally exploded! Everyone died apart from a few of the children. There are papers written on it!'

'Apart from Cummings,' pointed out Slane.

'Well, yes,' conceded Joseph. 'So it would appear, but as I said, that can be...' Joseph stopped, then turned to the board. He looked at the pictures of Cummings and the young girl. 'What aren't you telling me?'

'We would value your insight on this, Joseph,' said Slane. 'But we really do need you to sign this confidentiality document.'

'It won't be forever,' said Collins, his voice soft and damp, like he'd swallowed rotting wood. 'Once the case is completed you will be able to publish.'

Joseph blinked slowly and turned around. Collins was now standing next to Slane; almost the same height, but a third again as wide, and somehow more solid. As if he was made of something far denser than she was. Slane looked tense, the fingers on the hand holding the clipboard were white with pressure.

'What do you mean?' said Joseph.

'Just what I say.' Collins spread his fingers, palms out, the epitome of openness. If Joseph wasn't so tense himself he might have laughed. 'This is an ongoing investigation so, obviously, you are prohibited from divulging any details you have learnt thus far. If you choose to help us with your expertise, however, then I'm sure there is a paper in it for you.' Collins let the sentence hang.

'Or a book. With the names redacted, of course,' said Slane. 'You said to your secretary that you wanted to sort things out?'

Joseph looked from one to the other. Slane wore a strained smile, but it was only just staying on her face by its fingernails.

Collins was impossible to read; he'd been around the block a few times. But he was rubbing his Lego brick-like thumb against his finger. Back and forth. They're scared, Joseph realised. Scared, or something like scared. He glanced at Grant, pondering what they had said. The driver with the dead eyes had finished his call and was tapping out a message on his phone.

Joseph breathed in deeply. 'Why?'

'Why what, Joseph?' said Slane.

'Why do you need me so much that you're offering this? Publish new insights about The Fishermen? Surely you have people, specialists of your own? I'm an academic. Why do you want me?'

Slane shrugged. 'You're the man on the ground. When your lecture got flagged I looked into you; your history. It turns out that you're somewhat of a cult expert.'

Joseph shrugged in return. 'Not really. You need to go to America to become an expert. That's where the real work is done.'

'Don't be so modest! Work with the travellers in the eighties. The Lord's Army in Africa. The gang culture in Manchester in the nineties. You are well respected, Joseph. Why wouldn't we want your help?'

Joseph could see the tension in Collins and Slane as they waited for his response, and he found himself thinking: *I wonder what would happen if I said no?*

'The Fishermen? Still operational?' Joseph asked.

Slane gave a slight nod. Like an encouragement.

'Possibly,' qualified Collins.

'I'm sorry, Joseph, but we can't go any further without your signature. We can't make you sign. You are not part of the investigation, we merely want your insight. But the information is so sensitive...'

'And potentially could put a number of persons in danger,' said Collins.

Joseph looked at them both while the room ticked around them. 'A paper?' he said, thoughtfully.

'Or possibly a book. Probably a book. But not until after the case is finished,' said Slane. The smile was settling onto her face. Joseph regarded them both for a long moment, as if unsure, then seemed to make up his mind. He smiled.

'I'm going to need to phone my secretary, and I absolutely need to keep my hair appointment.' He felt the room relax around him. Joseph took the clipboard from Slane and reached into his jacket for a pen.

'What's so important about the haircut?' Collins asked.

Joseph signed his name in the box Slane had marked and handed the document back. 'A birthday present from my son. He made the appointment.'

Collins seemed puzzled. Before he could speak, Joseph continued. 'My son suffers from ASD. Autistic Spectrum Disorder. Dates. Times. Plans: these are all very important for him.' Joseph looked at them to see if they understood. The blank faces told him they did not. Subconsciously, he rubbed the side of his face, then ran his fingers through his hair. 'ASD presents itself in quite specific ways. One such is anxiety about things that would not really affect most people. Routines are one of the things that allow a person with ASD to function in everyday life. Always getting up at the same time. Going to work by the same route. Structure and ownership of the environment. These are the walls by which the ASD mind can contain the chaos of the world. If I were to miss the appointment, one of those walls collapses.' Joseph clenched his jaw. Put his hands in his pockets. Stared at Slane.

'Sorry,' Collins said, after a beat.

'That gives us a little time,' Slane broke the awkward silence that had developed. 'After which you will be in a better position to let us know if you can help us. We really are very grateful.' She turned and looked at Grant. 'Nothing from Fielding?' Grant shook his head.

'She's not answering. And I still can't raise Lawrence.'

Slane frowned.

'Okay, well we'll give it half an hour. If you haven't heard back by then you can check it out when you run Joseph in for his haircut.' She nodded at him, communicating more than she verbalised, then turned back to Joseph. 'Okay. Brace yourself.'

18
23RD OCTOBER

Jay watched Daisy as she walked down the narrow stone steps from Globe Street to the canal towpath. The little tunnel was so well hidden that unless you knew about it then it would never be spotted. Daisy and Jay had come across it on one of their place-hacking sojourns. It was part of their project of cataloguing the city; getting to feel confident. Contextual therapy.

In the beginning, it had given Jay a reason to spend time with Daisy. To bond. To win her trust. But now...

Jay felt another stab of guilt spasm through her.

No more, she promised herself. No more after today.

It was not even as if Jay thought she could develop a romantic relationship with the woman. Daisy was nonsexual. It was as if her mind hadn't followed her body into puberty. That whatever had happened to her had been so traumatic that she'd just stopped. Hadn't mentally wanted to walk through the door into adulthood. In fact, now she came to analyse it, Jay thought the feelings she had for Daisy were almost maternal.

'Jesus,' she muttered. 'I'm turning into my fucking mother.'

'Sorry?' said Daisy, over her shoulder, as she emerged out of the tunnel and into the late autumn sunlight.

'Nothing.' Jay paused as she came out of the darkness. The canal glittered in front of them, the uniformity of it offset by the wildflowers and grass that cradled its edge.

'It's beautiful, isn't it?'

'Yeah.' Jay scuffed her boots on the gravel, removing the dirt of the tunnel. 'And not a shopping trolley in sight.'

They started walking. Past the new-build offices, half-finished, and somehow seeming derelict before they were even occupied. Away from the station, the path was wide enough for them to walk side by side. Daisy stared directly in front of her, watching the swans. Her entire body language said that she didn't understand. Her shoulders were tight and she was making tiny movements with her head like she was having a conversation with her brain. The bit of it that was still in the past, replaying the tape. Trying to work out what had happened.

'Let's sit,' said Jay after a few minutes. 'My feet are fucking killing me after attempting to kick your door down when you didn't answer. Plus I need a smoke.'

Daisy nodded and sat down on the towpath, her feet dangling over the edge. Jay sat next to her and took out her tobacco tin. Began rolling herself a cigarette. She didn't want one. She didn't even smoke anymore, really. She'd only started again because the pressure of lying was too much. Once she had got it how she wanted, she pulled the Zippo out and flicked the wheel on her combats, igniting the wick.

'Come on, then,' she said, firing up the smoke. 'Tell me what's really bugging you.'

'What do you mean?' said Daisy, but she wasn't fooling anybody, least of all herself. The body language she was giving off, Jay thought even the swans knew something wasn't right.

'I mean you've had someone invade your space, fuck with

your head, and generally creep you to hell and back, so you should be all over the shop. You should be climbing the walls or packing a bag and zedding the place, but instead, you're walking the canal with me.'

Jay took another drag on her fag.

'Now I know I'm irresistible...' this raised a small smile from the woman next to her, '...but I'm not that irresistible. Something else must be bugging you. So what is it?'

Daisy didn't say anything. She just continued staring out over the grey water. Jay wondered if she'd gone too far; maybe she'd pushed so much that she'd finally pushed her away. Well if that was the case, then good. It would mean she didn't have to pretend anymore. Didn't have to feel like a prostitute to friendship.

'Daisy–'

'The door wasn't just locked.'

'What do you mean?'

'It was bolted as well. I know you saw that.'

Jay blinked. Here it was. The black hole at the centre of the morning. The thing they hadn't mentioned.

'Yes.' Jay took a slow drag of her cigarette. 'What do you think that means?'

When Daisy answered her voice was almost a whisper. Like she was hiding from it. 'Maybe there was no intruder.'

This, Jay understood, was the thing that was scaring her friend. More frightening than having her flat creeped. Than someone leaving a phone in her living room with a picture of a strange tattoo on its screen. More than whatever made her throw the phone at the wall. 'Maybe it was me and I've forgotten. I've been having blackouts recently...'

Jay reached out and placed her hand on top of Daisy's. 'Daisy, the meds you take. I know you feel you can't go to legit doctors, but buying them from the street is no good. Who knows what's in them? It wouldn't surprise me if they didn't fuck-up your short-term memory.'

'But what if it's more than that? It's not just that I zone out, Jay. There's whole chunks of time I can't remember! What if I'm... I don't know. Sleepwalking or something?'

Jay laughed. 'I think if you were zombie-ing all over Leeds, someone would have noticed you!'

Daisy nodded but Jay wondered. She remembered all the times she'd knocked on Daisy's door and got no answer. At the time she'd always put it down to Daisy not wanting to see anyone. The woman was a war zone to herself. She could only take a certain amount of time around other people before she shut down. But maybe it was more than that? Jay remembered reading something about fugues; the state when people do things. Go for walks, even drive cars, and then have no recollection of doing them.

'Look, Daisy.' Jay tightened her grip on the woman's arm then waited until Daisy turned and looked at her.

'The phone was real. Is real. And so was the photograph of the tattoo. I saw it. It had been downloaded. It hadn't just been photographed from the device. So even if you had been out taking pictures in your sleep,' she tried for a smile, 'which by the way is a non-starter cos you couldn't operate a smartphone to save your life...'

Daisy smiled wanly.

'...then that wasn't it. Somebody sent that as an attachment. It didn't download until you answered the phone. And you only answered the phone just before I came, yes?'

'Yes,' said Daisy in a small voice. 'But the bolts...'

'Fuck the bolts. Maybe the bolt-fairy did them. Let's leave the bolts for now. The only thing I've had to eat today is coffee and cigarettes. I'm starving!'

She stood and offered her hand. After a moment's hesitation, Daisy grasped it. Jay hauled her to her feet.

'Let's go and get some food.'

'Okay,' said Daisy. 'What shall we get?'

'We'll go straight for the important food groups and get chocolate,' said Jay firmly, then licked her lips. 'And possibly some form of marshmallow.'

19

Canal

Daisy Daisy Daisy.

Sometimes when I watch you it breaks my heart. Really. I can feel it folding and refolding inside of me, creasing until it just falls apart. Disintegrates like paper in water. Seeing you sitting there, with the weak sun washing your face, with your reflection rippling on the canal like you're not real. I want to remake you into what you could have been. Reshape you into what you should have been. What you will be.

I watch you with the policewoman and pretend that you aren't what you are. I make up whole alternative histories for you.

Like a childhood.

Like maybe you grew up with loving parents in some suburb somewhere. Ate fish fingers with ketchup sandwiches. Had posters in your room and joss sticks and dreamt of boys or girls and walked to school with your satchel on your back.

Gave away your virginity as a promise kept to yourself, rather than a price ripped.

I try to imagine all these things, but I can't.

Because I know they're not true.

Because I know you, Daisy.

I know everything about you.

Of course I do.

20

SEPTEMBER

'Thank you for agreeing to see me. I know what you've been through must have been a gruelling experience.'

Beata and the detective were sitting in a café near the bus station. The woman had approached Beata as she was on her way home, showing her ID and explaining that she had some follow-up questions about the dead man.

'I don't know how I can help. I've already told the officer who interviewed me everything I can remember.'

Beata shivered and took a sip of her hot chocolate. Outside the café, buses arrived and left, heading or returning from the rugged countryside that surrounded the city.

'It was so awful. That poor man.'

'And you didn't touch anything?' prompted the woman.

'No. Yes. I touched his arm to see if he was okay. I was concerned because I couldn't smell urine.'

'Urine?' The woman, Detective Slane, raised an eyebrow.

'I saw a patch of wet around him and thought it must be urine. You know how it is. Drinking to stay warm and then falling asleep.' Beata shrugged.

Slane nodded, her hands clasped around her own cup of coffee.

'Yes. Sadly the homeless situation is getting out of hand. They seem to drift here from all over.'

'God knows why. It's so bloody cold here! You'd think they'd have the sense to be homeless somewhere warm.'

Slane looked at her curiously. 'You don't like Leeds?'

'Oh, Leeds is nice enough. It's just where it is that's so bloody awful. It always rains! And it's not like normal rain in a normal country. It just seems to go right through your clothes like you are naked!'

Slane laughed, nodding. Beata felt herself warming to her.

'I know what you mean. I'm from the south of England. When I first came here I couldn't believe how cold it was. And how grimy the houses were. Like someone had forgotten to wash them a hundred years ago and then gave up.'

'Tell me about it! The stone on my flat looks like it's been eaten away by moths.'

'Beata, after what you experienced, it's common to feel...' the woman seemed to be searching for the right words. 'A little shaky. Sometimes days or even weeks later. As the full impact of what you've been through hits. This is also the time when memories, little details, come back into the mind that might have been hidden in the moment. Tell me, are you getting some support? Your boyfriend, perhaps?'

Beata stared at the woman. She thought about her boyfriend, and what he wanted to do to her. What he wanted his friends to do to her so he could earn some money. 'No help, No. I'm fine as I am.'

The woman clearly did not believe her but said nothing. Instead, she took out her tablet and began swiping. 'I understand from your interview that you said there was no one near the body when you found it?'

'That's right. I'd gone into an arcade for some shelter. When I saw the man, at least I thought it was a man, he looked so sad. He had this little tin cup by his hand. I remember thinking that he needed someone to change his luck, like me. So I decided to give a few pounds.'

'Very kind.' Slane smiled. 'And as you crossed over to him you didn't see anybody? Hear something, maybe?'

Beata shook her head. 'No, nothing.'

Slane nodded. 'The thing is, Beata, that according to the police report; from the first officers on scene and confirmed from the attending medical officer, the man could only just have died when you found him.'

Beata's eyes widened in shock. So this was why the woman was here.

'I swear I didn't do anything! I just work–'

'No, Beata, I'm sorry! You misunderstand, I'm not accusing you.' Slane reached over and touched her hand briefly. 'Far from it. We do not suspect you of anything other than being a decent citizen. What I'm saying is the murder was so fresh it seems possible that you might have seen the killer.'

Beata relaxed. 'As I said, the street was empty. The rain–'

'This is CCTV footage of the route you took from your previous job to the one you were heading for. Do you recognise it?'

Slane spun her tablet around for Beata to look at. She leant forward and saw herself hurrying past the Grand theatre. The camera was static so she wasn't in the shot for long.

'Hey, that's me!' she exclaimed, then looked up at the detective. 'The other officer, the one who interviewed me, never showed me this.'

Slane nodded.

'There have been more developments since your statement,

Beata. The identity of the homeless man has been ascertained, and the whole investigation has gone up a notch.'

Beata was intrigued. 'Who was he?'

Slane shook her head and tapped the computer tablet. 'I'm afraid I'm not allowed to tell you that. Suffice to say that it impelled us to look again at all the information streams we could. See here where the Uber passes you?'

Beata nodded, watching herself as a car stuttered past her on the screen in black and white. It was a different shot, from a different camera. Beata guessed that the whole city must be wired. She'd read somewhere that, after China, the UK was the most surveilled country in the world.

'We've tracked him and ruled him out. The same with some street cleaners and a prostitute. We haven't been able to find the clubbers, but by the way they were swaying as they walked we doubt that they were involved.'

As Slane talked she brought up various camera shots of Beata's journey. It was odd to think how much of her life had been archived without her knowing.

'In fact, the only person we failed to track down was the jogger who nearly ran you over,' said Slane mildly.

Beata remembered. There had been the youth in the hoodie and tracksuit. She had had to step off the curb to allow them to pass. As if on cue the incident repeated itself on Slane's tablet. Beata watched as, in starts and stutters, the jogger ran past her.

She swallowed as she felt a flutter of fear. 'You think that she's it? She's the killer?'

Slane said nothing, pausing the shot on the tablet. The jogger's face couldn't be seen from the angle of the camera. 'Let's just say that they are a person of interest.'

'She,' corrected Beata, staring at the still. 'It was a woman. Maybe thirty-five.'

'That's excellent, Beata,' said Slane, a twist of excitement in her voice. 'Are you sure? From the footage, it seems that you barely had time to view her.'

'I'm sure,' said Beata, nodding vigorously. 'I'm very good at faces. It was definitely a young woman. I thought she must be a student or something.'

Slane nodded, then reached into her jacket. She removed a photograph and showed it to Beata.

'Is this the woman, Beata? Is this the woman you saw?'

Beata looked at the photograph and swallowed. The slip of fear she had felt became a slow creep, numbing her. She nodded.

Slane looked at her a moment, her features unreadable, then put the photograph back in her pocket.

'Then I'm afraid, Beata, you are in terrible danger. So much so, in fact, that I might have to move you to a safe area, out of Leeds.'

21

23RD OCTOBER

'What's the session this afternoon? CBT? Place-solidity? What to store in the extra head?'

Jay and Daisy were sat in the churchyard off Briggate, eating chocolates from Charbonnel et Walker. The unkempt gravestones had long since lost the names of those buried beneath them and all the drunks were asleep against the church wall, steaming gently in the mid-morning sun. Jay thought they looked like statues, before they became stone. Sad and decaying, but in some odd way permanent and life-affirming. They always seemed to find some brightness in the day.

'CBT,' said Daisy. Cognitive Behavioural Therapy. A way of observing and cataloguing that allowed a person to break down their problems so they were easily manageable.

Jay thought Daisy might be a little beyond what CBT could do.

'Great,' she said through a mouthful of chocolate. 'At least it's not the one that makes you conjure the things that worry you, then make you bury them in a happy place.'

'You don't like that one?'

'I like the burying bit. It's the happy place that freaks me.'

'Finland,' said Daisy promptly.

Jay raised her eyebrows.

'Finland?'

'Happiest place on earth.'

Jay snorted, accidentally swallowing a piece of nut. 'According to who? The Finnish?' she spluttered.

'Followed by Denmark and Norway. All the cold places, mainly.'

'Makes sense,' said Jay, getting herself under control. 'Less insects. Less sand.'

'You don't like beaches?'

Jay snuck another chocolate. 'Oh I like beaches, fair enough. Windswept and wild with some pre-Raphaelite lady walking towards me with lust in her eyes.'

Daisy blushed, and Jay smiled.

'Don't worry, I'm not painting you in that picture. What I don't like is people all hot and oily, like chips ready for eating. All those summer holidays sitting on the beach makes me think of meat markets.'

'And that's why you live in Leeds, is it? No need for a bikini?'

Jay put another chocolate in her mouth, smiling around it.

'Exactly. A tent is the nearest you'd get to a bikini round here. The next best thing would be Alaska. Is that on the happy chart?'

Jay smiled at Daisy, then felt the smile slip off her face. The girl looked so sad.

'Daisy, what is it?'

'That's what it's like in my head. Like Alaska. Cold. Sometimes it's dark for months. Sometimes I wake up tired like I haven't been to sleep. By the time it gets to the afternoon I'm dead. Sometimes I dream when I'm awake.'

Jay didn't know what to say. It was the most Daisy had ever shared with her. If she had still been in the mindset of undercover police then it was the sort of thing her bosses would have been delighted with. It showed that Daisy was beginning to trust her.

Or beginning to unravel. Fall apart.

For something to do, Jay offered Daisy a chocolate, proffering the bag.

Daisy held her gaze for a moment, then looked down. She frowned.

'It's empty,' she said.

Jay looked. She was right. 'Ah. I wonder how that happened?'

'I didn't even get one!'

Jay nodded sadly. 'All gone.'

'And who do you think ate them all?'

'Well,' Jay mused, 'we *are* next to a church. Do you think that perhaps Jesus ate them?'

22

OCTOBER

Beata glanced at the church on Rider Street, taking the path that skirted through its grounds, her suitcase pulling at her arm. It was the shortest route to her rendezvous.

She grimaced to herself as she lugged the heavy case. She didn't think it looked like a church; not a proper one anyway. There was no steeple for a start. And it had a security guard. What sort of church had a security guard, for God's sake?

A community church, that's what they called it.

Not like home in Poland. You knew you were in a church there.

Not that Beata went to church. Not since she was a little girl.

Beata shivered as a bitter wind came around the corner and stabbed straight through her coat.

Bloody Leeds. She was glad she was leaving. The only reason she hadn't left already was she couldn't work out how to get her money without her shitty boyfriend finding out, but the woman – the detective – said she'd sort all that out.

Beata gathered her coat a little tighter around herself and walked across the car park towards the road. She had covered her hair with a scarf by way of disguise. She didn't expect her boyfriend to follow her but she wanted to be careful. Lately, he had been even more possessive than before. First, when she had found the murdered homeless man, her boyfriend had been delighted. He thought he might be able to sell her story. Beata fumed at the memory. It was her story! She'd found the body. If there was any money to be made it should be hers. But then he had started getting paranoid. Saying they were being watched. Saying that maybe they should go back to Poland.

Bloody idiot. It was all that Leeds skunk he smoked. Or all the vodka he drank or the bloody conspiracy theory documentaries he watched on YouTube.

Beata smiled to herself as she crossed over the road.

Although he was right, in a way. They probably were being watched. The woman said that she'd keep an eye on her, just in case. She said that as she'd practically witnessed the murder she might be in danger.

Which is why she was getting protection. Why she was slipping away in the middle of the night.

As she crested the hill she could see the high rise of the office buildings on the other side of Leeds, up near the university. In the night sky, they glittered like a future that would never quite happen. Cranes were festooned with twinkly lightings, as if metal Christmas trees. Beata paused to look at them. Felt the wind skimming the lines on her face, and gathering in the folds of her scarf. Felt a shiver of fear as the wind dropped, and a stillness came over the city.

She hurried on, lurching slightly sideways because of the weight of the case. She glanced at her watch. She was meeting one of the woman's detectives in five minutes, on the pedestrian bridge that spanned the A64; the motorway that cut through Leeds like a concrete river. Even at this time of night, she could hear it, with its constant stream of traffic. Where was everyone going, even so late, she wondered, then stopped wondering.

Anywhere away from Leeds, she answered herself. And that was fine with her. The woman would get her money and set her up with a new identity in a new town, and then her boyfriend would never find her and make her do things she would be ashamed of.

She could start again.

Ahead of her, she saw the bridge. Stood in the middle of it was a figure, smoking a cigarette.

Her contact.

The person who was going to take her to the policewoman, Slane.

Beata hurried on. As she drew nearer she saw that the person was wearing a windbreaker, with the hood pulled up to obscure their face. They were watching the traffic below. Beata nodded to herself. She'd seen enough films. She knew that undercover police had to protect their identity. She stepped onto the bridge and walked briskly to where the person stood.

'Hello, I'm Beata,' she said. 'I'm not late, am I?'

The person didn't say anything. Merely took another drag of their cigarette, then sent the butt spinning out over the chasm, down onto the traffic. Beata watched as it bounced off the roof of a car, sending sparks into the air.

'Detective Slane sent me,' she said, her voice uncertain. She felt a cold stab of air slip between her skin and her coat and snake its way down her spine. 'She said you'd take me somewhere safe?'

The figure nodded and, finally, turned to face her. Beata gasped. It was the jogger. The one she had seen just before finding the body of the homeless man. She had only a moment to wonder what was wrong with the woman's eyes before the hooded figure stepped forward and hoisted her over the rails of the bridge.

Beata didn't even have time to say 'why?' before her body smashed into the road fifteen meters below, killing her instantly.

23

3RD NOVEMBER

Slane placed the clipboard with the signed document in the filing cabinet and then walked toward the coffee machine. Joseph noticed she wasn't wearing socks. Her bare leg was visible between her trousers and brogues.

'Very stylish,' Joseph commented quietly.

'I'm sorry?' said the garden-fire voice of Collins, close to Joseph's ear.

Joseph gave a start; he had not heard the man approach him. For someone so heavy and solid he moved incredibly lightly. Joseph shook his head.

'It doesn't matter.' He turned and pointed at the board. 'I've signed your paper. Are you going to tell me why you think I can help you?'

'Walter Cummings and Heather Tayler ran the Surrey branch of The Fishermen.'

'I'm stunned, Inspector, that you have this much information,' said Joseph. 'It's incredible.' He subconsciously leaned forward, staring intently at the board. 'As far as I was aware, nobody knew any of the names of The Fishermen. The children that survived only ever called them Mother or Father.

Any interaction with the public, for supplies and such, was done by the men, and they all called themselves "Simon".'

'One of The fishermen met by Jesus on the sea of Galilee, yes,' said Collins.

Joseph gave a slight shake of his head in irritation; as if he wasn't used to being interrupted.

'Quite. And as all the houses were squatted, and their money came from private means, they never appeared on any kind of government record.'

'Completely off-grid, yes,' said Slane, joining them. She sipped her coffee. She was close enough for Joseph to smell her soap. No perfume, just the slightly antiseptic smell of a utilitarian cleanser. 'It couldn't happen these days, of course. Between the search for terrorists and Facebook, we pretty much know where everybody is all the time. In fact, with social media, we barely even need to search; people will just take photographs of themselves, geo-tag them, then post them in the public domain. Everyone with a mobile phone is an unpaid employee for GCHQ, basically.'

She paused, then smiled at Joseph. 'Except for your phone, of course. That won't even have an internet connection. All that is, is a phone.'

Joseph ignored the jibe. 'So how did you get them? How did you get the names?'

'When we searched through the wreckage of Damson Cottage we found some records that hadn't been destroyed.' Collins indicated the board, which showed a still from sometime before the explosion. 'The ground floor of the house was split into three main rooms. A living room, where we assume the video with Gemma was shot.'

Joseph felt a wave of nausea roll through him, as the image of the branded girl, silently screaming, flashed in front of him.

'A central hall, with stairs leading up to the first floor, and a large farmhouse kitchen and dining room. The two rooms correspond to the two windows.' Collins pointed to the right-hand corner of the building. 'There was a third small room that was connected to the kitchen, here. This room, as you see, had no window. It was originally a pantry or larder of some sort. It was annexed to the kitchen. Everything in it was slate. Shelves, worktops. That sort of thing. The house is nineteenth century, pre-electricity, so the room was designed to keep perishables cold, so they stayed edible as long as possible.'

'At the time of the explosion, it was being used as an office. We think they weren't quite ready for us. They knew we were coming, of course. They all did. That's why they blew themselves up; committed mass suicide. It's quite common, as far as these things go, apparently.'

Joseph nodded. 'Jonestown, and Waco. Heaven's Gate. Rather than having their alternative reality confronted, they choose to die instead. End their lives still in the bubble. Never having to face responsibility for their actions.' He turned to look at the two officers. 'What is unusual, however, is that they let all the children go. That they sent them out before blowing themselves and the houses up.'

'Agreed,' said Collins. 'I assume you've studied the papers on it? In your field, I imagine it's required reading.'

'I've read the available material, yes. What little there is. There's almost no extant evidence to consider. No official paper trail, due to them being,' he nodded at Collins, 'off-grid, as you call it. No household records, all destroyed, it was assumed, by the explosions. Anybody who met the occupants said they were pleasant, if a little shy. In fact, other than the surviving victims, there was almost no evidence they even existed – the photograph in my lecture was considered to be one of the few that remain. The locations they chose were remote, without being noticeably so.'

Slane nodded this time. 'Yes. In the Goldilocks zone.'

'I'm sorry?'

Slane held her hand out and tilted it back and forth. 'Not too hot and not too cold. Any nearer to a town or village and people might notice something odd. Any further away, too rural, and they might get people popping round whenever the weather was bad. Contrary to what people believe, the sparser the population, the more everybody knows everybody else's business.'

'I see. Well, quite. So nothing was really known about them. All the information we have came from the children.'

'Which was unreliable, as they were so damaged that they couldn't tell fact from fiction,' said Collins. 'The children had all been abducted at a young age, then broken down and rebuilt in the image The Fishermen saw fit.'

'If I remember correctly, they were all sent out of the houses naked before the explosion.' Joseph looked at the house on the screen. Even though there was nothing special about it; no outward expression of the evil that went on inside it, Joseph found it hard to look at. Hard to look at, and hard to look away from.

'Yes.' Collins walked to the trestle table as he spoke, and sat down in front of it.

The others joined him, barring Grant, who was typing on the keyboard. 'We think that it was meant to be like a birthing. That The Fishermen thought the children would be born into our society, then infect it with their ideals. They had all recently been branded on their backs.'

'Sick,' said Slane.

Joseph shook his head. 'Yes, but with a weird sort of logic.' Joseph's voice had taken on the characteristics that he used in lectures: authoritative, and didactic. 'You have to remember that these girls had been there for considerable lengths of time.

Sometimes even years.' While Joseph was talking, he noticed that Grant had projected a still of the girl from the swimming pool. She was standing close to Cummings, and looked small and vulnerable alongside the adult frame of the man. 'They had been moulded by abuse and pain until they began to associate the stimuli with love. To those girls, The Fishermen represented the law. Authority. Basic cult mentality. Control the environment and you control the person. Do it for long enough and they think it's the only way things can be. How was it that this information was never made available?'

The sudden change in direction would normally take a person a couple of seconds to assimilate. Slane responded almost immediately. As if she was expecting the question.

'What information, Joseph?'

'The names!' Irritation acidised Joseph's speech. 'If they were found in the room as you've said, why weren't the names released?' Joseph paused, trying to work through what he had learned. 'What else was found?'

'I'll tell you what wasn't found, Joseph,' said Slane softly.

Joseph focused his full attention on her. 'What?'

'Enough bodies.' Although Slane's tone was soft, the words cut through the room, deadening the air.

In the quiet after Slane had spoken, Joseph rubbed his head. His skull felt dry, as if the skin was shedding.

'Well, yes. You've already told me Cummings was found murdered in Leeds.'

'Last month, yes,' said Collins.

Joseph was mildly surprised to see him pull out a box-mod and vape a cloud of smoke into the air. 'Aren't you meant to do that outside?'

'Sorry,' said Collins, then: 'But you're an ex-smoker, no? If it bothers you, of course I'll step outside.' Collins began to stand, but Joseph waved him back down.

'No, it's fine. I just thought, government building and all that...' Joseph left the sentence hanging, but nobody said anything. Collins sucked in, then blew out another plume of vapour. Joseph closed his eyes, blocking out the room, trying to home-in on exactly what wasn't being said. The room ticked around them. After a few moments he had it.

'How did you know to look for him?' He pointed at the board. 'Walter Cummings. I mean he was just some street person. Murdered, yes, but probably not a priority. When he was found, I doubt anybody would connect him to The Fishermen.' Joseph paused, then stared at Collins. 'Unless they were looking for him.'

'That's right, Joseph,' said Slane. 'Like your lecture, when the discovery of Cummings' body showed up on the wire, his photograph was attached to the report, which raised a red flag with us.'

Joseph scratched his head harder. 'I don't understand. Why was there an "us" in the first place? Surely the traditional order is to set up a task force after the crime, not before it!'

'As we said, there weren't enough bodies,' said Slane. Joseph stopped scratching and looked at her, the penny finally dropping.

'You knew, didn't you?'

Slane gave a slight nod. 'The team that was working The Fishermen case catalogued the scene. Forensics. The bomb squad. Demolition experts. They were very excited when they found the material that failed to burn. It contained a list of all the members of the cult. Not their real names; just codenames. But it listed who was in which house. How many and so forth. Cummings had already been ID'd as the father of Damson Cottage, but when the team collected the remains found in the wreckage, Cummings' wasn't there. We assume he must have left before the explosion.'

Joseph stared at them, mouth slightly open. 'But why wasn't that information released? My God, that's massive!'

'It is not the way we would do things now, but at the time, it was considered better to contain the situation,' said Slane.

Joseph could see the discomfort on her face. 'Contain? What does that even mean? A serial child molester was allowed to roam free, with the public thinking that all The Fishermen were dead? That's...' Joseph waved his hands about in disbelief. 'Criminal.'

'Perhaps,' said Collins flatly. 'But the alternative was worse. Once the story broke, after the explosions, the public was in a frenzy. Of course they were. Child molesters, to use your term, living within the community. And not just one, but six houses. People they had sold goods to. Perhaps made small talk with in the street. People who didn't look like monsters, but just like them. The public was incensed. If it had got out that one of them was still loose, roaming the country, every stranger would have been a suspect. There would have been lynchings. You've seen what's happened with the vigilante paedophile-hunters in recent years? The innocent men whose lives have been ruined? Yes, they have caught a few, but others were mistaken. Remember Bijan Ebrahimi?'

Joseph nodded. 'The gardener from Bristol, yes.' Ebrahimi had been mistakenly identified as a paedophile, relentlessly persecuted, despite contacting the local police, and had been beaten by a neighbour so violently that he had died. Several neighbours then burned the body.

'Right. So we know what can happen. When the story of The Fishermen broke, all hell was let loose. There were rumours of sex cults cropping up everywhere. It was decided at a parliamentary level to keep a lid on it. Not to mention about any survivors. Attempt to find him clandestinely.'

'So that's why a task force was set up?'

'Yes. A small unit was established. Our primary task was to track down Cummings, but also to keep track of the girls who survived.'

'If "survived" is the right word,' commented Slane.

Collins gave a curt nod. 'Right. The girls were car crashes. Their heads were so messed that they could barely function. Then foster care or state children's homes. In one or two cases of the younger children, adoption. It was the nineties. Lots of cutbacks, and nobody wanted these girls. Too much of a reminder. One by one they went off the rails.'

'In the case of cults, with systematic and sustained physical and mental control, the rails are removed completely,' said Joseph.

'Okay. Anyway, that's what happened. We were set up and everything else was brushed under the carpet. After a few years with no leads, we were mothballed, and the girls that were still alive slid off the radar.'

'Until Cummings was found dead,' said Slane.

Joseph thought about it, looking from one to another. Then he shook his head. 'That still doesn't make sense. If you were mothballed then why did Cummings' murder send up a flare? There was no one to send a flare to.'

He looked at them, and after a beat Slane said, 'Because a flare had already been sent up. Two months prior to his murder, someone had been investigating The Fishermen.'

Joseph shrugged. 'So what? I don't see the connection. It's the age of Google. There must be dozens of students looking them up all the t–'

'Using their real names,' finished Slane.

Joseph shut his mouth. Started to say something, then reconsidered before finally saying a simple, 'What?'

'The person who was searching. They were searching using

the real names of The Fishermen. Cummings. Tayler. The others.'

Joseph narrowed his eyes.

'How? You said all the girls were sent out, and everybody else was blown up, except Cummings. How could anybody else be searching using their real names?' He thought for a moment. 'Unless it was one of the girls?'

'Exactly. Which is why we rebooted the unit. When Cummings turned up dead we were already on alert.'

'And when we found the girl–' Slane pointed at the whiteboard. At the cracked and faded picture of the young girl next to Walter Cummings. '–woman now, who had been looking up The Fishermen, we were completely on top of it. Right back in the game.'

'Until the woman who had found Walter, Beata Nowak, was thrown off a bridge in the centre of Leeds.'

Joseph stared at them, looking at first one, then the other. The silence stretched on, seemingly radiating out from Collins. Then Joseph looked down at the photograph on the table.

'The thing is, Joseph, Beata had given a positive identification of the main suspect in Walter's murder. Caught on CCTV running away from the scene.'

She pointed to the board. 'It was Daisy, Joseph. One of The Fishermen's mermaids.'

Joseph stared at her, unable to speak.

She nodded and pointed to the board again. On the screen was another CCTV shot. 'And this is the footage that started it all. When the original flag went up we followed the trail to various backroom public internet hubs around Leeds.'

'Never the same one. The searches were done from different venues,' said Collins.

'We pulled the video feed from a tattoo parlour that rented

internet access and we got lucky. There was some timestamped footage from when a couple of the searches were done.'

'Looking for The Fishermen,' said Joseph.

'Using their real names,' said Slane. 'Yes.'

Joseph looked at the screen. At the grainy black and white images of the person working the computers. Even though it was poor resolution and a wide-angled shot the person was instantly recognisable. 'Jesus.'

It was the girl.

Daisy.

The silence in the room solidified as Joseph thought of the implications.

Then, as if to fill a void, his phone rang.

24

23RD OCTOBER

It went wrong from the moment Jay and Daisy walked into the session.

Normally it was always the same people; women washed out from the burden of living, their faces coded with the pain of their past, like the lines of their skin were tattooed all the way through.

Occasionally there would be the odd new person; someone who had moved to the area to escape abuse or coercion. Or someone local whose life had taken a turn for the worse but had slipped through the cracks in the mainstream health provision system. God knew that mental health services were stretched to the max.

This time was different.

For a start, the session was being held in a new room. Jay could tell that this put Daisy on edge. Spaces were important. They signified safety. One of the first sessions they had done together consisted of counting the steps from the entrance to the door of the room.

'The final hurdle from the street to the workspace is often the hardest,' the therapist had told them. Then she had taken them all down to the pavement and they had step-counted the route to the room. Then they had done it again, cataloguing the doors and corridors they passed. Then again, listing the colours. And over and over, the entire session, until they had a map of the journey completely logged in their heads.

'So next time you will be able, as far as you can, to be in control of your environment.' She had beamed at them. 'And don't let it stop there. Breaking down the spaces in your day into mappable segments can be the first steps to controlling the way you think about the world. Putting the power back in your hands.'

Jay thought it was a little too much like giving in, but she could see the worth in the effect it had on Daisy. When she had first watched her in the street it was like watching a shadow. She seemed to slide through the city, trying hard not to make an impact. Like she didn't really exist.

Slowly, after a few contextual-space sessions, she began to assert herself. Become more tangible. Not like she was part of the city exactly but like she owned her journey through it.

So when they had arrived at the room supposed to be housing the session to find a sign saying it had moved, Daisy was already put on edge.

When they walked into the new room to find a new member, that anxiety only increased. The new woman didn't seem to fit, somehow. She sat at the back, but seemed to attract the gaze of the room like she was a magnet. There was something about her; an anger, or dismissal of her environment. Like she didn't want to be there.

Jay wondered if that was how she came across, when she first started.

The difference was, of course, Jay hadn't wanted to be there. She was undercover, doing a job.

She was a fake.

When the therapist came in and started drawing the blinds, Jay knew it was only going to get worse. All the sessions they attended were in light; either sunlight or artificial. Daisy never went anywhere with dimmed lighting. She didn't like her world to be blurry, or in gloom.

'I don't know who I am if I can't see myself,' she'd told Jay.

No sessions in the dark with candles. No sessions where you had to lie down. No sessions where you had to put your trust in someone else, like holding or catching or touching.

And no sessions involving regression. That was major.

'I'm not interested in going back, only forward. And I'm not interested in understanding; only coping.'

Jay got it. Not everybody needed to understand why something was. They just needed a way to be able to function with it.

'Why is she drawing the blinds?' whispered Daisy, a slight twist of panic in her voice.

Before Jay could answer, the therapist turned and addressed the group.

'Hello, everybody. As we have been forced out of our normal space today by a technical problem, I thought I'd turn the situation to our advantage by trying something new.'

Jay felt Daisy stiffen some more. Daisy didn't like new, or different, or spontaneity. She liked certainty, repetition, and mundanity. The boring cogs that meant the clock could keep on ticking.

'As you know, our normal session is all about control of our environment.' She smiled at them. In the gloom her teeth looked predatory. 'But as today's forced move has shown us; we can't always control that environment and so need to learn other techniques to help us stay in the driving seat.'

The woman reached into her bag and pulled out two tea lights. Daisy was almost concrete in her stiffness. Jay wondered if they should leave, but as the therapist lit the candles Daisy seemed to relax. Jay decided to hold off and see what played out.

'Now the biggest hurdle is being able to feel connected. That is why we do the step-counting and the place mapping. It allows us to feel grounded; not to the places themselves, per se, but to our relationship to them. But what happens when this is not possible? How do we secure our place setting when our environment changes beyond our control? That is what I'd like to focus on today.'

'I think she should have focused on securing the correct fucking room,' whispered Jay, but Daisy wasn't listening. Her whole attention seemed to be focused on the therapist.

'To demonstrate the technique I'm going to ask for one of you to share the space up here with me. I know this is different to how we would normally interact, but then...' her smile was warm and full and inclusive to everyone in the room as she took in her class, '...that's kind of my point!'

The therapist looked around the group, until her gaze settled on Daisy.

'Daisy,' she said gently. 'Would you help us out on this one? I think your particular concerns with space would be ideal to demonstrate the technique.'

To Jay's amazement Daisy smiled and stood, walking to the front of the room and joining the woman.

'Thank you, Daisy.' The woman's voice was calm and reassuring. To Jay it sounded like a countdown.

The therapist placed two chairs facing each other and sat down. After a moment's hesitation Daisy sat on the other.

'That's excellent.' The woman said encouragingly then turned to face the group.

'The biggest obstacle we face when finding ourselves in an unsecured environment is drifting. The feeling that we are not anchored to anything. We can't count or catalogue or spatially control. We feel like we are just flotsam washing in the swell of the city, with no agency or ability to determine.'

The therapist turned back and faced Daisy.

'May I?' she said, holding out a hand. After the briefest of pauses, Daisy nodded.

Everything felt wrong to Jay. The new room. The new member. The darkened setting and the breaking of a barrier they had never crossed before. The intrusion into personal space.

The woman gently took Daisy's hand. 'But of course, there is a stable space, an internal cityscape, if you will, that we carry about with us all the time. No matter where we are, or who we are with, there is a safe space for us to access. Does anybody know what I'm referring to?'

The room seemed to hold its breath. This was so far removed from anything they had done before that they had no reference.

'Yourself,' concluded the woman, smiling at Daisy. 'No matter where you are you always have yourself with you. That, in a way, is one of the fundamentals we need to inhabit. No matter what is done to you, and who has done it, you always have yourself. Your core being. No one can take that away.'

Daisy smiled at the woman. The woman smiled back, then looked down at her hand, the smile slipping slightly.

Even in the flickering light. Even in the safe setting, Jay could see that Daisy's grip on the woman was hard. More than hard. Her knuckles were clenched so tight they seemed to be popping. Jay knew that the therapist's bones must be gritting together, causing her significant pain.

The woman looked up from her hand and smiled at Daisy.

'It's all right, Daisy. There's nothing to fear. Inside of all of us is a central being of truth. The real us. If you can just learn to access that then you will always have a secure place. Somewhere you can call on when you need something extra.'

Daisy smiled wider and Jay stood. She could see that Daisy was only smiling with her mouth. Her eyes were cold, like buttons. Her eyes were merely reflecting, not seeing.

'I don't think...' began Jay, stepping forward.

'It's all right, Daisy. You just need to find your centre. I know you are just reacting to inner uncertainty. But the question you need to ask is,' the woman paused. Jay could tell she was in pain, but she was putting a brave face on it. Being professional. 'The question you need to ask is: do you really want to hurt me?'

Daisy blinked for a moment, then let go of the therapist's hand.

The woman smiled.

Then Daisy launched at her and the room exploded in pain.

25

23RD OCTOBER

'What the fuck happened back there, Daisy? You nearly beat the shit out of her!'

The whole room had watched as Daisy had straggled the therapist, raining punches down on her, while the woman screamed and tried to fend off the blows.

Jay and Daisy sat in the doorway opposite their apartment block. Jay smoked furiously, trying to calm herself down. She had had to pull Daisy off and away, shouting apologies into the shocked silence of the room. She had half carried, half dragged her through the streets. All the way Daisy had said nothing, just allowed herself to be led here, back to where they lived. Jay had expected to hear a police siren with every step. She looked at Daisy.

'Why the sodding hell did you hit her?'

Daisy said nothing. Just watched people walk past their building. Fat people. Thin people. People of different colours and social backgrounds. Young and old. Jay wasn't sure if Daisy even saw them.

Jay wondered if she should phone Slane. Things had

accelerated way beyond anything she could deal with. Beside her, Daisy took in a shuddering breath.

'It was what she said. It went straight through my brain.'

'What do you mean?'

'Do you really want to hurt me? It was what was playing down the phone when it rang again. This morning. When I threw it against the wall.'

Daisy's voice was monotone. Like her throat was just a mechanism. No need for emotion. Just paper to print on.

'Okay,' said Jay. 'That's weird, I guess, but she was just asking–'

'She said that deep down we've always got ourselves.'

Daisy continued as if Jay hadn't even spoken. 'That at the centre of ourselves is solidity.'

She turned and looked at Jay. Her heterochromia – the blue and the brown – made her look like she came from outer space.

'But I don't think I have a centre. I'm not even sure if there is such a thing as "me".'

'Oh, Daisy.' Jay tossed her cigarette and reached for the woman. Daisy pulled back.

'Daisy isn't even my real name. It was just the name they gave me.'

'What do you mean? Who?'

'The Fishers. The people who made me. I didn't have a name until I was five. Up to then I just had a number.'

Jay looked at her. At the girl who seemed to be only half in the present. It would have been better if Daisy had been crying, Jay thought. If there had been big slugs of tears leaking out of her eyes and sliding down her cheeks. Because then she might have been able to wipe them away, maybe hold her. Maybe help. Instead, there were just two different-coloured eyes, dry and dead and broken. Butterfly eyes, gassed and pinned to her face and left to desiccate.

Daisy blinked. 'They called me "fish",' she said, her voice flat and old and almost too quiet to hear. Jay saw a ruby jewel of blood slip down from her lip where Daisy was biting it; an alternative to tears. Deeper and thicker and harder to fathom.

'Don't,' she said softly. 'Don't hurt yourself, Daisy.'

'Why not? How else am I going to know I'm real?'

Jay stared at her, helpless.

26

23RD OCTOBER

Jay was sitting on Daisy's mattress. She was propped up against the internal wall watching her friend.

'I don't have too many memories of my childhood,' said Daisy. She had her back to Jay. She had taken off her coat, revealing a dark grey T-shirt, darker still where she had sweated between her shoulder blades. Jay could see the fine scars poking out of the neck of the garment, criss-crossing her skin like someone had covered her in a pain web. 'Little snatches, that's all. Like songs on the radio, when it goes in and out of signal. Do you know what I mean? Or like when you put on headphones to keep the world out, but little pieces of it seep in. Like a leaking bucket, only in reverse. Filling up instead of emptying out.'

Daisy was drawing on the whiteboard in her bedroom. It took Jay a minute to realise what it was. A portable radio, with headphones attached by a wire. Like a Walkman. Underneath she had written something, but the writing was too spidery for Jay to decipher without getting up and going nearer, and she didn't want to stop Daisy. Disturb her. It was like the woman was unwinding.

Girl:Broken

'Radios don't go out of signal anymore, Daisy,' said Jay. 'Everything is digital. They just buffer. Either there or not there.'

Daisy shrugged without turning around and continued drawing. Jay was finding it difficult to breathe.

'Whatever. Back then, they went out of signal. Or white noise would come through like it was snowing inside the radio. Or maybe it was the batteries running down. One of the first memories I have was my mother getting all her hair cut off, singing along to that song by Culture Club.'

'"Do You Really Want to Hurt Me?"' said Jay softly.

No wonder Daisy had exploded all over the therapist. It must have triggered something from her past. What the fuck had the woman thought she was doing?

Daisy ignored her like she wasn't there. 'I don't know how old I was. We never celebrated birthdays. Except the one where we were branded the first time.'

'Where were you living, Daisy?' Jay spoke quietly, like she was in a room of sleeping children. The word 'branded' felt like a stone dropped in a poisoned pond.

'I don't know. It had a big garden. In the summer I used to like sitting under the apple tree and watching the ants.'

Daisy paused, like the memory had overloaded her. After they had come into the apartment Daisy had dislocated. Gone into another place within herself. Jay felt like she was an observer of the inside of Daisy's head.

'I'm going to take a shower. Will you pour me some water?' she asked, before disappearing.

Jay watched as she left the room. Walked out into the corridor with steps that looked like she had learnt them from a book. Jay wanted to go outside right then. Phone her boss and tell her it was over. She couldn't do this anymore. Tell her that she thought Daisy was about to crack open. That she needed to bring her in for proper medical care.

But then she didn't want to leave Daisy alone. She seemed so fragile. Instead, she walked into the kitchen/living room and began looking in the doorless cupboards. Most were empty, but in one she found a stack of plastic cups. She removed two and filled them with water from the tap. Then she walked out of the living room and into the hall. Daisy was still in the shower so she placed the cups down carefully on the floor and walked to the flat entrance door. Undoing the locks she stepped out onto the landing and checked her phone for a signal. In her peripheral vision, she saw the door opposite close. The nosey neighbour. Jay made a mental note to question him later. Ask him if he'd seen anything unusual.

Like someone breaking into Daisy's flat maybe.

Or perhaps Daisy breaking out, she thought grimly.

She checked her phone.

Seeing full bars she typed out a message to Slane. She told her about the therapist, and the memories bleeding through from the past. She asked for assistance, explaining that she was out of her depth. No longer in control. Then she snapped the phone shut and went back inside. Jay picked up the cups, took a deep breath, and walked in.

Daisy was back, drawing on the whiteboard. Pouring out her pain.

'The memories are coming back. The garden wall was really high, and the only window I could look out of was the ground floor. But it was one of those houses where the garden was higher than the front of the house, so it kind of started halfway up the window. There was a sort of narrow run around the house at the back. Like a bank.'

Jay was momentarily confused, then realised Daisy was still talking about when she was young.

It took Jay a second to realise what she was drawing. It was

Girl:Broken

the mermaid from the phone. The tattoo that had been sent to her.

Jesus, was it only this morning? she wondered.

As Daisy drew, reaching up to complete the hair on her picture, her T-shirt rode up. On her skin, just above her boxers, Jay could see a smudge of blue. The mermaid Daisy had shown her earlier. They were clearly the same.

'Oh, Daisy,' she whispered, feeling tears form behind her eyes.

The old tattoo, older than could possibly be legal. Put on her as a stamp of ownership.

'I used to watch rats running in that little gap. The people in the house just put the bin bags outside, and the rats would come and gnaw at them. Every few weeks one of the Housemen would come and clear away the bags. Hose down the paving in the little gap. Then it would start again. The rubbish taken out. Old food. Fish and chip wrappers. Then the rats. Then the gnawing. I had a lot of time to watch.'

'Didn't you go to school? Didn't social services come round?'

'I don't think I even existed. Not on any record. My mum said I was made just for the house. That I was their mermaid. Their special magical creature that only they were allowed to see. And I think they were squatting, so no landlord or anything.'

Jay felt sick. She wanted to go to Daisy, and she wanted to run away, and she wanted to scream and hit someone. The men from Daisy's past maybe. Or Daisy's 'mother'. She'd waited so long for Daisy to open up; to break through, and now she didn't know what to do except listen.

'I had lots of free time. So I used to play games. Play games in my head. For hours and hours. Days and days. Isn't it funny how days seem to last forever when you're young? There was one of those portable cassette recorders in the house. It had headphones. Sometimes they let me wear them while I was being... changed.' Daisy spat the word out like it was poison. 'That was the best. It belonged to one of my catchers. One of The Fishermen. The one who marked us. He gave it to me as a present for my birthing day. I was listening to it when he did this.'

Daisy pulled neck of her T-shirt, exposing her shoulder.

Jay gasped.

The number '5' was scarified into her flesh, the scar a livid piece of knotted burn tissue. It was old and white, the skin red around it. Jay had no idea how much it must have hurt. How much Daisy must have screamed while the music played in her head, separating her.

Watching Daisy was like watching time shattering. Like watching the ghost of a little girl in a woman's body. Everything seemed to be coalescing into a singularity of pain and loss.

Although you can't lose something you never had, thought Jay, feeling the tears that slugged down her face, heavy and full.

'Changed?' she whispered. 'How were you changed?'

She didn't want to know, but she had to ask. She owed Daisy that.

'Into the Mermaid. There was a procedure. A becoming.'

Daisy put the finishing touches to her drawing, the line and the hook.

'It was...' Daisy paused in her work, looking up and to her left, as if searching for the right word or phrase. 'Unintelligible to me as a child. I know what it was now, of course. But back then... I don't know. I suppose I shattered; put myself in pieces. Tried to make everything work by making nothing real. When they did what they did to me. The physical things. I tried to pretend they were monsters. And that made it better. Because if I thought they were real people, the people I was with all the time, then I would have had no hope. No escape. So it was better if they were monsters. If they let me wear the headphones it was like I was on a ship.'

Jay felt a stab of pain and looked down at her hands. She was amazed to see that she had been clenching so hard that she had drawn blood. Perfect crescents of pierced skin on the mound of her thumb.

'Oh, Daisy,' whispered Jay again, so quietly that it caught in her throat. Never made it into the room. She tried again.

'Where was your mother? Why didn't she stop it?'

'My mother?' Daisy's face was a poppy field. Everything was dead and remembered at the same time.

'My mother was the one with the power. She was the one who controlled it all. I think I'll never stop dying, inside, from what she did to me. What she's still doing to me.'

Jay opened her arms, and Daisy fell into them, finally allowing the tears to come. Jay stroked her hair, feeling the woman's body break against her, like a tide that had been held back for far too long.

After what seemed an age, the crying slowed, and Jay laid her down on her bed. She felt so tired. Why did she feel so tired all of a sudden? Her friend needed her and she could barely keep her eyes open. She supposed it was the emotional release.

She lay down next to Daisy and stroked her hair.

'It's all right. I'm going to look after you now. It's going to be all right.'

The last thing Jay heard as she fell unconscious was Daisy's voice, soaked in sleep.

'Jay? When you came back in. Did you remember to lock the door?'

27

23RD OCTOBER: LATER

Daisy woke up wrong. She was sprawled on her mattress, shivering and light-headed. At least she supposed it was her mattress; her memories were flags, fluttering in the wind. She kept her eyes closed, trying to listen to the ticking of her apartment; work out what was off-kilter. Tried to remember what had happened before she went to sleep.

She bit her lip, tasting salt and lemons. The residue of evaporated tears and confessions. The air was thick; a storm yet to happen. There was a high smell of old pennies, a smell that tugged at her, triggering alarm bells in her brain. In her body. Fight or flight. She could feel the material of her boxers and T-shirt sticking to her skin with cold sweat.

Daisy opened her eyes.

The room was dark, with a wash of red and blue light metronomically illuminating the wall. The images she'd drawn the previous day on the whiteboard seemed to appear, then disappear, as the light stuttered; a sped-up lighthouse of warning.

Daisy felt wrong, dislocated like she'd been mind-mugged,

or someone had climbed inside her head and used it for a funhouse. She tried to concentrate.

Jay.

Somewhere deep in the apartment complex, Daisy heard the faint sound of a buzzer, signalling a door opening. The mattress beneath her felt damp. Damp and cold and a million miles away from where she wanted to be. There was a weight on her back. Limp and still and warm.

Jay, she remembered. She'd lain down next to her. Protected her. Tried to make her feel safe.

Daisy could feel Jay's arm on her side. Her hand circling her waist. The trickle of liquid sliding from the fingers and across her belly, following the line of her boxers. Daisy held her own hand in front of her face. Even in the strange repeating light, she could tell. Even in the fug of her mind.

It was covered in blood.

Daisy felt like her head was full of insects. Stuffed full. Overfull. So full they were creating pressure, but there was nowhere to go. All they could do was click and buzz. Gently, Daisy reached round and down and lifted Jay's arm off her. There was no resistance. Daisy got up. As she separated from the bed there was a slight ripping sound; the skin unsticking from the sheet. Daisy stayed staring straight ahead, not letting the fear-spiders out of her head. She concentrated on counting.

Breaths. The revolution of the red and blue light. The sound of steps being climbed from the lobby.

Jay's phone was by the side of the mattress, its screen glowing.

'Jay?' The word sounded like it came from someone else. It was faltering and hopeless and didn't sound like a question. The smartphone's glow seemed, somehow, to be all she could concentrate on. She looked at the words on the small screen. It was a text conversation to the emergency services.

my name is daisy and they're going to kill me.

    Daisy's face crinkled in confusion as she read her name.

not just me. the policewoman. Jay

    Policewoman? Daisy's head hurt. She couldn't turn around. See what was on the bed behind her.

999: we have a fix on you. If you are in danger please find a secure place to hide

so much blood. where can I hide?

999: somewhere safe. Can you state your name?

daisy. please come. I think she is dead

999: who? What is the emergency?

I don't think she's breathing

999: is there someone with you? Are you in danger?

you need to come. now. fast

999: what is your emergency?

    Daisy let the phone fall from her hand. She didn't hear the sound it made when it hit the wooden floor. The buzzing was too loud. Too loud but also far away. She turned around, twisting her upper body so she could see the bed behind her. See Jay. Daisy's breath caught, and she blinked slowly.

Jay was a horror film. Her hair was stuck to her face in strands. Stuck by blood, Daisy guessed. Some liquid that should be inside the body, not outside. Her face was swollen. Her clothes were soaked in rust. Except it wasn't rust. One of her legs seemed to be at a strange angle.

'Jay,' Daisy whispered. She didn't cry. She was pretty sure she had no tears left. She just stared at Jay's ruined body.

'I'm so sorry,' she said. In the back of her mind, she heard the pattern of the building. The people outside. She felt disembodied. Someone who could only watch events. Not control. Not change. She looked on as her hand reached forward. Stroked the face of her friend. Gentle, gentle strokes, brushing the sticky hair from her face. Jay's mouth was slightly open, with a span of saliva across the entrance, like the skin of a drum. As Daisy watched, the skin rose, became concave, then popped.

Daisy stopped stroking. Blinked. Felt the flesh beneath her hand.

Warm.

Saw the cuts around Jay's neck.

Bleeding. Still bleeding.

Watched as the bubble of saliva formed, then again popped.

Breathing.

Alive.

Daisy stared at her.

Red. Blue. Black. Red. Blue. Black. The light washed over the wall like a tide. She leant forward and kissed Jay's hand.

'I'll be back,' she whispered. 'I'll be back for you.'

And then she grabbed her clothes from the floor and ran.

When the emergency services kicked the door in, five minutes later, they found Jay beaten but alive. Outside, through the open window, the storm finally broke, and the skies started screaming water onto the concrete pavement.

28

3RD NOVEMBER

Joseph pulled the phone out of his pocket and pressed the green button, putting the device to his ear.

'Good morning, Professor Skinner, can I help you? Oh, Mark! How are you?' Joseph held the phone away from his ear and covered the mouthpiece. 'It's my son, Mark. I won't be a moment.'

Slane smiled and nodded, but didn't get up to give him privacy. Collins stood and went to talk with Grant. Joseph continued with his phone call.

'Where are you? Are you studying hard?' He listened to the answer. 'That's great. Well, I've been tied up here too, but I haven't forgotten.' He glanced at his watch and frowned. 'No, of *course* I'll make it! Calm down, Mark, I'm only...' Joseph looked at Slane and whispered, 'City centre?'

She held up one hand, fingers splayed. Joseph nodded his thanks. 'Five minutes away. Once the cut is done I'll get the barber to take a picture and send it to you as proof, okay?'

Joseph smiled and nodded. 'Right. I've got to go, Mark, but we'll meet up for tea later. Say six, tonight? Great. See you later. I love you.'

Joseph ended the call, frowning at the screen as he did so.

'Hardly any charge left.' He turned to the detectives. 'Look, I'm really sorry, but I've got to go. Mark...' Joseph paused, his expression clearly trying to work out how to put into words the importance of making the appointment.

'It's okay, Joseph. Grant will drive you there, and then meet you after, and bring you back. That is if you wish to. There's no obligation.'

'You still haven't told me what you want. Presumably you have this poor girl, Daisy, under surveillance?'

'We did, but then she half-killed our operative and absconded,' said Slane. 'Now we have no idea where she is.'

Joseph looked at the officers.

'You're kidding me.'

'Sadly not. Thus far she has put two people in hospital – a police officer and a therapist – and two people in the morgue. Daisy is a bomb, professor. The Fishermen shaped and primed her years ago, and now she's gone off.'

'Like a sleeper,' he mused.

'Exactly. And what we need you to do is retro engineer her.'

'I'm sorry?'

'We need to find her, Joseph, urgently. And to do that we need to understand her. We need someone to take all the information we have and convert it into a map. A way of decoding where she might be. What she might do.'

'If you want the job, that is,' chimed in Collins.

'Are you kidding me?' Joseph said. 'You're basically giving me the opportunity of my academic career! To study a product of The Fishermen...'

'Plus the chance to help save a young person from doing more damage,' reminded Slane.

'Yes, of course,' said Joseph. 'And you can get all the data together for when I come back? Where Daisy has been visiting?

The towns she was in beforehand? What she looked up in the internet cafés? Everything you can about her "becoming"?'

Grant had already donned his jacket and was holding Joseph's coat open. Joseph nodded in thanks.

'It will all be waiting for you, along with a complete psychological profile of the officer. We think they may have developed a bond. We think Daisy may in fact still be in touch.'

'Really? What does he say about it? The officer?'

Slane smiled thinly. 'She. And she's not saying very much at the moment. We'll explain it all when you come back. We've booked you into the Nesser Hotel for two nights. If it takes longer then we will extend, of course.'

'And you'll pay my consultancy fee? I'm sorry I have to ask, but I'll have to get Hilda to cancel my engagements.'

Slane waved her hand dismissively. 'If you give Grant your details it will be in your bank account by the time you return.'

Joseph nodded. 'Great. Then I'm in.'

∼

Slane watched as the two men left. Once the door had closed she turned to Collins. 'What do you think?'

'I think he's an arsehole.' Collins sipped his drink, swallowed and grimaced. 'But then, academics always are.'

'Yes, but what do you think, with regard to us?'

Collins looked at her and smiled. It was not a pleasant smile. 'I think he'll do nicely.'

Slane nodded. 'Yes. But I still got Grant to slip a tracker in Skinner's coat. I want to make sure he does what he says he's doing. Autistic son or not; the information we fed him should set him on fire.'

Collins shrugged. 'Grant needed to go in anyhow. It's odd we haven't heard back from Lawrence. Fielding looked in the tattooist's, but no go. She's gone to the flat, to see if he left a message there.'

'Let's hope he's found her. Found them both. Then we can put an end to this fuck-up.'

Collins smiled. 'Amen to that.'

∽

Joseph sat in the front passenger seat, next to Grant. If anything, the rain was harder now, the windscreen wipers metronoming their journey into Leeds city centre. Joseph casually looked at the streets as they drove past.

'How long have you worked with the unit?' Joseph asked the driver, making conversation.

'I'm sorry, sir.' Grant kept his dead eyes on the road; he didn't sound sorry at all. 'I'm not permitted to discuss the case, or any aspects of the investigation. That includes operational structures and personnel.'

'Right,' said Joseph, blinking. 'That's me told then.' He pulled his phone out of his jacket. 'I'll just let Mark know that – damn!' The phone was dead, completely out of charge. He shook it, as if that might make it work. 'Bugger.' He turned slightly toward the driver. 'I don't suppose I could borrow yours, could I?'

'Sorry. For work use, I'm afraid. All our calls are logged and checked.'

Joseph sighed. 'Fair enough.'

They spent the last few minutes of the drive in silence. When eventually they pulled up outside of the Corn Exchange, Joseph said, 'Shall I meet you back here in an hour? Or if you give me the address of the incident building I could get a taxi.'

Grant shook his head. 'I'll meet you here. One hour long enough?'

Joseph smiled sadly and patted his hair. 'Yes, I'm afraid it is. There isn't much to cut, these days.' Joseph unbuckled the seat belt and opened the door. Unlike the rear, the front door had a handle on the inside. He hauled himself out. Just before shutting the door, he paused, then bent down to address the detective. 'I might nip into the market.' He pointed at the indoor market across the road. 'I was in there early this morning; there was one of those phone kiosks. Do you think they might stock chargers that would fit my phone?'

The driver shrugged. 'No idea, sir.'

'Worth a try. See you back here in an hour.' He shut the door and watched as the car pulled away and drove along Duncan Street, in the direction of the Corn Exchange. Joseph stayed watching a moment, then crossed the road and entered the narrow alley of Central Arcade, heading for King Koby's hair salon. As he did, he took his phone out of his pocket. He flipped the power button, turning the device on. Despite what he had said to the officer, it still had some life. He dialled a number.

'It's me,' he said when it was answered.

'Of course it's fucking you. Who else would it be?' said the agitated voice on the other end.

Joseph smiled. 'You know you swear too much?'

'No I don't. I swear just the right amount. What do you think of Slane?'

Joseph's smile slipped off his face as the image of the little girl being burnt flicked across his vision.

'I think you're right. She's as evil as they come.'

End of Part One

PART II

JAY

29

25TH OCTOBER

'Jay? Jay, are you awake?'

The voice was weak but insistent... like it came from far away but was running fast. It created an itch in her head like someone was scratching her brain. Jay decided to ignore it and burrowed deeper into sleep.

'Jay. Can she hear me?' Louder this time. 'You said she should be coming round. Are you sure she can hear me?'

'There's no physical reason why not. The injuries are severe, but none should affect her hearing.'

This voice was different. Jay liked it. There was a warmth to it, and a certainty that was reassuring. A man's voice. Nurse? Doctor?

Jay broke into consciousness and became aware of her body like she'd gatecrashed a bad party: she immediately wanted to leave. She tried to open her eyes but then gasped as the light hit them. A river of pain burst its banks in her chest and leg. She wanted to get up, to flee, but she thought if she moved she might vomit.

'What injuries?' she croaked.

'Excellent!' the male voice said. 'Welcome back to the land of the living, Ms Starling. Please don't try to move or open your eyes. Would you like some water?'

'Thank God! I'm sorry, Jay, but you've been in the wars. You were knocked unconscious during the attack. The doctors have said that there is no permanent brain damage, but you're going to feel a bit battered for a few days.' The female voice again. Not a doctor.

Jay kept her eyes closed, trying to place the voice. Her head felt like it had gone through a tumble dryer. She was having trouble making connections.

'Where the fuck am I?' she said, then winced. Her throat felt like it had been sandpapered. She felt a hand behind her head, lifting it. A few moments later a straw was placed in her mouth. She sucked gratefully, feeling the cold liquid ease the pain. After a few gulps it was removed.

'Slowly. You've been nil by mouth, so we'll have to wean you back on. Liquids, to begin with. My name is Doctor Malik. Do you understand what I am saying to you?'

Jay ignored him and moved her fingers, feeling the hospital bed beneath her. At least she guessed it was a hospital bed. She definitely wasn't at home. The sheet was thin and scratchy, and felt like it would combust if she moved her hand across it too fast. She breathed in slowly, through her nose.

'Yes, I understand you. Jesus fucking Christ, I hurt,' she rasped. The water had helped, but her mouth still felt like someone had stored a vacuum cleaner in it. Switched on.

'Try not to talk yet. We've been swabbing your mouth to keep it moist, but even so it will feel strange.'

'No fucking shit,' said Jay, ignoring the voice's advice. She was pleased to find her own a little stronger.

'Also, try not to swear. I'll leave you in the nurse's capable hands and come back when she's settled you. I'll do a proper assessment then.'

'Where am I?' Jay licked her lips, feeling the cracks.

'Leeds General, love. How are you fettling?' A third voice. Female, but different. Kind. Northern. Leeds vowels. A nurse, Jay guessed. Too kind to be a doctor. 'Brain a bit big for the skull, is it? Just think of it as the Devil's hangover!' The woman cackled, the sound slightly wheezy.

Definitely a nurse. The familiarity of the language. The dark humour. The tiredness at the edge of her voice like a tide coming in.

Jay nodded carefully, her vision clearing with each second. 'I can do that. Could you bring me a vodka? That's what I normally do to cure it.'

Her weak joke earned her a chuckle. 'Try not to move, love. Your face looks like it's been clogged on.'

'A boot will do that,' said the other woman.

Inspector Slane, Jay's battered brain supplied the name. Her boss. The police inspector who ran her undercover operation.

Jay turned and looked at her. The woman's face was full of concern.

'What do you remember, Jay? When we arrived the uniforms were already there. They had received a 999 and broken down the door.'

Despite the blurred vision, Jay could see something off about Slane. Like she was annoyed rather than concerned. Like she was only just containing her anger.

'I don't know; it's all jumbled up.'

Images swirled in Jay's brain.

Daisy beating up the therapist.

Her mother angry at her when she'd been suspended from the force, Jay unable to tell her it was a subterfuge.

Barefaced lying to her work colleagues when she'd gone undercover for Slane.

All the deceit with Daisy.

The phone with the mermaid image lying broken on the woman's living room floor like an insect that had been stamped on again and again.

'Daisy,' she said.

'Missing. When the emergency services broke down the door she'd already gone out of the window.'

'What?'

Jay finally focused on her boss. The woman stared down at her, tramlines of worry on her face.

'What do you remember, Jay? Daisy beat you half to death. Did she find out you were a police officer? Is that why she did this and ran?'

'What?' she said again, her thoughts snagging on images and half-memories. 'Daisy didn't... she was telling me... she couldn't...'

The words dried up as the image of Daisy astride the therapist returned.

Slane held her gaze. 'I'm afraid she did. So badly the paramedics actually thought you were dead. And we're worried that she might hurt somebody else: has already done, in fact.'

Jay couldn't process. The more she came to, the more pain she was in. 'Fuck,' she whispered.

'What?' Slane. 'Do you remember something?'

Jay shook her head. Slowly. 'Sorry. Everything is still messed up. Daisy was a mess. The therapy session had really upset her.'

Slane snorted. 'Not as much as she upset the therapist. I've seen the footage. If you hadn't pulled her off we could be looking at another murder.'

Jay was hurting. Her body felt like someone had used it for scrubbing down an abattoir. Her ribs hurt and her head hurt and her heart simply couldn't relate to what her boss was saying. That Daisy had assaulted her for some reason. That she had... what, had some sort of episode?

Daisy's words came back to her. *I have these blackouts. Like I'm sleepwalking or something.*

Jay turned and looked at Slane. 'What do you mean, another murder?'

Slane glanced at the doctor and nurse, clearly uncomfortable. 'It seems that Daisy might be responsible for the murder of a homeless man a month ago. Possibly the murder of the witness to the murder too.'

'I don't believe it,' said Jay flatly.

Slane said nothing, merely stared at her, concern on her face.

'Right!' said the nurse, brightly, slipping a rubber sleeve over Jay's arm. 'This might feel a bit tight.' She flicked a switch and Jay felt pressure as the tube expanded. 'Used to have a load here back in the nineties. Always very polite. Just wanted a better world,' the nurse said amiably. 'The way it is now I think they had it about right. Maybe it's time for them to make a comeback.'

She paused while she looked at the machine. Then smiled at Jay. 'Only maybe with more personal hygiene. All good on the blood pressure front!'

'Sorry, but what are you talking about?' said Slane. There was a slight sneer to her that the nurse chose to ignore.

'Crusties!' She beamed, pointing at Jay's dreads, with their metal skull sleeves. Then she looked at Slane and stopped smiling. 'Now the officer's awake the doctor will want to do a full assessment and judge what pain management she requires. I'll let you know when she is well enough for visitors.'

'I don't–' began Slane, but the nurse was having none of it. 'My ward, my rules. No more questions until the doctor has seen her. Girl's had a nasty head trauma! Ribs prob'ly cracked too. Not to mention the knee. Lucky to be alive and still with most of her marbles, she is! Let her rest, let the specialist see her, and then we can make a visiting plan. Till then back off, okay?' A steel timbre had come into the nurse's voice and her body language seemed to have weaponised. Not just any nurse, thought Jay. Head nurse, or maybe Sister. Jay silently thanked her, wondering how much compassion she could convey with a few blinks and a wiggle of her dreads. Enough, apparently, because the nurse winked at her and began shutting the curtain around the bed.

'Just make sure you think of what happened that night, when Daisy hit you. Try to remember, Jay. It's important,' said Slane. Getting the last word in before the curtain closed.

'She wouldn't,' Jay whispered again, but this time not out of doubt, but gentleness. She thought of the way Daisy had lain down next to her, pressing herself against her like a second skin.

Jay opened her eyes, remembering the last thing Daisy had said to her.

Did you lock the door?

Jay thought back, through the jumble. Through the fog of the beating and the weirdness of the drawings and the horror of what Daisy was telling her about her childhood. Thought back, catalogued, separated and dialled into her actions.

Jay blinked.

'I'm not sure,' she said. 'But I don't think so. I don't think I did.'

Then she closed her eyes and went to sleep.

30

28TH OCTOBER

'Hello, Jay. My name is Doctor Hall. How do you feel about me removing the strapping around your ribs?'

'I don't know, Doctor Hall. How do you feel about me screaming in agony, then hitting you?'

The specialist, who looked about twelve to Jay, laughed nervously.

'Really, Miss... um, Jay, as I'm sure you know the hospital comes down very hard on the mistreatment of its sta–'

Jay smiled at him.

'Oh, you're joking,' he said, his tone mildly disapproving.

'Yes, sorry. It's how I relieve tension. Tell me. Are you quite blurry in real life?'

'I beg your pardon?'

'My vision,' she explained. 'Everything's still a bit fuzzy, doctor.'

'Oh, I see! Of course! Well, you received a blunt force trauma to the side of the head,' he tapped his own head, just above the temple. 'So it's only to be expected, really. You'll find that in a day or two the vision should settle down and you will make a full recovery.'

Jay felt relief flush through her. 'Thank fuck for that.'

The specialist wrinkled his nose at the cussing, but let it pass. 'Actually, you were very lucky.'

'Really? I don't feel lucky. I feel like I've been run over.'

Jay touched her head, feeling stitching and ripped flesh. The lump felt enormous under her fingers.

'Oh you are!' said the doctor happily. 'If the blow had been any harder there is a good chance you would have been dead.'

Jay stopped feeling her head and looked at him. 'You're shitting me?'

'Please don't swear. And no, I'm not. That particular area is a weak spot, and one good kick can traumatise the brain to a fatal degree. Whoever did this to you had serious intentions on your life. You really are very lucky.'

An image of Daisy, barefooted, drawing on her whiteboard, flashed through Jay's mind.

'I'm sorry for the swearing. I'll try not to do it again. Can you tell what size?'

'Size?'

'The shoe. Is there an imprint or something on my head? Can you tell what size boot it was that kicked my head in?'

'Ah, I understand.' The specialist looked at Jay's head thoughtfully. 'That's not the sort of question we normally get asked. Will I have brain damage? How bad is the scarring? Those are more the sort of thing.'

'How bad *is* the scarring,' she asked, interested. 'Am I going to have like a cool sci-fi rip in my head?'

'Do you *want* a cool sci-fi rip in your head?'

'Who wouldn't? The girls will go wild.'

Doctor Hall blinked, then smiled. 'Let's check the ribs out first, shall we?'

'You didn't answer my question. About the boot size.'

'Right.' He looked at her head again. 'From the head trauma

I can only really tell you about the front of the boot. It must have been steel-toe-capped because of the damage. I can't tell the size though.'

Jay sighed.

'However, as whoever attacked you also stamped repeatedly on your chest, cracking your ribs, I can safely say the indent formed is around an eight.'

Jay blinked, seeing Daisy's small bare feet again, no more than a size five.

'Maybe a nine.'

She turned and treated the doctor to a dazzling smile.

'You're right; I am lucky. You can remove the strapping now, I promise I won't hit you.'

∼

'The doctors say the leg isn't broken and that you should be able to walk without the crutches in a day or two. Three at the outside.' Slane was pacing the room, occasionally glancing at Jay.

'Fab, then I'll be able to lurch around the room like a zombie. Where's Daisy?'

'I've already told you, Jay, we don't know.' Slane spoke slowly, as if talking to a child. 'When the uniforms arrived she had already gone.'

'But if she'd done this...' Jay pointed at her injuries. 'She must have been covered in blood. There would be biological data points all over the window. The fire escape. You must be able to tell where she went.'

Slane shook her head, clearly frustrated. 'You'd think, wouldn't you? She went out of the window; it's the only explanation. The door was not only locked but bolted from the inside. The officers had to use a battering ram to break it down. So the only way she could have left is through the window.'

'Why were they even there?' said Jay. 'The uniforms? If Daisy assaulted me and then ran, why did she call the police?'

'She didn't,' said Slane, surprised. 'The call was phoned in by a neighbour. He heard screaming, a fight he thought, and dialled 999. Why would you think she called the police?'

Jay touched her head, shaking it slowly. 'I just assumed. I can't believe she'd–'

'I'm sorry, Jay.'

Slane stopped pacing and sat by her bed.

'It's my fault. When we recruited you for surveillance of Daisy I never realised she was so disturbed. I should have, of course. God knows after what was done to her it's not surprising, but we just didn't understand.'

'And what was done to her, exactly? She was beginning to tell me that last day. About the house she was kept in when she was a child. The Fishermen.'

Slane gazed intently at her. There was an eagerness in her expression. 'So you said in your last message. The one you sent before...' Slane nodded at Jay's injuries. 'Can you remember what she told you? Did she remember any of the cult members? We think she must have seen one of them; someone who survived somehow. We think that's what must have ignited her psychosis.'

Jay shook her head. 'Sorry, I can only remember snatches. Daisy drawing a mermaid. Something about a song.'

Slane sighed and nodded, standing. 'Well, hopefully, as you recover, more of your memory will return. Until then you should rest.'

'Why is there a guard outside my door?'

Slane wrinkled her brow in confusion. 'I'm sorry?'

'The policeman. I see him standing there when the doctors and nurses come in. Why is he there?'

'Grant? I know you don't want to accept it, Jay, but Daisy is a very sick woman. She nearly killed you, and we have no idea where she is. The fact that she had evaded us for so long means she's resourceful. There is a chance she may come here.'

'You think I'm in danger?'

Slane took a step forward. 'Jay, we've already messed up and put you in jeopardy once. I don't intend to do it again. Once you're fit enough we'll move you to a safe environment. Until then...' She smiled and shrugged.

Jay nodded. 'Do you know what happened to my phone?'

Slane paused and looked at her. Jay thought there was a slight calculating coldness in her gaze.

'It wasn't with you. We think Daisy must have taken it.'

'And the other phone? The one she threw against the wall?'

'We're having our tech guys analyse it. See if there is anything salvageable.'

Jay nodded and sighed, closing her eyes. 'I'm tired now, and my vision is blurred. I'd like to rest, if that's okay?'

'Oh, of course you must be. I'll leave you now. But if you do remember anything...'

'I'll let Grant at the door know.' Jay smiled wanly.

Once Slane had left, the smile slipped off Jay's face like it had been pushed.

With great effort she climbed out of bed and limped to the little sink, leaving her crutches by the bedside table. She tried a few gentle exercises, holding on to the sink. Her knee hurt, but it was bearable, especially with the pills the doctor had prescribed her. Gritting her teeth, Jay walked to the bed and back, limping badly, but still mobile.

When she got back to the sink she poured a glass of water and sipped at it thoughtfully, looking at herself in the mirror. After a few minutes she limped back to the bed and sat down. She opened the bedside drawer and took out her smart pocket watch. Slane had said her phone had gone, presumably taken by Daisy, but the woman clearly hadn't known she had an ancillary unit. She supposed she wouldn't associate the fob watch with a connected device. Had she known, she would have understood that Jay could read any texts that had been sent to or from her phone.

She reread the message sent just before the police had come. The message sent from her phone while she lay unconscious in a bolted flat.

my name is daisy and they're going to kill me.

not just me. the policewoman. Jay

999: we have a fix on you. If you are in danger please find a secure place to hide

so much blood. where can I hide?

999: somewhere safe. Can you state your name?

daisy. please come. I think she is dead

999: who? What is the emergency?

I don't think she's breathing

999: is there someone with you? Are you in danger?

you need to come. now. fast

999: what is your emergency?

Jay read through the text thread, trying to make sense of it. Why had Slane lied? Why had she said Daisy hadn't called the police? And why had she said Daisy had beaten her up?

Jay lay back down on the bed and thought about the guard on the door. Thought about whether it was to keep Daisy out, or to keep her in.

As she fell asleep another thought came to her as well.

Maybe I'm in danger.

∼

'You never explained to me what put you onto Daisy in the first place. Why it was so important to keep the surveillance secret.'

Slane sighed as if the question bored her. The inspector had become more and more distant as Jay asked her questions.

'I'm afraid it's a little above your clearance level, Constable. Especially as you're no longer an active player in the operation.'

'What operation? As far as I can see, without Daisy there is no operation.'

Slane smiled thinly. 'There are several other lines of enquiry. We are chasing down suspect internet searches carried out in various spots around the city centre. Cafés. Libraries.'

'She doesn't know how to use the internet.'

'So she told you. We believe differently. It was internet traffic that first identified her. That and...'

'And what?'

'Like I said. Above your clearance.'

'Why haven't the police come to see me?'

Slane paused.

'I'm not sure what you mean, Jay. We are the police.'

'I mean the uniformed police. The regular police.'

'This investigation is very sensitive. There is a public protection dimension to the information surrounding it. That's why you had to sign the non-disclosure form when you joined us.'

'Right.'

Jay rubbed a hand across her face.

'Sorry. The pain makes me grouchy, and the pills make me fuzzy. Between them I keep on forgetting things.'

Like Daisy, she thought.

'I understand.' Slane switched on one of her smiles. 'But don't worry. Grant – the guard who's protecting you – has gone to check out a safe house. We'll be moving you tonight. Once you're there you'll be completely secure.'

Slane's smile got wider. 'Nobody will know where you are.'

Jay felt a chill of fear spread through her. 'Who's guarding me now, if Grant has gone off to check out this safe house?'

'Don't worry. We've hired one of the hospital security, *pro tem*. No one will get through.'

And I bet I won't get out, thought Jay, grimly.

'That's good news,' was all she said.

Slane stood. 'Try to get some rest, Jay. Hopefully, by tomorrow you'll be clear-headed and we'll do a proper interrogation, and this will all be over.'

Slane nodded once, smiled, and left. Jay decided it was the first real smile she'd seen her do, and it filled her with dread. As did the use of the word 'proper': it conjured up images of hot coals.

'I don't trust you a fucking inch,' she whispered.

∼

'That's the first I've heard of it. I'm sure you must be mistaken.' Doctor Hall looked at her in surprise, one eyebrow raised. Jay was impressed and wondered if he practised in front of a mirror. He had come in to change the dressing on her ribs. She nodded.

'That's what she said. Apparently, I'm being taken off-ward tonight. Somewhere more secure.'

'No one's informed me. I shall have to–'

'Don't worry. I probably got the wrong end of the stick,' she said, cutting him off. 'I don't suppose you could arrange for a wheelchair to be sent up here?' She pulled open her drawer. Inside was a home-rolled cigarette she'd bummed off the nurse. 'I've given up. Decided to make a clean break after the, um, incident. This is the only one I have. Now I know that I'm not going to die, I thought I might...?'

If the surgeon disapproved he hid it well. 'I'm sure that can be arranged, Jay.' Doctor Hall stood. 'I am really pleased with your recovery. But you don't really need to be pushed–'

'I know, Liam, but it would make me feel special.' He looked at her quizzically.

'How did you know my na–'

'Name tag.'

He looked down at his name tag, containing his details and hospital ID.

'Oh. Right. Then good. I'm on nights as well today. I'll come in and check on you later.' He smiled distractedly and walked towards the door.

'Hey, Liam?'

'Yes?'

'I'm interested. Were my bloods done when I was brought in?'

'Your bloods? What do you mean?'

'When I arrived, I guess it was by ambulance?'

'Yes.'

'And Inspector Slane turned up later? Not with the police who came with the medics?'

'That's right.'

'I'm guessing no one knew what had happened to me at that time? That all avenues must have been considered?'

'What are you getting at, Jay?'

Jay held his gaze.

'I'm just wondering if my blood was checked for drugs. In case there had been foul play. Surely that would have been done. Check for rape drugs and whatnot?'

'I'm not sure,' he said after a long beat. 'I'll check.'

31

29TH OCTOBER

'What the fuck do you think's going to happen? Someone's going to come along and kidnap the wheelchair-bound hot lesbian chick in a nightie and waistcoat from the front of the hospital whilst you chat up the receptionist? Please. Stop reading the melodramas outside my door and get some perspective!'

Jay smiled at the stand-in guard, wagging her cigarette in her fingers. She had done a speed-bonding job on him as he'd wheeled her down through to the hospital entrance to smoke her cigarette.

The stand-in guard looked uneasy. 'I'm not sure. That inspector is pretty scary.'

'Or do you think I'm going to jump up and leg it in an Uber, so that I can stop the torture-doctors from experimenting on me any further like I'm in an episode of *American Horror Story*? Thanks for the lend of your phone, by the way; my girlfriend will be worried stiff. The boss hasn't let me be in contact. Between you and me I think she's not down with the queers.'

The guard rolled his eyes.

'What are people like? I'm not too keen on Inspector Slane.

Two years I've been here, and nobody has talked down to me like her.'

'That, Derrick, is because she's a bit of a wanker.'

'And that monster who was with her.'

'Grant,' supplied Jay.

Derrick nodded.

'He gave me a right grilling. Complete bastard. Like you're in any position to run away. You can't even walk!'

'Bastard, indeed.' She cupped her hand around her roll-up as Derrick flicked his Zippo. 'Bastard from planet Bastard. Don't let the fuckers grind you down, that's what I say. Anyhow, I really appreciate you letting me text my girl. I'll be quick and I'll wipe the message off your phone afterwards. No one will know.'

'No sweat. I don't understand why the inspector won't just let you talk to her. It's not as if you're some big security risk, is it? She must be worried stiff. Your girlfriend, that is.'

Jay nodded, trying to remember the last time she had actually had a girlfriend.

Too long, she decided.

'Cheers, Derrick. Now go and see what luck you can get with the hot chick handling the phone at reception.'

'Lucy.' The security guard smiled. 'Okay, but you'll be able to see me through the glass doors, yeah? Just wave when you've finished.'

'Sure,' said Jay, taking the offered mobile, then looking up at him, wide-eyed. 'You'll need to unlock it first.'

'What? Oh, yeah. Sorry.' He leant forward and swiped a pattern on the home screen, opening up the device, then sauntered toward the automatic doors to the hospital reception. Jay watched him enter and strike up a conversation with the receptionist, then Jay turned her attention to the phone.

'Thank fuck you're an android boy, Derrick,' she muttered, referring to the operating system. She checked the signal bar

Girl:Broken

and saw she had data connection, allowing her to access the internet. Glancing around her to make sure no one was near, she opened up the Play Store and downloaded Uber, the taxi app. She verified it using Derrick's email and phone number.

'Really, Derrick,' she whispered. 'If you are going to put your entire life on your phone at least have passwords.' As she suspected, once the guard had unlocked the device she had access to everything on it. When the app was live she ordered a car to pick her up from the entrance to the hospital, around the corner from where she was, and put a random address as the destination. The app told her that a car was 0.9 miles away and would be with her in four minutes. It even supplied her with a map showing the position in real time.

'Step one,' muttered Jay, checking that Derrick was still usefully occupied. He glanced up at her and waved. She gave him the thumbs up and held up her hand, fingers outstretched, indicating that she'd like five more minutes. He nodded and turned back to the receptionist.

'Juicy Lucy must be quite something,' Jay said under her breath. She looked around at her fellow smokers. It was something to see. There were people attached to drips, on stands with little wheels on them. People, like her, in wheelchairs. Men in dressing gowns and women with coats thrown over nighties. All sucking away. To Jay it looked completely desperate. She saw one young woman, clearly just having given birth, dragging so hard she looked like unhappiness was all her life consisted of. Checking that Derrick was still occupied, Jay reached down, hitched up her hospital nightie and unrolled the legs of her trousers, covering the bruising.

'Here, love!' The unpregnant girl looked up from whatever horror was playing in her mind and stared at Jay. Jay stood and tucked her nightie into her combats. It now resembled a pirate shirt. Jay felt the urge to swagger. 'I was just keeping this warm,' she said, indicating the wheelchair. 'You look like you need it more than me.' The girl glared at her for a moment, then gratefully sat down. Jay turned the chair slightly so that it was facing away from the door, then handed the girl a note from her pocket.

'Could you give this to my mate when he comes back? Tell him I've just nipped to the loo. Since the birth, my pelvic floor has completely cocked off.'

'Tell me about it,' said the girl, absently taking the note, her concentration on her cigarette and the years of possible incontinence ahead of her. 'I'm having to wear special bloody pants!'

Jay smiled in sympathy, then walked swiftly away, chin down, counting in her head. At any second she expected a shout from Derrick. She was convinced her crappy plan was going to be discovered, right up to when she turned the corner and saw the Uber idling just outside the hospital grounds. Jay gave it a wave and hurried over. As she neared she saw that her luck was holding; that the driver was a woman. Jay opened the back passenger door and slid in.

'Cheers,' she said, pulling on her seat belt. The car slid smoothly away.

'No problem, love. Layton Avenue, is it?' Jay could see the destination she had given flashing on the car's navigation panel, along with the route to get there. It gave an ETA of seventeen minutes. Jay slumped her shoulders and looked at the driver. When the car stopped at a junction, the driver glanced in the mirror.

'Jesus, love, what happened to you? Did you have a fight with a bus?'

'No. Just with a man who wouldn't take no for an answer.'

'Right.' The driver nodded, turning back to the road.

'Gotcha.' She slid quietly through the traffic, onto the inner circle road.

'In fact,' said Jay. 'It was him who made me order the car. He wants me to come back to him. Says he's really sorry. Never meant to do it.' Jay kept her eyes focused on the passing scenery, pinching her top lip between her teeth The driver looked at her worriedly in the mirror as she drove.

'Come on, love, you don't want to put up with that! I saw a programme on it. Coercive Abuse, it was called. Something like that.' She tapped the screen of the satnav. The little picture of the house. 'Is that him. Is that where you're going?'

Jay gave a small shudder, and nodded. She swiped the phone into life and deleted the Uber account.

'Or at least that's where he thinks I'm going. I had to tap it in because we've got a linked account. He could see what I'd done. Like he always can.' Jay held her breath, seeing if the woman would get it. The pain in her leg ripped into her, and she took the bottle of pills the specialist had given her out of the waistcoat and popped the lid. Under the sad gaze of the driver, she flipped a couple into her hand and dry swallowed them. Derrick would almost certainly have returned by now. Jay reckoned she'd have maybe five minutes of him too embarrassed to call it in, hoping against hope there was a safe explanation. Then maybe another ten minutes for them to check on hospital pick-ups. Buses. Black cabs.

If they were smart they'd track the phone.

Jay thought of Slane; how she'd been used.

They were smart.

Jay wound down the window and threw the phone out. She watched as it smashed on the road behind them.

The driver, whose name tag said 'Brenda', smiled at her and said, 'He can't see you now, can he?'

Jay shook her head and smiled bravely back. 'I don't suppose you could drop me at the Corn Exchange, could you? I've got a friend who works there. She'll take me in. He doesn't know about her.'

'Of course, love.'

Jay felt a surge of gratitude.

'And I know it's a huge ask, but could you drive on to Heaton Park? It's just up from the road I tapped in? Say you dropped me there?'

'Keep him off the scent, yeah?'

Jay nodded. Under interrogation, she was sure the woman would say where she actually dropped her, but it was all about worst-case scenarios. All about maximising the time.

And it wasn't as if she knew anybody at the Corn Exchange anyhow.

'Cheers. I just want to lie low for a bit. Make some choices. You know what I mean?'

The truth of what she said shone through, and the driver nodded and drove.

Four minutes later she stopped outside the Corn Exchange. Jay got out, wincing with the pain, but noting it was already beginning to recede, the little tablets doing the heavy lifting for her.

'Hey!' said the driver.

Jay froze and looked back down at Brenda.

The driver held out her hand. 'This is a roll of pound coins.'

Jay saw what looked like a plain packet of polos.

'Keep it in your pocket. Next time you're in trouble hold it in your fist.' The woman placed it in the palm of her hand and made a fist around it, demonstrating. 'He or anyone else comes near you, smash them in the face. It'll break their jaw big time.' She opened her fist and offered the roll. Jay looked at her. Thought of a woman in a city picking up men. Even with the app. Even with all the checks and balances it must take nerve.

Jay nodded and took the roll. 'Thanks.'

'No problem. Hope you get fled.'

Jay stood and slammed the door. She watched the Uber drive away, disappearing into the Leeds traffic. She looked at the Corn Exchange for a second, then turned and limped her way to the indoor market.

32

29TH OCTOBER

When Jay entered, she was momentarily stunned by the noise. After the quiet of the hospital, it was almost overwhelming. The pills she had taken for her pain deadened it a little, but she still felt like she was being sonically crushed. Also, the sheer bustle of the place was intimidating, with people pushing past each other in a hurry to reach the next bargain.

Hunching her shoulders, she hobbled down the stone lanes created by the stalls until she found herself in a quieter part of the market. She skimmed past the grey stalls, with their none-brand goods and a fug of industrial-strength skunk smoke hovering above them, towards the Moroccan café she used to frequent when she first went on the beat. Opposite was a phone repair kiosk; a grey-market establishment that had one foot in the legitimate repair business, and the other in the highly suspect practice of being able to unlock any phone, no questions asked. *We unlock fones while u w8!* the legend above the bead-strings, that served as a door, declared in old-skool speak.

Jay smiled; she used to visit here too. Whenever she locked herself out of her phone or had problems rooting it. She passed through the curtain and entered the tiny store, glancing casually about. There was only one other customer; a young man with tweed drainpipe trousers and a mock Victorian black creeper jacket. He was deep in discussion with the owner about UI skins and crypto hard-vaults: Jay slid in and pretended to view the phone cases that lined one entire wall.

Five minutes later, when the man finally left, Jay turned and limped to the desk. The owner, a thin man with shiny skin and scraped back hair, was fiddling with an open phone, a watch-screwdriver in one long-fingered hand.

'Hello, Beemer; how's it going?' she said softly.

The young man, nicknamed after the car he told everyone he was going to own, looked up at her. It took him a couple of beats to place her, then he smiled and stuck out his fist. She smiled back and raised her own, gently bumping.

'Crap, what the fuck happened to you?' His smile slipped as he took the rest of her in. 'You been in the wars and no mistake, Jay.'

'And the rest,' she agreed. 'Look, Beemer, any chance of closing the gates for five minutes? I've got myself in the middle of a shitstorm, and I need some help.'

He searched her eyes, and looked at her battered body again, then nodded sharply. Lifting the hinged counter, he edged past her and pulled down the roller door. A few years earlier, when she was still a beat officer, the young man had got himself into a fix; nothing serious, but he had pissed off a few nasty people. She had smoothed things over.

It was something an officer on the street learnt to do; bend a few rules when a greater good can be achieved.

Plus, you never knew when you needed a favour down the line.

The door secure, he came back and looked at her, concern stamped on his face.

'Jesus, Jay, who fucked you? You given up on girls and started dating lorries?'

Jay smiled. She was beginning to feel light-headed from the pills and the adrenaline. She reckoned that Derrick would have reported her by now. Although she wasn't technically under arrest, and was just meant to have a watch for her own protection, she knew that it would be reported back to Slane. She didn't know how much time she had so she laid it on the line.

'Something like that. I need a cold phone and some travelling money. I have to hole up for a few days, and I can't go back to my flat. I know it's a lot to ask, but–'

'No sweat.' Beemer held up his hand, stopping her in mid flow.

Jay felt like crying. She'd been holding it together and now... she looked down. The youth's hand was on her arm, warm and solid.

'If you hadn't sorted me out I'd be in jail or a wheelchair by now. I owe you, Jay.'

She looked up and smiled at him, thinking of how genuine he was compared to Slane.

'Nah, you'd've been fine, Clarence.'

The man winced at the use of his real name. Jay reached forward and clasped his wrist. 'But thank you. I'll pay you back in a few weeks.'

'No need,' he said, his smile full and front of house; the gold in it almost dazzling her. 'When you can, yeah?' He held up his hand, with his fingers splayed. 'Burn Street in five, okay?'

Then he walked past her, back to the roller doors, and heaved them up.

Jay shoved her hands in her pockets and limped out. She made her way to the bottom of the market, exiting through the outdoor section. She turned left, passing the food stall selling stuff that purported to be meat in bread rolls, and made her way to Burn Street, the name coined by the locals due to the fire that decimated it. All that remained was a facade; like a veneer. The front brickwork was held up with stanchions and braces; nothing solid. Behind them was a wasteland of broken bricks and twisted metal, a playground for children and lo-fi criminals.

Checking that no one was paying her any attention, Jay stepped through one of the many gaps in the security fencing and stood in the shadow of the scaffolded wall. Due to the rain, there was nobody about. Jay slid down against the wall, weariness taking her the adrenaline left her body. She closed her eyes for a second.

∽

'Jesus, maybe you should go to a hospital, instead of hiding out!'

Jay opened her eyes. Beemer was standing over her, a look of concern on his face. Over his shoulder he had an Adidas holdall.

She smiled at him. Even that small action sent sharp thorns of pain into her. 'I've been there; it's fucking rubbish. I'm pretty certain someone was going to hurt me.'

'What, more than you are now? You know, you swear more than anyone I know.' He reached down, hand outstretched. She grabbed it and hauled herself up. She actually felt her muscles creak.

'Well, if you're good at something...'

He smiled, handing her the bag. 'It's not much. I got you a clone-phone so there's no way to be tracked. There are some clothes and shit, a preloaded cash card and some paper money; not much.' Beemer shuffled from foot to foot. Although he acted tough, he was just a kid.

She patted him on the arm. 'It's more than enough, Clarence. I'm really grateful. I'll try to make it straight with you soon.'

'As I said, no need.' He looked at her sadly, then turned and walked away.

She watched him until he was through the fencing, then pulled the zip on the bag and looked inside. There was a pair of cut-off jogging pants, a green hoodie and a fishing hat; the circular soft-brimmed headwear favoured by eighties rappers, that could be rolled into a back pocket. She pulled the hoodie out and slipped it over her waistcoat, wincing as she did so, then crammed the hat on her head, tucking her dreads under.

'I look like a fucking raver,' she muttered.

She rummaged in the bag again, pulled out the phone and pocketed it. She put the slim roll of notes in a different pocket. Then she shouldered the bag and made her way out of the derelict land and headed for the bus station, trying not to limp.

Once inside the building, she visited the toilets and changed into the jogging pants, transferring the money and phone, and putting her combats in the sports bag. She looked at her battered face in the mirror. The bruising had gone down but the eyes looked like they came from outer space. The pupils were massive from the painkillers and the sockets sunken from fear and pain and tiredness.

'Definitely look like a raver,' she said. 'Plus I'm talking to myself, so I'm definitely on drugs.'

She gave a little giggle and felt a tear slip out of her eye.

Pulling a pair of shades out of the backpack she left the toilets and studied the electronic board. She looked at the names; cities and towns, from London to Blackpool. From here she could go anywhere. She sighed, feeling sad and alone, and then limped her way to the correct gate.

She could go anywhere, but she really had nowhere to go. She needed to find Daisy. She needed to rewind her life and try to set things right.

She needed to find out why Slane seemed to be setting them up. There was something going on that she was missing.

And then she felt it. The thing she needed to keep her going. To fire her engine.

She felt anger.

Glancing at the board, she got on the bus.

∼

Jay looked at her reflection in the window as the bus's engine sparked into life. Worms of Leeds-rain, heavy with a hundred years of industrial soot, oozed down its surface, ribboning her ghost-face. She could feel the throb of the bus vibrating her seat as the vehicle left the station, pulling at her muscles, sending ripples of pain through her.

Jay sighed and looked out of the window. She watched the city centre turn from tower blocks and shops to industry and decay; building sites and abandoned churches, like history that refused to understand itself. Zombie buildings, clearly dead and unused but still standing; still telegraphing their past as if it was present.

She sat on the bus, watching the city slip away like it was made of nothing. Watched the green and the grey of the Yorkshire landscape take over like it was made of forever. Out of Leeds. Through Oakwood and beyond. Past Wetherby and north, towards York.

She'd signed into her WhatsApp and left a message with her mother, saying she was going away. Then she'd signed out and deleted the app. If she was being monitored then at least her mother would be safe. There was something about the way Slane had talked about debriefing that had terrified her.

Next, Jay started working the phone, swiping and pinching and searching. She opened a separate window and messaged through Element – the encrypted peer-to-peer service that only the sender and receiver could open – the only person from work she thought she could trust. There was an outside chance he might help her, even after the bridge-burning Slane had insisted on before she joined their team.

'Of course she did,' Jay muttered, seeing it all in a new light.

Then she'd checked into Doctor Hall's medical notes. With his full name and ID she'd skimmed from his tag accessing his computer had been a doddle.

She quickly scanned what had been written. True to his word he had checked back through her admittance.

And discovered what had been redacted.

What had been found in her bloodstream.

She opened another screen to look up the drugs that had been identified.

'Well, well. No wonder I passed out.'

And just how much trouble am I in? she wondered. *What's really going on?*

She exited his notes, then she messaged the only person who could really help her now. Help her hide. Help her heal. The only person she could really, really trust.

And then she sank back in her seat and closed her eyes, floating in a pharmaceutical fug until the bus arrived at where she needed to get off.

33

30TH OCTOBER

Fulford, Nr York

Jay came to slowly, warm in the duvet she had wrapped herself in the previous night when she had arrived. The bed was rocking slightly and, for a moment, she felt protected, like when she was little.

She revelled in it, snuggling deeper into the warmth until a noise from outside brought her fully awake. It took her a moment to identify it.

A duck.

Jay stared at the roof a few feet above her head. Wooden and warped and very close. It took her a moment to recall where she was, and why her body felt like it had been to a party without her brain.

'Quack,' she said, quietly, mimicking the duck.

She sat up gingerly, checking into her body for any new horrors. The painkillers had worn off, and her mind was clear of the fog that had enveloped it when she had limped off the bus the previous night. Even in her befuddlement, it had not taken her long to find the canal, and the key to the narrowboat was where her mother had said it was, when she had messaged her the second time. Not on WhatsApp, but on Signal.

'Quack quack,' whispered Jay, standing up, her head inches away from the roof of the boat. The duck didn't answer. Her mother, who had not acknowledged the first message, when she had said she was going away, had responded almost immediately to the Signal message. Jay had said where she was, and where she was heading. Her mother had sent directions as to where the boat was moored and how to access the key-safe hidden off the towpath.

When Jay had arrived, late at night, with the weather seemingly taking a personal interest in her fucked-upery, she had lit the wood-burning stove, dry swallowed a double dose of painkillers, and buried herself in the duvet. The gentle motion of the boat had rocked her to sleep in zero seconds flat.

And now she was awake.

Outside the duck quacked again.

'That's what I'm talking about,' whispered Jay. 'Up and quacking. Ready to rock.'

Although she wondered if she *was* up to it. She felt like she might have run out of body-road.

'Get a grip,' she said softly.

The houseboat was warm, the ghost of the fire still ticking over. Gently, Jay stripped off her clothes, and limped down the single walkway of the vessel to the shower. It was a walk-in with a sliding door, a hole in the floor which ran the used water into the canal. Looking at the shower shelf, Jay could see that it was stocked with green products. Honey and oatmeal soap. Tisserand body wash. A flannel that looked like it previously covered a sheep. She picked up the body wash. Looked at the label.

A unique collaboration combining Tisserand's botanical expertise with the rich heritage of the National Trust

'Oh dear,' she said.

Jay stepped inside.

Five minutes later, when she was finished, she limped to the oak drawers by the fold-down bed she had slept in, and searched through them.

'The underwear better not be knitted by the fucking National Trust,' she said, pulling out cotton boxers, a black vest and some walking socks. In another drawer, she found some black corduroy plus-two trousers. She held them up, gazing at them incredulously. Instead of a zip, they had exposed sixpence coins as buttons, with no cover flap. Similarly, the fasteners just below the knee were also coins. Jay looked at the label.

Bilitiz:4girlz

'Right,' she said, climbing into them and buttoning them up. They were slightly too big for her, so she rummaged around until she found a belt. Finishing off with a flannel shirt, she shuffled over to the desk and sat down. The desk faced a rectangular window. Jay pulled the curtain back and got her look at the canal.

A light mist drifted just above its surface, lit and diffused by a low sun, indicating that it was early morning. She couldn't see any other boats, just a dirty swan gliding past with no interest in her. Possibly on purpose.

'Big sodding duck,' Jay whispered, staring, then looked down at the desk. Despite being made of traditional materials the design of the structure was modern, with a monitor and a sliding drawer containing the keyboard. Jay reached forward and fired up the computer, tapping in the password her mother had sent her the previous day. Then, while Jay waited for the device to boot up, she rummaged through the drawers, searching for tobacco. All she found was a CND membership card, a Pride bracelet, and what seemed to be hundreds of identical keys. Sighing, she shut the drawers and looked at the walls of the narrowboat. Above the tiny sink was a picture of Che, fist raised in military salute; and a poster of Tanita Tikaram, hair cut in the style of Elvis Presley, staring past the camera.

'Okedoke,' said Jay looking at the posters thoughtfully. 'All this and the National Trust?' She was pulled from her thoughts by a notification bell on the computer, indicating an incoming Signal message. Jay pressed the button, accepting the call.

'Whose boat am I on, Mother?' she said without preamble when the familiar face appeared. ''Cause it appears to belong to a lesbian militant who loves the environment and wishes to protect the heritage of our great nation.' She paused for a moment. 'And why haven't I met her?'

Her mother looked out at her from the monitor. Even with the slightly stuttering image produced by the ever-refreshing connection, it broke Jay's heart. Since she'd last seen her mother someone appeared to have driven worry-trucks across her face, cutting deep lines into her skin.

'Jesus, Mum, you look like shit. I'm so sorry.'

Her mother smiled, slicing another corner off Jay's self-control. 'Sayings about kettles spring to mind, Jaseran. Along with colours. Black, for example.'

'It's just Jay now, Mum,' said Jay softly. 'I changed it, remember?'

Her mother looked sad for a moment. Sadder. Then she smiled. 'But you kept the first letter, didn't you? Used it as the complete thing. Thank you for that. Although I think you could do with the full name now.'

Jay's mouth twitched. She used to hate her name. That's why she'd changed it. She didn't want it nailed to her, for all to see.

'You remember what it means, don't you?'

'Of course I fucking do! It was my name!' If her mother was fazed by her swearing, she didn't show it.

'Yes. Well, you should try to wear it, love. It's why I named you. And it was such a lovely naming ceremony! I–' Her mother's voice cracked. Like a teacup she was holding too tight. 'Oh, Jay. What have they done to you? Nobody would tell me anything! After you got suspended they said you went away! That they didn't know where you were!'

'Lies. All lies, Mum.' She swallowed. 'And not just them. Me too. I've been lying to you. From the beginning. I thought it was the right thing, but it's all fucked up!' Jay could feel tears forming behind her eyes.

'I was never suspended. Just sent undercover. Transferred to a different unit.' She shook her head before her mother could say anything. 'Except I think I was set up. Chosen to do something I hadn't signed up to. There was something hooky about it from the beginning. And then Daisy went missing and people started dying...' Jay paused, as the confusion and concern on her mother's face increased. She realised that her mother knew nothing of what had happened to her. She felt a stab of guilt.

'Look, Mum. Thank you for doing this.' She gestured with her hand, careful not to put too much pressure on her ribs. 'I'm not sure where else I would've gone. Whose is it, anyway? The boat?'

Her mother smiled. 'No one you know. A university student with rich parents. She's taking a term out to do some research with the WWF.'

'Right. Lesbian militant who loves the environment and wishes to protect the heritage of our great nation.'

'WWF as in wrestling. She's the daughter of an old friend and has gone to assess the patriarchal gaze of female sports within the American rust belt. They won't mind you staying there.'

'The patriarchal gaze, right. What old friend? I thought you severed ties with your old life when you lawyered up?'

'You never sever ties with your old life. There's only one life,' said her mother, her gaze steady.

Jay looked at her. Saw the hardness of a life spent campaigning; first on one side of the divide as an agitator; then on the other as a witness. She nodded.

'Yes. Right.' Jay didn't know what else to say.

Her mother leant forward.

'You used to have outdoor eyes, Jay. When you were young.' Her mother's own eyes shone as she spoke, her face juddering slightly on the screen. With a start of alarm, Jay saw that she was trying not to cry. 'Outdoor eyes. Outdoor smile. Outdoor body. Now look at you. You look like there isn't a secret you don't know, like you set everything on fire just to see yourself. I can't even tell what you're thinking, and I used to be able to tell what had happened to you by looking. Or at least I thought I did. I'm so sorry if it's my fault.'

'What do you mean?'

'The life I led; before. The travelling and the prison. The protests and the...' She shrugged. 'I just wanted to make a difference.'

Jay's heart broke, glittered into a thousand pieces as she watched her mother cry, unhidden. She leaned forward. Gently stroked the screen.

'It's okay, Mum,' she whispered. 'It was just me. Being,' she shrugged. 'Not getting it. Being too fragile.'

'Don't be sorry, love. Just let me in! Let me be a mother. Let me help!'

Jay smiled, and sat back. Outside the duck quacked again.

'I thought you'd never ask,' she said.

And Jay began to tell her story.

∽

By the time Jay had finished she was famished, and her body was on fire. She had been sitting in front of the computer for more than an hour, laying it all down, and her bones felt like they were welded together.

'Look, Mum,' she said. 'I need to move about, or I'm going to seize up.'

Her mother waved her away. 'Go! Have a walk by the canal, if you think it's safe.'

'It is. No one knows I'm here. If you're sure no one can connect you to the boat...?'

'Hundred per cent. Let me think about what you've said. Try to see a way I can help.' She smiled at her daughter through the screen, the lines of worry reverting to a lattice of laughter lines. 'Bizarrely I have to say I'm very happy.'

'How?'

'When Inspector Slane got in touch she said that you had become depressed, and that she was worried about your mental state. She said you blame yourself for wrecking the investigation. Thought you might be suicidal.'

'What a fuckbucket.'

'Exactly. A perfect summation of your Inspector Slane. Very rude. She wouldn't even give me her first name.'

'When?' Jay asked, alarm cutting through her pain. 'When did she get hold of you?'

'Yesterday. Before you messaged me.'

Her mother's face had changed at the mention of Slane. Hardened. Become colder, stronger, as if she'd just unzipped an extra part of herself. Jay was suddenly reminded of exactly what her mother was. Of all the years of hardship and sacrifice it had taken her to get from where she once was to where she was now. And why she'd felt so inadequate next to her.

'Yeah, well,' she said, jaw clenched. 'I'm sure they didn't give you the runaround. What did you say?'

'I said that we'd had a massive falling out, and I would be the last person you'd contact in a crisis. I have to say she seemed under quite a bit of pressure. I also have to say she didn't seem to know who I am, which is a bit of an error.'

'What do you mean?'

Her mother beamed at her. 'I mean that nobody fucks with my daughter.'

Before she could say anything that might embarrass herself, Jay nodded, and killed the connection.

She stayed looking at the dead screen a moment, then stood and limped to the fridge and surveyed the contents. Inside was a bottle of Tequila, a lime and a collection of energy drinks. There was also a paperback copy of *Orlando*, by Virginia Woolf. The cover had a picture of Tilda Swinton on it, androgynous and overtly sexual at the same time. Jay leant forward, one hip against the door, and stroked the cover. It was cold and dry and felt like it should be in jail.

'Must be one hot fucking book.' Jay reached past it and pulled out a Red Bull. She thought for a moment, then pulled out the lime, the tequila and the book.

'In for a penny.' Jay limped to the bed. Now that she had moved she felt the limp was easing up; that the pain in her ribs was probably the worst thing. She found a glass and mixed herself a drink.

'Who needs painkillers?' she sneered, settling down and opening the book. For the first time since regaining consciousness in the hospital, she felt safe. Felt like she was wrestling back some control. She looked out of the window. The swan failed to look back at her.

'I'm going to sort this out,' she whispered. 'And when I do, someone is going to get a nasty surprise.' She took a sip of her drink, then put it on the little shelf by the window and closed her eyes.

Five seconds later she was asleep.

～

Jay snapped out of sleep, the notification chime on her new phone indicating she had received a message. She groggily checked her watch and realised that she had slept through the entire morning and half of the afternoon. She looked at the book, open at the first page and balanced on her chest. She stroked its cover sympathetically.

'Maybe you were in the fridge too long.' She checked to see who had messaged her; smiled when she saw it was her mother.

She read the text.

Don't panic – he's very nice

Jay squinted at the message, sleep shredding from her.
'What the fuck?'

I thought about what you said, and got in contact with an old friend

Jay read the words with increasing alarm.

He's agreed to help and should be with you pm

'Pm? What does pm mean?'
Jay swung out of bed and slammed her feet into her boots. After lacing them up she continued reading.

He's an expert in cults. He's also had experience with the law. He should at least be able to give practical advice.

Jay read the rest of the message, then looked up. Outside, she could hear the sound of a car pulling up; the slam of a door as someone got out.

'You don't fuck about, Mother, do you?'

His name is Joseph.

34

30TH OCTOBER

Jay stared wearily out of the window of Joseph's car and watched the landscape change as they turned off the A19, and headed into the Yorkshire Moors National Park. They had only moved forward forty miles north of York, away from the canal, but seemed to have slipped back a hundred years. All the houses were built like they'd either been grown from the ground or put there, stone by stone, as some sort of war against nature. With each mile the car encroached onto the moor, the moor seemed to strip another layer of culture away.

'Christ, do people live here on purpose, or is it some sort of punishment?' she wondered out loud.

'It is quite remote. But surprisingly diverse, and beautiful in a brutal way, once you get tuned into it.'

Jay snorted. 'If you say so, Heathcliff.'

'Wrong moor.'

Jay ignored him, and stared some more out of the window, not seeing. Instead she was going over the recent past; sifting and cataloguing. Making tables and counting steps. Daisy-ing herself up, she thought grimly.

'What I don't understand is how they know what they know,

or can do what they do, if they're not legit.' She was talking out loud, but mostly to herself.

'What do you mean?' Joseph scanned the road, which with each turning became narrower and narrower. Every year the number of road accidents involving deer increased.

'They recruited me, didn't they? F-branch. It wasn't as if they flipped me in a bar or anything.'

During the journey, Jay had told her story for the second time in a day. It felt like she was beating herself up with personal information.

'They went through my inspector. They must have had access to my psych evaluation: knew I was the kind of person who could get close to Daisy.' At the thought of Daisy, Jay felt her chest tighten. Felt a squall of sad rain pass over her heart.

'I'm not sure they can be F-branch,' said Joseph thoughtfully.

'Why not?'

'As far as I know, F-branch were disbanded in the eighties. They were kind of a precursor to the Special Demonstration Squad.'

Jay's nose wrinkled, as if they were passing a sewerage plant. 'Fuckers.'

'Apparently so.'

The SDS were notorious for their methods of infiltrating suspect groups considered dangerous. They had finally been disbanded after being exposed for stealing dead children's identities to use as their own, and going so deep in their cover that they actually married and, in some cases, had children with the people they were investigating.

Jay felt a coldness seep into her tired bones. 'But they approached me through my boss,' she insisted. 'So they must be on the up?'

Joseph drove, quiet, as if mulling it over. 'Maybe they kept a skeleton force on. For cases that hadn't been closed.'

They drove in silence for a while.

'You know, from what you've told me, you have to entertain the possibility that she is responsible, or at least culpable, for some of the events you describe. Daisy, I mean.'

Joseph carefully did not use the word 'murder'. Or point out that when the police arrived, Jay was found alone in Daisy's bed, looking like a human punching bag.

Jay shook her head violently.

'No. I got to know her. She's damaged, yes. If even half the things she talked about that night were true, who wouldn't be? But no way was she capable of murder. Killing a witness? Why? None of it makes sense. Plus I was drugged. Why would she drug me?'

And, more importantly, how was I drugged? she thought.

Jay placed her hands in her pocket and tightened her jaw. She desperately wanted a cigarette, but Joseph was an ex-smoker and would not let her light up, even with the window down.

'You said Inspector Slane told you Daisy was part of a cult, The Fishermen,' he confirmed.

Jay nodded. 'Daisy said the same. That she'd been there since she was a child.'

Jay gave an involuntary shiver.

'But from the way Daisy described it, she was a prisoner, not an inductee. She mentioned a mother and father, but it was more like a house matron or something. On the bus I tried to look them up. The Fishermen. See if I could work out the structure. There was hardly anything online.'

Joseph nodded, keeping his eyes on the narrow road. 'That's because all of the members died, blowing themselves up in a suspected suicide pact. There was no one left to document what they did. Some scraps were pieced together by the girls they abused, but they were so young, and so damaged, that much of their testimony was considered unreliable.'

They drove along in silence for a while. As the light began to bleed from the sky the colour of the moor began to fade. What had once been green became grey. In the distance Jay could see a storm; rain falling like dirty ash from the blue-black cloud. She guessed it might be twenty miles away. The moor was so barren, the distance was hard to judge.

'All I'm saying is that Daisy might have been so traumatised by the events in their houses, that she might have developed some form of psychosis. If she was doing internet searches–'

'And that's another thing,' interrupted Jay. 'Not only was there fuck-all about them on the internet, but Daisy is about as computer literate as a hedge. No way would she know how to do a sophisticated search, or any sort of search.'

'Okay, but...' Joseph didn't know what else to say, so let his sentence fizzle out.

After a few more tense miles, Jay said, 'So how did you meet my mother, anyhow?'

'She was part of a paper I was writing,' said Joseph, happy to be on safer ground. 'I was doing a follow-up on the Greenham Common peace movement. As you probably know your mother was there in the nineteen eighties, along with thousands of other women, protesting against the nuclear missiles being imported from America.'

'I don't remember, but she's told me all about it.'

Joseph hesitated. 'But you know you were born there?'

'How could I forget, with my mother banging on about it all the time.' Jay kept her eyes on the passing moor, letting the uniformity of it zen out her mind. She didn't want to think too much about what had happened: the rift that had opened up between them.

'I can imagine. You were only one of a handful who were actually delivered on site. In some circles, you were quite famous.'

'That's why I changed my name,' Jay said bluntly. 'To make a separation from my mother. Look, can we stop so I can have a smoke? I need to stretch my leg before I start screaming.'

Joseph didn't say anything else; just pulled in at the next lay-by and eased the car to a stop. Jay undid her seat belt, pulled the handle and lurched out. Joseph held on to the steering wheel for a few moments, then got out and joined her. She was sitting on a rock, leg outstretched, facing the expanse of desolate moorland and smoking furiously.

'Sometimes you can see birds of prey hunting from here,' he said, sitting down beside her. 'This is just the right time, as the light fades.'

'Whooperty-fucking-doo.'

'Look, I'm sorry, but you did ask. Perhaps I shouldn't have mentioned about where you were b–'

'No, I'm sorry.' Jay sighed, wiping her hand through her hair, like she was brushing it with the cigarette. 'You were very kind to come and get me. So was my mum for asking you. I guess I'm feeling a bit ripped-up at the moment. I feel so guilty. And worried. I'm going out of my mind trying to work out who to trust and how to go forward. If Slane recruited me through my boss, then I don't know if I can trust him.' Jay sucked on her cigarette like it was thrown rope. As the day died she felt the wind pick up; cold and bitter from the nearby North Sea. She shivered and wrapped an arm around herself. 'Him or any other police officer. I don't know what they – Slane and Grant – have said after I legged it from the hospital. For all I know there might be a warrant out for me.'

Joseph nodded but didn't look at her; stayed staring out at the moor.

'As you know, after Greenham, your mother joined the travelling community, ending up being part of the so-called

Battle of the Beanfield at Stonehenge, in 1985. You would have been about three.'

'I don't remember it.' Jay threw her cigarette away and wrapped her other arm around herself. Joseph suspected it had more to do with protection than warding off the cold.

'There were six hundred new-age travellers, and thirteen hundred police officers with riot gear,' Joseph said. 'In a standoff at Stonehenge. It is disputed who threw the first punch, so to speak, but it was an event that changed your mother's life.'

'We never spoke about it,' insisted Jay.

'Witnessing the clubbing of pregnant women by the state had a profound effect on her. The beating of children too, it was alleged.'

Jay said nothing; just hugged herself tighter.

'That was when she gave you your name, Jaseran. Literally "chain mail" in old French. Protection. That is also when she left the community and went to university, eventually became what she is now, a campaigning lawyer for human rights.'

'Old news,' said Jay; but inside she felt an aching, one that had been there so long she couldn't remember a time when it wasn't there.

'Of course.' Joseph nodded again. 'Anyhow, I liked your mother, and we stayed in touch. Occasionally our paths crossed. A lot of the work I do ends up having a human rights dimension.'

'Sorry, Joseph. I'm a right cow sometimes, especially when it comes to my mother. I am really grateful to you and honestly, if you caught me when I wasn't completely having my melons twisted, I'm really quite funny.'

'Do you always swear this much?'

Jay smiled, giving him the first genuine sign of pleasure he had seen on her. The effect was electric. She seemed to fizz with life. 'Fuck, no. I've cut down just for you.'

'Okay.'

'To be polite.'

Joseph didn't say anything else after that; just smiled, stood, and got back in the car.

After a moment, Jay followed.

35

30TH OCTOBER

Grize Cottage

When they arrived at Joseph's cottage, Jay had a bath while he lit the Esse stove in the kitchen. By the time she finished and came back out wearing the pyjamas he had left out, the room was warm and welcoming. As she sat down in front of the burning box of the stove Joseph handed her a cup of coffee.

'Instant, I'm afraid. I don't spend enough time here to bother with ground; always away in-field or at conferences.'

'I don't care, as long as it's got caffeine in it.' Jay took the offered cup and sipped the hot liquid.

Joseph smiled. 'Good. I've put your clothes in the wash. They'll be ready in about an hour.'

'Thank you, but they're not my clothes. They belong to the woman whose boat it was. As soon as possible I need to pick up some cargos.'

'We can do that in town.'

He handed her a leaflet. She took it and looked at the cover.

'The Magpie Café : the finest fish and chips in Whitby,' she read, then looked at him, her expression neutral.

'Fact,' said Joseph. 'They serve over thirty different fish and edible ocean miscellanea there.'

Jay raised an eyebrow at him and flicked through the menu.

'Well done; you've just given me a first. I don't think I've ever heard the words "edible ocean miscellanea" put together before.'

'You're welcome; I thought we could go there later if you want? When we pick up some clothes.'

Jay smiled and shook her head. 'You've been really kind, Joseph, but I just want to get my head down for now and try to work out what I'm going to do.'

'Fair enough.' Joseph pulled up a chair and sat down next to her. 'Good idea. We'll have a few cups of coffee and see if we can come up with a plan.'

'No, Joseph. You've already been sterling, getting me here so I can sort my head out.'

'And then what? You've said you can't trust your former colleagues. How old was your chief inspector, by the way?'

Jay's forehead creased. 'Why do you ask?'

Joseph sighed. 'The police force wasn't always like it is now. Back in the day it was more like a club. In some areas, anyway. That's why the Met in London were so corrupt. Or Manchester. If this Slane and your Chief go back a ways…?'

Jay's eyes widened. 'That's exactly what she said. That they knew each other from the old days.'

Joseph nodded. 'Before you get your head down I want you to give me names of everyone you can think of who you've met, or Slane has told you about. I'm going to get a colleague to do some digging, strictly off-campus. Don't worry; she won't raise any flags.' Joseph reassured her when he saw the concern stamped on Jay's face.

'How do you know?'

'Because the person I'm talking about is used to dealing with secret organisations who are paranoid.'

Jay shook her head. 'Really kind, but it's too much, Joseph. I'm sure I'll be able to come up with–'

He cut her off. 'You don't know where Daisy is. You think that Slane and co are somehow nefarious, but you don't know in what way. What exactly is it you're going to come up with?'

Jay looked at him. 'Nefarious? What does that even mean?'

Joseph stared back at her, a thoughtful expression on his face. 'You know, I'm not entirely sure. I think it means "up to no fucking good".'

Jay burst out laughing.

'Seriously,' he said. 'You need some help. Your mother called me and I'm here. Let me help.'

'What is it with you and my mother? Were you an item or something?' Jay suddenly looked terrified. 'Oh God, you're not my father, are you?'

'No, no, nothing like that!'

'Thank fuck for that! No offence, but I don't think I can take any more.'

'No, don't worry. But there is one thing I haven't told you about your mother.'

Jay took a sip of her coffee, burning the roof of her mouth. She studied the menu of the café just to have something to focus on. She sighed. 'Go on then.'

'The battle, at Stonehenge. I was there.'

Jay turned and looked at him, surprised. 'I don't remember you.'

'Why would you? You don't remember anything, do you?'

Jay blushed. 'What I mean is she never talked about you,' she said, covering.

'Of course. No reason why she should, plus she's a lawyer;

they never talk. Anyhow, I was there, documenting the community. I was doing a paper on counter-culture movements. When it all...' he made a gesture with his hand as if throwing something away, '...went south. It was really hard-school. There was fighting everywhere. Blood, mud and screaming. It was insane. There were children there and the batons never even slowed. I'm sure most of the police were as careful as they could be, but there were just so many. A kind of primitive miasma seemed to take hold. Anyhow, I slipped, and a policeman came running towards me. He had a baton in his hand and this vacant look on his face, like he'd gone away and left someone else in charge; someone much more primal. It was terrible. I put my arms over my head to protect myself but he just kicked me. My hands shot down to cover my side. It was instinctual. I couldn't help it. Then I saw him standing over me, with this weird nobody-home grin on his face, and the baton raised above his head.'

'What happened,' Jay asked, gripped, the coffee in her hand forgotten.

'Your mother,' Joseph said simply. 'She had you clamped tight to her side. She was trying to find a way out, to get you safe. But she still paused long enough to kick the policeman hard enough in the balls to make him fall to the ground like someone had cut his strings.'

Jay looked at him, mouth wide open. 'Well, well. Go, Mum,' she whispered, turning to stare into the fire.

'Quite. Anyhow, ever since then I've been waiting for a chance to pay her back. I'm convinced if it hadn't been for your mother, I would have died in that field, or at least been knocked into brain damage. The look in that policeman's eyes was...' Joseph ran out of words. He just sat, looking into the past.

'Okay, you can help.' Jay held out her hand. Gently, Joseph

shook it. 'Although I'm not sure how. And only if you can answer a question.'

'What?'

Jay held up the menu from the Magpie Café, and pointed at a dish halfway down. 'What the fuck is "Woof"?'

Joseph laughed. 'Woof? Finest eating fish in the world.'

36

31ST OCTOBER

Grize Cottage

When Jay walked into the kitchen the Esse stove was already lit, the wood crackling in the firebox. On top, sizzling in a pan sitting on one of the hobs, eggs and bacon were frying. The smell of cheap burnt coffee, mixed with cooking fat and charcoal, was almost overpowering.

'Morning!' Joseph was sat at the farmhouse table. In front of him was a shiny plate, shiny from the grease that was all that remained of his breakfast. Jay felt her stomach flip, and tried to breathe through her mouth.

'Morning. Were you planning to have a heart attack before, or after, you help me? I only ask, because I know a really nice doctor.'

Jay walked gingerly over to the stove and poured herself a coffee from the saucepan on the hob next to the frying pan. Although her body was healing fast she was still tender in the places she had been hit.

She walked to the table and sat down opposite Joseph.

'Funny,' he said. 'But seriously, I've been doing some investigating.' He pointed at the laptop next to him.

'What, on the internet?' Alarmed, Jay also saw a top-range mobile phone plugged into it. She looked out of the kitchen window, across the windswept moorland, half expecting to see Collins hanging out of a helicopter. She realised it was nonsense but her heart rate increased nevertheless.

Joseph smiled and said, 'Don't worry; I told you last night. No breadcrumbs to follow. I use a satellite broadband service with VPN, which makes my IP address appear as if it is coming from somewhere else.'

'I know what a VPN is,' said Jay, relaxing a little. 'I am in the police force. We have whole courses on internet crime.' She felt a slight stab as she wondered if that was still true. That she was a police officer. She appraised Joseph, looking again at his set-up. 'And anyhow why would you even need this, Mr Snowden?'

'Not all cults are scary sex death God-y ones. And the Snowden jibe isn't far off. I'm currently working on a paper about Hacktivists.'

Jay gave a whistle. 'I'm impressed. But then, if you have a good grasp of the internet mechanisms then VPN is only half of it.' She nodded at his laptop. 'If you're looking, then, if what they said was in any way true, they'll see it. Even if they don't know who it is, they'll know someone is interested. Whatever you said last night you can't stop a flare from your searches.'

'Exactly!' Joseph beamed.

Jay shook her head, baffled. 'Go on then, tell me. I can see you're dying to.'

Joseph grinned at her.

'I peer-to-peered a few contacts last night. Directly contacted them. No way for it to be traced. It seems that your Slane has been sending up her own flares.'

'What do you mean?'

'Trying to find Daisy by leaving Fishermen trails. Things she really shouldn't know unless she is an expert. More than an expert, in fact.'

'If she was part of F-branch–'

'There's something going on here. More than an escaped member of an old cult. Something that seems to suggest a cover-up of monumental scale.'

'What do you mean?'

'I've trawled back through the news media outlets, including online and blog sites, and no connection has been made between the death of the homeless man and the woman who found him. Also, there is no mention of Daisy anywhere.'

Jay looked thoughtfully at him. 'That's... interesting.'

'Moreover, no mention at all has been made of The Fishermen; at least not in the context of the murders.'

Jay stared at the wood in the stove; at the flames licking around and seemingly through them.

'Which I take to mean,' continued Joseph. 'That either there is no connection, or the connection is being suppressed.'

'By the police?'

'Doesn't the whole thing strike you as some form of set-up?' said Joseph. 'Getting you to follow Daisy. Watching her fall apart and become unstable.'

'But she did beat up the therapist. I saw her.'

Joseph nodded. The previous night Jay had run through everything she could remember with him.

'I've been thinking about that too. You said they had CCTV footage?'

Jay nodded.

'That's what Slane said.'

'In a private therapy session?'

Jay nodded again, slower.

'In a meeting room that neither of you had visited before?'

Jay just stared at him.

'Where there was a new member and the therapist somehow knew a phrase that would set Daisy off.'

The room ticked around them as what Joseph said sank in.

'The fucking bastards,' said Jay. 'It *was* a set-up!'

'Looks that way to me.'

Jay stood and limped around the room. 'But why? Why are they, whoever they are, going to all this trouble?'

'That's the million-dollar question, isn't it? Come and look at this.'

Jay came and sat back down next to Joseph. On the laptop screen were images of old newspaper stories, archived online.

'What's this?' Jay asked, peering at the screen.

'Articles of The Fishermen, from back when it all came out.'

Joseph reverse-pinched the screen, expanding a section.

Police Net Sex Cult in Multiple House Explosions!

Beneath the headline was a grainy picture of officers sifting through the debris of what remained of a cottage.

'All The Fishermen houses were blown up or burnt down simultaneously, apparently. The thinking was that they wished to remain a mystery. Retain the truth they had built their philosophy on. It's not uncommon. That's what happened with Jonestown. If the cult member is made to confront the unreality of their belief system, then it all collapses. Better to die a believer, than be forced to accept the horror of what you have done.'

Jay read over his shoulder. 'So they all blew up at once? The only survivors were the girls? The victims?'

'Yes. One permanent girl, or fish, per house, with others moved between them, for reasons that died with the abusers.'

'What do you mean, "exactly"?'

Joseph looked confused.

'When I first came in, and I said you might attract attention with your search, you said "exactly". Why?'

'Oh, I see! Yes. Well, I thought that if the police, the traditional police, aren't in The Fishermen loop, so to speak, then the only people who would be flagged by the search would be your mysterious new friends, or Daisy herself.'

'She doesn't even know how to operate a phone,' insisted Jay.

'Perhaps.' Joseph looked sceptical. 'So, assuming they're still using whatever algorithm to highlight relevant searches, they should know that someone is interested. If there was a time factor, which I'm assuming there is, as you felt in imminent peril before you ran, then this,' he pointed to his laptop, 'should only exacerbate the situation.'

'And how does that help, exactly?'

'A colleague of mine is giving a lecture at Leeds University on Friday. I messaged her this morning and pulled in a favour.'

Jay looked at him, feeling cogs being turned that were out of her control. 'What have you done, Joseph?'

'Called in a favour, as I said. Doctor Rowe, who was going to be teaching about social coercion in the public sphere, has, unfortunately, had to pull out. Luckily, she has suggested to the university administration that my current lecture would be a suitable replacement.'

'I'm not sure I understand.'

'My lecture includes a section on cults. It is quite easy for me to incorporate some data on The Fishermen. All lectures are posted in the cloud before they are actually given. This allows the students to be informed, and so prepare before the address. It is all there on the internet prior to the lecture.' He looked at her expectantly.

'So you think Collins and Slane will clock it,' she said, working it out.

Joseph nodded. 'If, like you say, they were trying to, for reasons completely beyond me, pin these deaths on Daisy, then they need to find her. If I put enough detail in, and they are desperate enough, they may want to find out what I know. Any mention of The Fishermen will seem either a suspicious coincidence, or fortuitous. Either way, they'd need to check it out.'

Jay thought it over, trying to see how any advantage could be gained.

After a few minutes Joseph said, 'Well? What do you think?'

Jay stood and took her plate to the sink. 'I think I need to think about it. I need a walk.' She glanced out of the window. 'It's tenting it down outside; do you think I could borrow a coat?'

~

Jay lay on the wet grass, its toughness causing a spring in the ground that was surprisingly comfortable. She was in a slight dip in the moor, protected from the wind, but not the rain. She stared up at the sky, letting the water run down her face and hair. The clouds seemed to be hurtling across the sky, as if they had somewhere to go. Towards something or away from something, Jay thought, opening her mouth slightly and letting the rain trickle in. She was surprised to find it salty, but then remembered she was only a few miles from the coast. She licked her lips.

'How did they get into the flat, Daisy, when it was locked from the inside?' Jay whispered to the sky.

'How did they drug us?' She closed her eyes and swallowed a little of the rain. It was gentle out of the wind. Separate. Like a space in a moment.

Girl:Broken

She thought of Slane. Of her recruitment.

'What do you actually want? Who are you?' Jay opened her eyes.

'Why is Daisy so important? Important enough to kill?'

Jay stayed mulling over these questions.

'Or maybe not kill. Maybe fuck over then kidnap.'

After a while she got up and limped back to the house.

She didn't even realise she was crying.

'Okay,' she said, walking into the kitchen. Joseph looked up from his laptop. He was answering a query from Doctor Rowe. Jay looked insane. Her hair had bits of grass stuck in it, she was dripping water like it was a race, and her eyes were on fire.

'Nice swim?'

'Absolutely.'

'Okay, what?' he questioned, referring to her first comment when she had entered the room.

'Okay, I can think of a way it can help. Several ways, in fact. If they go for it then it will keep them busy. If they do actually want something they will need to take you somewhere secure. Maybe show you footage of Daisy and the therapist. Convince you it's the real deal. If they need your help they'll want you to know they are legit; that means showing you an office.' She waved her hands. 'It's all a bit of a long shot, but it's worth a go. Headquarters. Something. And that means computers.'

'So what?' Joseph looked at his laptop, then back at Jay.

Jay grinned at him, making her look totally demented. 'And you're going to have to lose your fancy phone.' She paused, and looked at him for a moment. 'And get a haircut.'

37

31ST OCTOBER

Grize Cottage

Jay stood in the small bathroom regarding herself in the mirror. She was surprised to find she was happy. Not because something had happened, but because she was moving; being proactive. The last week, since she'd been attacked, had been awful, like she hadn't been herself. Like she'd been someone weaker. And before, when she'd been befriending Daisy. She had felt like she was a cancer; something corrosive and damaging rather than productive and helpful. The relationship they were developing built on lies and deceit. When she had first been approached by Slane she had felt special. Important. Like she was singled out for her talent. Now she felt that she had been lying to herself: that she had been singled out for her vulnerability. For her fragility, recognisable by Daisy, so she would be able to slide behind Daisy's defences. So she could be set up.

She refused to believe what Slane had said; that Daisy had

committed the murders. Beaten her up. Jay knew in her bones it wasn't true.

She looked at her reflection. She had borrowed Joseph's clippers, which hung loosely in her hand. The bruises on her face had faded enough to be hidden by foundation, and her limp had almost gone. Her ribs hurt but so what?

Pain was life.

Although Joseph said that there appeared to be no active search for her, Jay wasn't convinced. There may not be a full-on image recognition on CCTV hunt for her, but Slane and Collins knew she had run. That she was no longer their puppet. That she was now the enemy.

She held up her dreads, then placed the clippers right at the base. Five minutes later she barely recognised herself. With the DIY suede cut, the hollow cheeks and the fight-song eyes she looked like a stranger. She smiled a predatory smile. A stranger who was no longer hiding.

'Fuck you, Slane,' she said forcefully. There were strands of hair on her shoulder from her rough cut.

Still smiling, she stepped into the shower, and turned the dial to 'cold'.

As she washed her fear and guilt away she heard the distant sound of Joseph's phone ringing.

When she was clean and dressed she came downstairs, knocked, and entered his study.

Joseph was standing by the window, gazing out at the dying day. He turned, took in Jay's DIY haircut, and smiled.

'Nice hack-job. That was Leeds University. It looks like I'm going to be giving a lecture on Friday. They tried to reach me electronically, but I explained about the connection out here.'

'That it's fucking rubbish?' she said, ignoring the hair barb and eyeing the electronic kit he had set up on his table. She thought it must rival GCHQ.

'Quite. So I'll need to go into Whitby and dial into the web; do some research and pick up some information that's being sent. File my lecture.'

Jay picked up the leaflet from his desk, containing the menu of the Magpie Café.

'And we can get some Woof?'

'Woof?' he repeated.

'Woof. So you can prove it exists.'

Joseph Skinner smiled widely.

'Absolutely.'

38

3RD NOVEMBER

York to Leeds train

'So we're clear on the plan?' Jay said for the tenth time. Her feet tapped a frenetic beat on the floor of the train, adrenalin flooding her body, possibly not helped by the nuclear-strength coffee she had bought at York Station. They had driven in from the cottage whilst it was still dark and caught the five thirty-five express to Leeds. Joseph sat quietly by her side, gazing out at the rain as it scraped its way across the window.

'Yes, we're clear. As clear as we can be, anyway. It all depends if they turn up, doesn't it?'

'They'll turn up.' Jay clenched her fist, willing it to be true. 'Don't forget to go to the market first, so that you clock Clarence's kiosk. It will look more authentic if you can say that you saw it before. And when you do pick up the dummy charger, don't call him Clarence; he'll kill me.'

'I know, get a cup of tea at the Moroccan stand, and glance

over.' He sighed. Jay and he had been through the plan, such as it was, endlessly the night before.

'And remember not to act too eager,' she reminded him. 'They can't suspect that you know anything.' Joseph didn't bother replying, realising that Jay was talking more to herself than to him. Calming herself down and psyching herself up at the same time. 'And remember to draw attention to the phone.'

'It's not a phone.' Joseph sounded genuinely upset. 'It's a relic. I feel like an idiot.'

'Yes, well they'll probably search you when you first go in. That's why we need the excuse of the haircut. How long is your lecture?'

'An hour and a half.'

Jay nodded. They had already discussed it but she wanted Joseph to say it again. To make him think through it all.

'Right. So I'll give it another hour after that; long enough for you to get where they need you if they turn up. Then I'll ring you. You'll need to pretend I'm somebody else.'

'Obviously.' The affront in Joseph's voice was honey-thick, making him sound like a teenager. 'And what are you going to be doing?'

'I'm going to go to Daisy's flat. I need to get a look at it and try to work out how they gained entry.'

'Actually, I've had a thought about that. About how the door could be bolted from the inside without it being done by Daisy.'

Jay shook her head. 'There wasn't anybody hiding inside. She doesn't have any doors or hidden areas. There's nowhere to conceal yourself. We'd have seen them.'

'That's not my thought.'

'Oh. Sorry. Go on then. I'm all ears.'

'You are with no hair.'

She hit him. 'Fuck off. Tell me your brilliant idea.'

'You said the door was wooden, yes?'

'And?'

'And the bolts were metal?'

'Yes. Where are you going with this, Joseph?'

'Magnets,' he said firmly.

She looked at him. Several seconds ticked by. 'Magnets,' she said finally.

'Electromagnets. Powered by electricity. You get them from specialist shops. They could be used to slide back the bolts. Even through a thick wooden door. I've seen it done.'

Jay stared at him, trying to decide if the pressure had been too much. He smiled back at her. 'Where?' she said, finally.

Joseph looked away, mumbling something.

'I'm sorry? Where did you see this done?'

'On YouTube. On a programme about how illusionists do their tricks.'

Jay didn't really know what to say.

'What?' said Joseph under her scrutiny. 'It was really interesting. It's how they used to get the spirits to move the puck on Ouija boards.'

'I think you might need to get out more, Joseph.'

'It was just a thought.'

Joseph turned away and looked out of the window, clearly hurt.

'No. It's good to think out of the box. Magnets. Of course. I should have thought of it myself.'

'If you're going to make fun–'

Jay smiled and patted his shoulder. 'Look, I'm sorry. I'm just quite wired. I'm worried someone might recognise me, or I might not be able to figure it out.' She shook her head. 'Or I've got it all wrong somehow, and Daisy is actually–'

'You haven't,' said Joseph, placing a hand on her arm. The corded muscle under her sleeve jumped and jittered at his touch.

'I just need to go to her flat. I've got a spare key at mine. She gave me one in case of emergencies.' Jay's stomach tightened at the guilt she felt. 'Because she thought I was her friend.'

'You were her friend,' said Joseph, his voice firm. 'You *are* her friend. This Slane... she's setting her up for murder. With the lie about who called in the police she was setting her up for *your* murder too.'

Jay nodded. Daisy had been the one to call for an ambulance before she disappeared.

'Okay, but you'll be careful? I don't think I could face your mother if–'

'I'll be careful, Joseph. I need to find Daisy, and I need to know what happened. The only way to achieve both things is to be careful.' She looked at him, her eyes clear. 'And possibly violent. Hopefully violent. Whoever beat me up...' She left the sentence hanging, but her intention couldn't have been more telegraphed.

They looked at each other. Above them, the crackle of the intercom came into life.

We are now approaching Leeds Central Station, where this train will terminate. Please make sure you have all your belongings with you, and on behalf of the on-train staff, I hope you have enjoyed your trip with Northern Rail, and have a pleasant continuing journey. All alight at Leeds Central, as this train will terminate here.

'I think you mean the journey will terminate, not the train,' muttered Joseph absently, staring out at the driving rain that lashed at the platform as it swung into view.

Beside him, Jay stood and retrieved her bag from the overhead shelf. In it was a baseball bat bought from a sports shop in Whitby, a hammer and chisel, in case the locks on either Daisy's or her flat had been replaced, and a change of clothing, in case she needed to suddenly look different.

Once the train had stopped and the passengers began to

leave, Joseph stood, clutching his briefcase. Together they shuffled off the train. Joseph followed Jay through the automatic turnstile and stayed behind her as they walked with the rest of the passengers to the station's exit. He scanned the concourse as he walked, looking for policemen, or not-policemen. Looking for danger.

When they reached the exit, Joseph pulled the piece of paper out of his pocket to check on directions. He wished he had his smartphone with him, so he could just pull up a map.

'Which way to your lecture?' Jay slung the rucksack onto her back. Pulled a pre-rolled cigarette out of her top pocket and slotted it into the corner of her mouth. He squinted at the paper.

'Right,' he said.

Jay fired up her cigarette, blowing smoke into the rain. She pointed across the taxi lane in front of them. On the other side was a structure housing steps that led down to the road below the station.

'That's me.' She turned to Joseph, then, unexpectedly, hugged him tightly. 'Good luck,' she whispered in his ear. 'And thank you.' She gave him one last squeeze, then broke off abruptly and walked away, limping slightly, across the road and down the steps. Joseph watched her go, hoping with all his heart that she would be all right. Safe.

Then, pulling his coat tight around himself, he turned right, around the bend and headed for the Corn Exchange, then on to the market.

END OF PART TWO

PART III

JOSEPH

39

3RD NOVEMBER

'Welcome to King Koby, brother. Take a seat. Brett's just finishing off; he'll be with you in a short while.' The Dean-ager with the quiff and the stubble beard smiled brilliantly and pointed at an industrial-looking wooden bench against the wall. Joseph couldn't remember when he'd last seen so many gold teeth. Latvia, maybe. Or Georgia. Somewhere Eastern European. Back in the nineties. He nodded his thanks, walked over, and sat down.

On the sound system, some grime was being pumped out; low and dirty, the female rapper toasting about choice, and who owned her body: it was clearly her. Opposite him were four nineteen-fifties barber chairs occupied by four young men, being barbered within an inch of their lives by four other young men. Bare Edison light bulbs hung from the roof on thick black industrial cables, with no attempt at gentrification. The walls were uniform with white tiling in the style of a hospital sub-basement from the nineteenth century, save from the four giant mirrors in front of the chairs.

Joseph settled into the bench, letting the atmosphere wash

over him. Giving himself space to think about Slane and Collins. About The Fishermen.

And Jay.

She was so different from her mother, yet exactly the same. It was like looking through a backwards mirror. Seeing the old woman he knew in the young face he did not.

And despite her swearing and rebel attitude, she was so vulnerable. Joseph felt a genuine protection toward her, and not just because of the debt he owed her mother. The way she seemed to be empathising with the girl, Daisy, was amazing. Having to deal with all the conflicting roles she had given herself. Protector. Friend. Witness. Traitor. And somehow, from sheer willpower, she was holding the storm within her.

'It's Joseph, yeah?'

Joseph came out of his reverie to find one of the barbers standing by him, a gentle smile on his face. 'I'm Brett. I'm going to be doing for you today, if that's cool?' Brett was wearing a pair of black dungarees, no socks, lobe plugs, and had enough tattoos to send Ray Bradbury on a drinking spree.

Joseph smiled back. 'That's great, thank you.' He got up and walked the few feet to sit down in the barber's chair. The music had changed to Billie Holiday. On the counter in front of the mirror were all the accoutrements of a hipster hair establishment. *King of Shaves* oil and talc. *Monkey* pomades. Joseph spotted one bottle worryingly called Head Lube. Brett stood behind him and started gently examining his hair.

'What would you like me to do today, Joseph?' he said, his eyes never leaving the hair.

Joseph didn't really want a haircut, but it was needed for their plan. An excuse to come back into town.

'Um, maybe just a trim?' There seemed to be so much testosterone in the room that Joseph was surprised there was no one fighting. The thought suddenly fired off a spark in his brain. He smiled and looked around.

'You know, Brett, this place reminds me of a film. *Fight Club*. Have you seen it?'

Brett grinned like Joseph had just made his day. 'Sure, Joseph. And do you know what the first rule of Fight Club is?' Brett turned and addressed the entire room. 'Guys? Do we know what the first rule of Fight Club is?'

In unison, the barbers answered. 'The first rule of Fight Club is... Good Hair!' A couple of them bumped fists. Joseph realised he had stumbled on an in-joke.

'Now if you just want a trim, that's cool, but you know, Joseph, I'd love to put a fade in. Give you a bit of a forties vibe.' He pulled out a wooden-framed hand mirror and gave Joseph a view of the back of his own head. 'We could crop and chop here, then fade it up to the top, see? We could crew up the sides and leave the front a bit punky. Kind of giving the finger to the corporate world, while owning the boardroom. Do you get me?'

Joseph looked at him in the reflection of the mirror, translating. 'Do you mean a short back and sides, filling out the middle so I don't look bald?' Joseph said evenly.

'Bang on, brother.' Brett put the mirror back. 'Only with a twist, yeah? Now have you ever thought about having a beard?'

Joseph smiled. 'No beard.'

As Brett worked, Joseph thought about The Fishermen. About the abuse and destruction they had caused, back in the day. And not just in the day, he mused. Abuse was like a truck: it just kept on rolling, causing more destruction; wrecking more lives. The lives of the families who lost their children to it. The families of the abused and the abusers both; resulting in having to live outside of the norms acceptable to society. Pretending to take part in the day-to-day mechanics of living, but rotting inside, festering and decaying until the shell, one day, collapses.

'So they thought that becoming fish was the more likely option. How batshit is that?'

Joseph blinked and looked back out of himself at the reflection of Brett in the giant mirror.

'I'm sorry?'

'The birds. What people used to think they did.'

'Brett, sorry but I blanked out for a minute. What are you talking about?'

Brett nodded. 'It's the sound of the snips. It *zens* you straight into the inner-self. A metal mantra, you get me?'

'Sure. What about the birds?'

'It was on the radio. I like to listen to podcasts when I'm cleaning up. Documentaries and stuff. Keeps the brain from getting split ends.'

'Right. You mentioned fish?'

'And mermaids, yeah.'

Joseph felt a push at the back of the brain, like someone had greased it and pulled a lever. The sound of the snipping all around him took on a sinister tone. 'What about them?'

'It's just mental, isn't it? What the guy said. On the radio. That back in the day, the sixteenth century, they didn't know about birds migrating and that. They saw all these birds in the countryside then...' he snipped his snips for emphasis, '...one day they all disappeared. Like overnight. Migration, yeah?'

'And?' Joseph put an encouraging smile on his face.

'And they couldn't work out where they all went! Little things flying thousands of miles to Africa? Madness!'

Joseph waited.

'So what they thought was that the birds had turned into fish! Became like special fish that hibernated at the bottom of rivers and ponds. That one day they all transformed. Became something else. Like a disguise against nature.'

Joseph felt his phone vibrate in his pocket, indicating that he had received a text.

Brett put some Pomade in Joseph's hair, applying the finishing touches. Then he brushed him down, removing the last of the cut, and taking off the grey smock he had wrapped round him to protect his clothes from the cut hair. Joseph stood.

'How so?' he asked.

'They transform, don't they? They used to be human but then transform. Have to live in an environment that isn't theirs.'

Joseph wasn't completely following Brett's reasoning, but that didn't matter. He was following his own.

'Birds into fish? Like the people think they can change into something they're not? Is that it?'

Brett smiled. 'That's it. Mad, yeah? All the things we used to believe.'

'Totally. Brett, you've made my day. How much for the hair?'

Brett told him. Joseph thought it was cheap and left a good tip.

'Best haircut I've ever had,' he said.

'What it's all about.'

'One thing, Brett,' Joseph asked as he was leaving.

The barber raised one perfectly pierced eyebrow.

'All this,' he waved around him, taking in the whole shop, 'this set-up. With the brotherhood thing. And all the accoutrements. It's all very masculine. What about the girls?'

Brett, still smiling, opened his arms wide. 'Everyone needs a space, man. Where they can relax. A time out. A safe zone.'

Now it was Joseph's turn to raise an eyebrow. Except he couldn't. It was not a skill he'd ever learned. Instead, both went up.

'And where do the girls relax? Where do they get their zen?'

Still smiling, Brett reached under the reception counter and handed Joseph a card. It was made from thick, rough cardboard, downmarket-expensive. On the front was a black-and-white picture. Like a stencil. It showed a girl with a heart tattoo on her neck and a fifties quiff. Like a female James Dean. A cigarette dangled out of her mouth. Joseph turned the card over.

> *From midnight every Saturday*
> *Queen Koby*
> *Because everyone counts*

Joseph looked at the card a moment, then up at Brett.

'Two faces of the same love, you get me?' said the barber.

Joseph placed the card in the top pocket of his jacket.

'Thank you, Brett. For the haircut and the chat. It's been a real experience.'

Joseph smiled and left. He walked down the stairs and out of the arcade onto New Market Street.

Joseph entered the market proper and walked down the rows between the stalls.

He located the phone shop that he had seen earlier, owned by Jay's friend, and walked through the beaded entrance into the kiosk.

40

3RD NOVEMBER

Jay watched the security door to the flats she and Daisy shared. Used to share, she reminded herself. She smoked her cigarette thoughtfully, trying to decide the best way in. The rain was lighter, but still persisted, and the sky had turned the colours of a moth's wing; all blues and purples as the weak sun tried to work its way through the thick clouds.

The only traffic on the road to speak of was industrial; small municipal gutter cleaners, with yellow flashing lights and weary drivers; delivery vans and early worker taxis. Every few minutes the door would open and an occupant would emerge, either on their way to work or for a run, weighed down with personal monitors and arm strengthening bars. Jay watched as they jogged away, the outer door slowly swinging shut behind them.

She decided to try to catch the door next time someone came through.

'It always works on the TV.' She threw her butt down by her feet and pulled her cap low over her head. Swinging the rucksack over one shoulder, to make it look more sporty, she stepped out of the doorway and onto the pavement. She was about to cross the road when she stopped, something nagging at her mind. Something from now, but also something from before. She turned and slowly walked back to the doorway, and squatted down.

The building behind was obviously in disuse; the doorway was shabby; the door itself was riveted closed with sturdy metal bands to deter squatting. Jay guessed that the street cleaners never made it to this particular space. She could see the cigarette she had tossed, its end still feebly glowing. She watched as it slowly died. On the scabby floor next to it were other cigarette butts. Not hers.

Although all packaging to cigarettes had become generic, the labelling on the cigarette itself was still individual. Jay examined the floor of the doorway. In the light of the street lamps, dozens of similar butts could be seen, half hidden amongst the dirt and old cans that had shored up in the doorway. Jay stared thoughtfully for a moment, picturing somebody watching the block of flats.

Maybe watching Daisy. Maybe following her.

'I really was a gullible tosser,' Jay muttered.

She turned and walked across the road. Sheltering under the awning of the shop next door, she pulled out her phone and held it to her ear.

After a few minutes, she saw the door to the flats swing outward. She talked into the dead device.

'Yes, could I have a cab, please? I need to go to the Sainsbury's on Wood Street.'

In her peripheral vision, she saw a figure emerge, already accelerating into a jog, headphones on and eyes fixed on a distant goal.

'Yes, it's Stacy; could I have my normal driver please?'

Although the woman jogging past her probably couldn't hear, Jay worked on the principle that you never knew. She continued her imaginary conversation until the woman was a few feet past her, then swiftly stepped back and caught the door before it closed. She slipped into the vestibule and quickly scanned the lobby beyond the glass internal door. There was a man – no one she recognised – descending the stairs, office trousers tucked into his socks, and a waterproof hi-vis jacket. His bike helmet was already on, with the LED light glowing.

Jay faced the street and began to do stretches. She hoped the light was too dim, and the man too preoccupied, to notice that she was in combats rather than jogging pants. By the time he passed her she was fully into character; alternatively pulling each knee up to her chest, in preparation for her imaginary run. Not that she needed to; he never gave her a second glance. As he exited the building and turned left out of sight, she had snagged the inner door and entered the foyer.

Well that nearly fucked my knee all over again. She grimaced, taking the stairs at a steady lurch, head down. The pain was like someone had stuffed a bunch of keys behind her kneecap and was merrily jangling them. She glanced at the clock on the wall. Joseph would have finished his lecture by now. Jay walked past the landing that gave access to the floor containing Daisy's flat, barely giving it a glance. The corridor was empty, all the doors closed. The entrance to Daisy's flat had yellow police warning tape across it in haphazard diagonals.

At least there's no actual police sitting outside, thought Jay, as she ascended the stairs to the next floor. The corridor here was also deserted. Jay mouthed a quiet thanks under her breath and quickly made her way to her flat. She tried the door on the off-chance that it was unlocked, left open by a careless tech guy. The handle turned but the door stayed firm. Jay sighed and walked towards the window at the end of the lobby. The day beyond the glass was grey; the street lights having been turned off. Next to the window was a poster-sized print in a frame. It showed a generic mill in a generic countryside in non-threatening colours. Jay guessed there were a million of them in hotels and building lobbies up and down the country, mass-produced to be something neutral to put on a wall. She gently pulled the bottom of the painting frame away from the wall and reached behind the picture. Feeling the smooth back of the frame, Jay kept a constant eye on the flat doors, ready to drop to her knee and pretend to do her shoe up should one of them open. She felt a knot of tension undo itself when her fingers brushed against the spare key she had taped there.

'Bingo,' she whispered, pulling it loose and quickly walking to her door, inserting the key, and letting herself in. Once the door was closed, and she was safely inside, she turned and put her eye to the security lens. She stayed there a full ten seconds, but none of the doors to the other flats opened. She sighed, guessing she was safe.

For now.

Jay turned and walked down the short hall. Like Daisy's flat, her apartment consisted of the hallway, with the bathroom and bedroom on either side, and the kitchen/living area reached through a doorway at the end of the hall. It took her brain a moment to catch up with her eyes.

'Well, fuck a duck,' she said quietly. Even from this distance, she could see that her flat was in pieces. She silently lowered her rucksack and removed the baseball bat. Leaving the holdall on the ground she slowly walked forward, placing her weight on the balls of her feet. Through the open door at the end of the hall, she could see that her kitchen had been taken apart; cutlery and crockery strewn on every surface. As she passed her bedroom she saw that her bed was stripped, the duvet ripped and left on the floor. The cupboard doors had been forcibly pulled off the hinges, with her clothes half out, like they were making a bid for escape. Even her mattress had been cut open.

No way was this the police, she thought, continuing silently down the hall. Even if they'd ransacked the place they would have put it back together. Catalogued everything and signed it all off. Jay paused outside the door to the living space, cocking her head, listening for sounds of occupation; breathing or creeping. Air movement or the special stillness you get when someone is trying to be quiet. Out of the silence came nothing but more silence. She lowered the bat and stepped in.

'Well, well.' She gazed around the room at the mess. Nothing seemed to have been left unbroken. Jay edged into the centre, turning in amazement as she did so. Not only had her flat been creeped, it had been broken apart.

'What could you possibly want?' she wondered aloud, convinced that no one was in her flat. She shook her head slightly as she assessed the damage which, she decided after a moment's viewing of the carnage, was complete.

'Lucky I wasn't paying for it.' She grimaced. Slane had set her up in the flat when she had first taken the surveillance job. It was she, heading the task force as Jay had been led to believe, who had paid for and managed the lease. Her eyes widened as she stared at the devastation.

Which meant that Slane would have a spare key.

'Not Slane,' she mused, walking slowly back out of the room. 'She was more on the management side. More white shirt than this.' She nodded to herself. 'Which means someone else. Maybe Grant. Maybe somebody new.'

She saw that her laptop was missing. It was a work item; where she typed up her reports. It made sense they would take it, removing any evidence.

She walked into the bathroom, leaving the bat resting against the wall; not needed but within easy reach if someone entered the flat. The bathroom was in the same state as the living room, torn apart in a frenzy of mindless searching. Seeing the same devastation, Jay wracked her brains, trying to think who knew where she had lived.

Other than Daisy.

Jay shook her head, not going there. She opened the medicine cabinet above the sink, already expecting it to be empty. She was right. All the normal paraphernalia was on the bathroom floor: paracetamol, tampons, Deep Heat, with its contents squeezed onto the tiled floor.

But not Daisy's spare keys. She kept them on a hook at the back of the cabinet, but the hook was empty.

'Of course it is.' Jay sighed, looking at the complete lack of keys in front of her. 'That would just be too easy.' She sat on the edge of the bath, deciding what to do.

After a few minutes, she stood. She couldn't think of anything else other than busting the lock of Daisy's flat. She needed to get in there; needed to look at the wall again.

But she had to wait until the building was quieter.

Once everyone had gone to work.

Jay walked out of the bathroom, picked up the bat and replaced it in the rucksack. An hour later she slipped out of the flat and quietly shut the door.

∽

This was going to be noisy.

Jay wondered if she could pretend she was a maintenance worker, or someone from the force, brought in to do follow-up work on the flat. Looking at herself briefly, she doubted it. What she looked like, with her rucksack and combats and hoodie, was suspicious. What she would look like, if she was spotted kneeling down with a hammer and chisel against the lock, would be a burglar. Shrugging inwardly, seeing no other way round it, she stepped off the stairway and crossed the landing to Daisy's flat.

So far so good. Jay had waited long enough, upstairs in her bomb-flat, for the rest of the office workers to have left, giving herself the best chance of breaking in undisturbed. She reckoned she could, once she started, be done and in the flat within thirty seconds. She took a deep breath, taking one last look to make sure she was alone.

Thirty seconds of luck, that's all she needed. It wasn't too much to ask for. She knelt down in front of the door, miming tying her shoes whilst examining the lock. It was broken from when the door had been forcibly opened by the emergency services on the night of her attack. A new clasp and padlock had been fitted. Jay reached into her rucksack for the hammer.

'Excuse me, can I help you?'

Jay froze, then slowly removed her hand, straightening as she did so.

'I'm sorry, but the lady who lives there is away at the moment. Is there something you wanted?'

Jay turned around, a smile stitched to her face. She got ready to say that she was a journalist. That she was hoping to do a follow-up story on the incident, but as the person who had challenged her came into view, she knew it wouldn't wash.

'Oh, it's you!'

Jay saw with relief that it was the man from the flat opposite. The peeping tom who was always trying to scope a look at any woman walking by.

He stared at her, mouth slightly open, amazed.

'Sorry! I didn't recognise you without the...' he raised his hands to his hair, '...hair.'

'Yeah, well I decided to go for a new look,' she said, wondering what the hell she was going to say when he asked her why she was there. She was about to make her excuses and leg it when his face broke into a smile.

'Actually, this is amazing! I've been wondering how to get in touch with you!' He jerked his thumb up, indicating his flat. 'Your friend, the one who's missing? Daisy?'

Jay felt her breath catch. 'Yes?'

'She left something for you. With me.' He took a step back, opening his door wide. 'I'm not sure what it is, it's in an envelope. An address maybe? She seemed such a nice girl, I didn't want to give it to the police. She said she was sure that you'd pop by.'

Jay broke into a smile. 'That's the best news I've had all week.'

The man grinned widely, showing his yellow teeth. He was in a T-shirt and jeans, with no shoes on. Jay guessed he didn't get out much.

'Great!' His forehead creased in confusion or concentration. 'Actually, I didn't think it likely you'd be calling around anytime soon. You were in the hospital...?'

'They released me,' she said, smiling and picking up her rucksack.

'Oh,' said the man, his features clearing. 'Well, that's good.'

He looked her up and down. She hoped to fuck her nipples weren't poking out.

'It's on my desk, somewhere. Would you like to come in while I find it?'

'Thanks.' Jay nodded and walked toward him. The man turned and stepped back into his flat.

'Great. I can maybe make you a cup of tea, and then–'

He half-turned back to her but didn't get any further because Jay smashed him around the head with the baseball bat.

41

Quickly, she dragged the man's prone body into the flat and shut the door.

'That's for staring at my tits,' she said, looking through the spyhole. The corridor was empty. 'And for making me look stupid for not working it out earlier.'

She knelt and examined his head. The swelling where she'd hit him was already impressive. She imagined, when he regained consciousness, he was going to be in considerable pain.

'Good. You deserve it.' She got a firm grip under his armpits and manhandled him down the hall and into the room at the bottom. The set-up was pretty much the same as her and Daisy's. She dumped him on the floor and started opening drawers, searching for something to tie him up with. On the third try, she found a roll of gaffer tape. She pulled it out and looked at it.

'What is it with gaffer tape?' she pondered. 'It's always fucking gaffer tape. Is there an evil-criminal school you all go to or something?'

Swiftly, she secured his arms and legs with the tape, then stuck a strip over his mouth for good measure. Checking that he could still breathe, she walked to the bathroom and searched through the medicine cabinet above the sink. She looked at the contents, speed-reading the labels on the bottles.

Fentanyl.

Midazolam.

'You total bastard.' She recognised the names from the doctor's report on her blood samples.

As well as the bottles, there was a plastic container of cotton buds. She grabbed the items and closed the cabinet, catching a slice of her reflection on its mirror as she did so.

'I wouldn't mess with me,' she said as she stared at herself. She wasn't sure she liked what she saw; with the shaved head and the tight skin, she looked dangerous. On top of that, the way her eyes blazed, she looked insane.

As she turned to leave the bathroom there was a sharp knock on the front door. Jay froze. She stayed still and held her breath. The knocking began again, louder and more insistent. She tiptoed to the door jamb and turned her face away, listening. After a few seconds, the knocking stopped. Jay stayed still, praying that whoever was outside didn't have a key; she'd left the baseball bat in the living room. She waited a full five minutes before she was sure that whoever it was had gone. Breathing a sigh of relief, she walked back into the living room, past the unconscious man, and poured herself a glass of water at the sink. She drank half, then walked back and squatted in front of him. His eyes were closed, and he was breathing steadily. She smiled.

'Stop pretending you're unconscious, fuckface. You're six inches nearer the door than you were when I went out. What were you trying to do, get their attention?' She threw the remainder of the water in his face. With his mouth taped he couldn't splutter, snorting water out of his nose instead. His eyes flew open and stared wildly at her. She sat down cross-legged in front of him. It sent welcoming spears of pain through her knee.

Good. She wanted the focus the sensation brought.

'I was trying to think who could possibly rip up my flat so much,' she said conversationally. 'Because it couldn't be the police, and I don't think Grant or Slane have it in them. No one really knows where I live, you see?' She winked at him.

'And I was trying to think who would know when Daisy was out, for the planting of evidence and general fucking about. Who could maybe go in and paint something on the plastic cups that would contaminate the water? Something to knock us unconscious.' She paused and held up a bottle she had got from the cabinet. It contained a clear liquid. Jay shook it. From her other pocket, she brought the cotton buds.

'Just wipe the stuff on the rim, yeah? Once it was dry, who would know?'

The man's eyes looked wildly around.

'Tell me, what's Midazolam?' She raised her eyes inquiringly. 'Or Fentanyl?' She leaned forward and ripped the tape covering the man's mouth.

'Actually, don't worry; I know. I know because I saw them listed as being in my bloodstream from when you put me in the hospital, so I looked them up. You fucking drugged us, you complete wanker.'

The man stared wide-eyed at her.

'Or how about this one: what's your real name?' She reached into her rucksack and pulled out the hammer. 'I should warn you; I don't really mind if you don't tell me. I've been itching to smash someone's teeth in ever since I was beaten up.'

The man stared at her a beat, then said, 'Lawrence. My name is Lawrence.'

Jay smiled widely. 'That's great, Lawrence. Now tell me where you keep the keys to Daisy's flat. You must have them.'

'I'm not going to tell you anything–'

Jay brought the hammer whistling down, missing the side of his head by inches.

'Stop messing about, Lawrence. We both know you're going to tell me where they are. It's just a matter of how many teeth you do it with.'

Lawrence looked into her eyes and saw the truth. He swallowed and nodded.

'They're in the kitchen drawer, but it won't do you any good.'

Jay put the tape back over his mouth and stood. She pulled her phone out of her pocket and dialled Joseph's number.

'Good morning. Professor Skinner speaking. May I help you?' Joseph's voice sounded slightly metallic, coming from the small phone speaker.

'It's me. Can you talk? Did they turn up?' Jay stayed looking at Lawrence while she spoke. She had fitted a Bluetooth EarPod in her ear so she could keep her hands free. Although Lawrence was gaffer'd up she didn't know his skill sets. He might actually have some.

'Ah, Hilda, how are you?' said Joseph, his voice warm. Then his voice became slightly more distant as he pulled the phone away to talk to someone else: 'Sorry, it's my secretary, I won't be a minute.'

'Hilda!' said Jay, smiling. 'Your secretary, Hilda? You used that name deliberately to humiliate me, didn't you?'

'Very well, thank you. The students seemed to enjoy it at any rate. Actually, rather excitingly, I've been picked up by the police!'

'What, the *police* police?'

'No, nothing like that; they just want my opinion on something. In a professional capacity.'

'Right,' said Jay, relaxing. 'It's all shaping up. It's confirmed. Daisy and me, we were drugged. And we were right about it being more than just Slane and Grant. The guy from across Daisy's flat is with them, Lawrence–'

'Yes. I understand, and you're right, he is,' interrupted Joseph.

Jay blinked, then realised Joseph was confirming that he'd heard the name; that Slane must have mentioned him.

'Okay,' she said. 'Do you know where you are?' Jay heard Joseph talking to Slane and someone else; a man. He asked them where he should send the bill.

Clever, she thought. She listened hard and heard the man fob him off.

'Okay,' she said, thinking. 'Do you know how many people we're talking about?'

'I'll keep a track of my hours. Hopefully no more than five.'

Five people.

'What? Yes, I won't forget. Noon. It's written in my diary. Okay. You have to go now, Hilda, I'm busy. I'll see you later.'

Joseph crashed the call on her.

Jay looked thoughtfully at Lawrence. Then she swiped up Google on her phone. She looked at the label on the bottle, and tapped it in. After a moment the search engine found what she wanted. She looked at the bound man.

'It says here that Midazolam can induce sleep. It also says that it can disorientate, and affect the memory. That it can interfere with the ability to even create memories.'

Hopefully not more than five.

You have to go now, Hilda.

Joseph telling her she may have company soon.

Like the person who was knocking at the door.

'Where's Daisy?' she asked Lawrence brightly, removing the tape then stepping back.

'We don't know. Look, it's not what you think. Daisy's dangerous. What was done to her–'

'I know what was done to her. I've been given a crash course on what was fucking done to her.'

Lawrence shook his head. 'You don't know anything.'

'Why did you drug us? Why did you plant the phone and set her up?'

'What? Look, just untie me a little. I can't feel my hands. Let me sit up and I'll tell you everything.'

Jay shook her head. 'Are they on their way?' she asked, raising her eyebrows at the bound man. 'Is that why you're so chatty? Were you meant to check in, and now they are coming to see why the silence? Is that it?'

Jay walked over to the kitchen. She opened the cutlery drawer. Behind the knives, there were Daisy's keys, just as he said. Jay picked them up.

'I'm going to go now, Lawrence, but I've got a problem. I really don't want you telling anybody where I am.'

Lawrence's eyes bulged in fear. Sweat popped out on his forehead. 'Wait–'

Jay stuck the tape back over his mouth and began to walk to the door. Then she stopped and looked at him, tilting her head.

'Do you think that's enough?' she questioned herself. 'Or will you work it loose?'

Lawrence nodded his head. Then shook it. Jay tutted, deep in thought.

'But what if they ring, or knock? You'd be able to do something. Hit the table with your leg. Mumble loudly. Something.'

She scrunched up her face, searching for a solution. Then her features cleared, and she smiled at him.

'I know!' she said, brightly. She reached into her rucksack. Lawrence shook his head violently, trying to scream.

Jay pulled the baseball bat out. 'If I smash your head in, you won't be able to make a peep, will you? Everybody happy.'

42

Jay looked through the security hole, checking the coast was clear, then let herself out of Lawrence's flat.

Behind her, the man lay unconscious on the floor, bound and gagged and gently bleeding.

Jay didn't feel a pang of guilt. Each time she had hit him she had seen Daisy's face.

Daisy, who had spent her entire life being abused, then ran so far away she didn't even know who she was.

Jay locked the door, pocketed the keys, and walked across the landing to Daisy's flat.

She'd been so stupid.

They'd put her undercover. Got her a flat in Daisy's block.

Of course they'd put someone else there too. Someone they could trust. Someone who knew what was going on.

Because Jay had not been there to watch Daisy. Anybody could have done that.

Most of Leeds was wired for visuals. If they wanted, they could have done the whole thing remotely.

If they were legitimate.

If they were really on the level.

Jay shook her head.

She'd been so dazzled by the idea of working undercover that she'd never questioned the legitimacy of it.

Of *course* it was shit. Shit polished to such a degree that it shone, but shit nevertheless.

It didn't take much.

The nod from her boss, who knew Slane from the old days.

Just enough information to make her feel in the loop; like she was an asset in a team.

And she'd supplied the rest.

She felt her face burn with shame.

Jay looked around quickly, then slipped into Daisy's flat.

Once inside, she let out a shallow breath. Now that she had separated herself from the lies she felt the full weight of guilt. She'd abused her friendship with the woman. Worse, she'd put her in danger.

And on some level, Daisy had known she was fake, Jay realised.

Hence the message to 999, calling her a policewoman. Present tense.

Hence not telling her everything. Not completely trusting her.

Hence running away again; hiding from whoever was trying to set her up for murder.

Is there somewhere safe you can hide?

And not taking Jay with her.

The detective took a shaky breath and walked down the narrow corridor to Daisy's bedroom.

The place was a slasher film.

The stuffing from the mattress was strewn all over the floor where the insides of the bed had been removed. The act was so violent that it took Jay's breath away. Why would someone take a knife to the bed like that? What could they possibly think was hidden?

Nothing, Jay realised. They just did it to control where Daisy had lain. Destroy, symbolically, the place she might have felt safe.

'You really are over the fucking rainbow, aren't you?' she whispered to the room. The madness of the action filled the space. All the space.

The whiteboard had been wiped clean of Daisy's drawing of the mermaid and covered with expletives. Statements of intention involving burning and breaking. Ripping and gagging. Crude pictures of Daisy in bondage. At least Jay assumed they were meant to be Daisy. They looked like they'd been drawn by a lunatic.

Daisy having sex with fish. With men. With women.

Except, of course, it wasn't sex.

Sex required choice and agreement.

It was rape.

Systematic, insane, depraved abuse of one human being by another.

Jay studied the pictures. She could tell they were Daisy because of the eyes. Two different colours like she was two different people in one body. Sometimes she had legs and sometimes a tail like a mermaid.

But always the heterochromia.

The blue and the brown.

'What does it mean?' she whispered, staring at the insanity on the wall.

'What is it you wanted from her?'

Jay was concentrating so hard on the pictures that the ringing of her phone shocked her, its tone causing her to start.

She quickly took it out and swiped it open.

'It's me.'

Joseph, ringing her. Which meant the first part of their plan had worked. Jay smiled.

'Of course it's fucking you. Who else would it be?'

'You know you swear too much?'

'No, I don't. I swear just the right amount. What do you think of Slane?'

'I think you're right. She's as evil as they come.'

Jay looked at the drawings on the whiteboard.

'Oh, she's much more than that. Do they know where Daisy is?'

'No, and they're blaming her for two murders. One of them is an ex-member of The Fishermen called Walter Cummings.'

Jay shook her head in confusion. 'I thought you said they were all dead?'

'They were. Or supposed to be. There's something very wrong here, Jay. Something they are not telling me.'

'Do you think we should pull it now? Risk it and get the cops in?'

'No. They're so sure of themselves. They haven't mentioned you at all. It's like you're not even a problem. I suspect they have some form of warning set up with the police. Maybe your old boss. Some network that's been there since the bad old days. I think we should go with our original plan. They're going to let something slip. I can feel it. Plus, you were right. Their computer set-up is mobile. It should be open to what we thought.'

'Okay, but be careful. I found the spy in the flat, by the way. The person who had been watching us.'

'Really? I hope you didn't do anything–'

'It's fine. I've immobilised him.'

'How?'

'I tied him up a little.'

'Okay.'

'And hit him with a baseball bat.'

'Right.'

'A lot.'

'Is he alive?'

'Of course he's fucking alive. I'm not stupid.'

Jay pictured the unmoving man and wondered if that was true. She decided she didn't care.

'Do you know how they managed to bolt the flat to set Daisy up?'

Jay shook her head, frustrated. When she'd entered it was clear the door had been battered in, the bolts broken and hanging off the frame.

'No. I'm working on it.'

'Look, Jay. Daisy... what The Fishermen did. She's really damaged. It's possible that she doesn't even know who she is some of the time. That she might have to hide inside of herself. Protect herself.'

Jay didn't say anything. The silence down the line said it all.

'She might not be what you think she is, is all I'm saying.'

Joseph's voice was gentle.

Jay swallowed the pain in her chest. 'As I said, I'm not stupid. I've got to go.'

'Me too. I need to get a haircut and a charger.'

Jay smiled, the dangerous moment passed. 'Don't forget to send a picture.'

'Will do.'

Joseph hung up.

'Of course I know Daisy is broken. I'm not bloody stupid,' Jay muttered again.

Which was when the person charged out of the bathroom and kicked her in the kneecap, proving that she was very stupid indeed.

Jay screamed and collapsed to the floor.

43

'Wow, it rains more here than it does on the moor. Is it like this all the time?'

The distance between the car and the roller door was only fifteen meters or so, but Joseph could tell he was going to get soaked. The driver, Grant, who had picked him up after the haircut, shrugged.

'I wouldn't know, sir. If you run, I'm sure you'll miss the worst of it.'

'You're not coming in?'

Grant shook his head.

'Just returning you, sir. I'm requested elsewhere.'

'Right. Well, thank you.' Joseph looked at the rain bouncing off the concrete, then, resigning himself to a soaking, opened the door and made a run for it.

Once he was in the shelter of the broken awning he turned and watched the saloon car make a slow circle and head out the way they had come.

Joseph took a breath. He really didn't want to go back in, but the plan he and Jay had concocted required it. He just hoped she was all right.

Wiping the rain from his head, Joseph turned and entered the building. In the debris-strewn corridor, the smell of urine had intensified, the rain somehow reinvigorating the acrid odour. Joseph breathed shallowly as he made his way to the large incident room. Inside, Slane and Collins were seated in front of the Smart Board, deep in conversation. On one of the computer screens was a satellite map of Leeds centre. As he entered, the two officers ceased their conversation and looked at him. Slane smiled broadly.

'Ah, Joseph. How was the haircut?'

'As you can see; pointless.' He took off his coat. 'The rain here is unreal. Still, I went to the market afterwards and managed to get a charger–' Joseph waved the plastic bag he was carrying, '–so there's a positive. I'll be able to put some power into the phone so I can contact Mark.' Joseph pulled the sealed charger out of the plastic bag and looked expectantly at them. 'Tell him about my hair. Where can I plug it in?'

'You could just use my phone if you like,' said Slane.

Joseph shook his head.

'Remember I told you about Mark's ASD? He wouldn't answer a strange number.'

'Could I see that, please?' said Collins, standing and walking over to Joseph. Puzzled, Joseph handed it to him. Collins took the package, turning it over several times to check that it was fully sealed.

'I was quite lucky, actually,' Joseph explained while Collins conducted his examination. 'The man in the kiosk said this is the last one he had.' Joseph laughed, slightly embarrassed. 'In fact, he told me it had been in there a couple of years! No one, apparently, has phones like mine anymore.'

Satisfied, Collins handed it back. 'You can plug it in over there.' He pointed at a socket under the far trestle table.

'Thanks.' Joseph pushed the charger out of the plastic and

cardboard packaging. He walked over and plugged it in, then connected his phone into the other end. The device made a cheery *beep*, and a green light came on, indicating it was working. Joseph stood and walked back to the detectives.

'Okay, I'm all yours. Can I take some notes as we talk?' Joseph went to open his work case, but Slane shook her head.

'Not yet, if that's all right, Joseph. Once we've fully briefed you, and you know that you can help us, then a portfolio will be issued to you, with all the relevant intel.'

'Fair enough.' Joseph nodded.

'The first thing you need to know is just how we managed to infiltrate The Fishermen. Once you understand that, you'll see why it is vital that we find Daisy, and get her somewhere safe.'

'I'm all ears, Inspector.'

Slane looked at him intently. Joseph was amazed. Everything about her seemed sincere. If he didn't know better he would have said she was exactly what she said she was; a civil servant trying to do a difficult job.

Which is what made her so terrifying.

'Back at the end of the eighties, when The Fishermen came to our attention, the police force was not like it is now.'

Joseph was uncomfortably aware that he had said almost exactly the same sentence to Jay two days earlier.

'I know. Cliques and cabals within the different departments. Much more of a blurring between what was criminal and what was the law.'

'Yes. The law was something to be enforced, not followed. As long as a result was achieved, the methods were somewhat irrelevant, hence the heavy reliance on informants and the somewhat blasé attitude to undercover work.'

'How do you mean?'

'Oh come on, Joseph! You know how it was. Policemen and women – although mainly men – who went so far undercover that they had families. Children even. They were given immunity by the state because they needed to fit in. Some even committed crimes so they could be accepted. Did initiation beating in gangs. Went on burglaries.'

Joseph nodded. 'I get it. A wild-west culture quite rightly consigned to the past. There have even been prosecutions recently. What has this got to do with The Fishermen?'

Slane just stared at him.

'What?' he said.

'Deep, deep cover.'

Joseph felt his flesh crawl. 'No.'

'Yes, I'm afraid so, Joseph. It was considered the only way.'

Joseph looked from one officer to another, disbelieving.

'But nobody would have sanctioned it!'

'But they did. The Fishermen were considered a threat to society. They were founded and fuelled by a middle-class ideology that struck right at the heart of England. They were the precursors of the movements against what became a deep state. They were anti-establishment and educated enough to be considered a threat to the moral fibre if they ever went mainstream. Do you remember what it was like, back then? With the IRA blowing up pubs and the coal strikes and AIDs described as a punishment from God? The general public were considered malleable.'

'They were child abusers!' Joseph practically shouted.

'When we first looked into them we didn't know that. And when it became clear that they weren't just a paedophile ring – that they had an ideology – well... it became even more important that we understood them,' said Slane.

'And their set-up was tight,' added Collins. 'They kept themselves in cells, with only one or two members moving between the houses. No charismatic God-head. Hardly anybody knew the entire operation. They were priming themselves for a moral change in our society. If they'd survived into the digital age...'

'But we've seen the footage, Slane! We watched it not two hours ago: it was horrific! How could anyone think they could infiltrate that?'

'How do you think we got the footage?' Slane said mildly.

Joseph looked at her, open-mouthed, and felt himself collapse a little.

There it was. The thing that hadn't made sense. The reason for the operation to be so off-grid.

'You had someone on the inside,' he said simply.

Slane nodded. 'Walter Cummings was an undercover police officer. He was sent in to provide valuable intel on what was considered, at the time, a national threat. Many of the members of The Fishermen were recruited at university. They would, one day, have connections to the government. To state. To the medical profession.'

'But a *police officer*,' whispered Joseph. 'You must have known that to be accepted into such a group he would have had to–'

'It was believed they could infiltrate without participation. Just watch from the sidelines, as it were. Do menial jobs to show their support, but nothing... unsavoury.'

Joseph couldn't believe what he was hearing.

'And it was worth it in the end.'

'Worth it? What could possibly be worth it?'

Joseph felt ill with disgust. His skin felt like it was contaminated, just sitting listening to this woman.

'It was Walter who gave us the information we needed to finally shut them down.'

Joseph was staring at the Smart Board. At the pictures of Walter and Daisy. Joseph turned back to Slane, his expression beyond sorrow.

'What do you mean?'

'I mean, Joseph, The Fishermen didn't commit mass-suicide, sending the girls out in a final act of mercy or social seeding.'

She smiled her binary smile. Joseph wondered how he had ever thought she was a normal human being.

'I'm not following.'

'They didn't blow themselves up, Joseph. We blew them up. We set explosives in all their houses, got the children out, and blew them all to hell. That was the intel Walter managed to get to us. The whereabouts of all the houses.'

44

Jay collapsed to the floor, pain exploding in her leg where she had been kicked.

The woman stood over her and, for a brief second, Jay thought it was Daisy. She was around the same size, wearing cargos and a hoodie. Her hair was cut in a similar style. Her eyes were heterochromatic.

But her face was a mask of anger and old hatred, like it had been baked-in over the years.

'What the fuck are you doing here? Slane said you'd be long gone.'

The woman's mouth twisted into a sneer, like Jay was a piece of shit that had got stuck to her shoe. The resemblance to Daisy disappeared like a mirage as if it had never been there. The woman raised her foot and brought it down on Jay's chest. Hard.

Jay screamed, but the only sound that came out was a whistle of air like she was leaking.

'Doesn't matter. You're not going anywhere now. I reckon I've fucked up your knee good and proper.'

The woman smiled. Her teeth were yellow, with gum decay clearly visible.

Girl:Broken

Jay's knee was a volcano. It was the same one that had been hit before, the night Daisy had gone. She suspected the woman was right and it was proper fucked; possibly even dislocated. Pain ran up her leg and into her hip.

But excruciating pain in one knee probably meant her other knee worked just fine.

Jay brought her boot up and kicked the woman in the crotch with all her force. She actually saw her lift off the ground a little, before collapsing on the floor. Jay crawled on top of the woman and headbutted her in the face. The nose exploded in blood and cartilage, flattening with a crunch. Jay felt it shatter. The reverberation sent a shockwave of pain from her head to her ribs.

'That's for making me feel stupid for not checking the bathroom,' she said, then headbutted her again. Jay had long ago learnt the lesson of overkill. That way they couldn't give you any surprises. The woman's eyes glazed over, then rolled back. Jay thought she might have dislocated a retina when she saw something slip out, then realised it was a contact lens.

Blue.

Jay rolled off the woman, breathing heavily.

'Fake eyes. Fake Daisy. What the fuck?'

After a minute Jay eased onto her stomach and pulled herself up onto her good knee. Her entire left leg was on fire, apart from the knee that had been kicked, which was worryingly empty of any feeling at all and seemed to be swelling in front of her eyes. It was amazing. It was as if it was being inflated.

Using the wall as support, she hauled herself to her feet.

Or foot, as it turned out.

She stayed very still until the room stopped swimming in front of her.

There was no way she was going to be able to put any serious weight on her leg. She lurched to her bag and fished out the painkillers the doctor had given her and dry swallowed a handful. As lightning flashes of agony telegraphed through her body she thought of taking the tablets she'd found in Lawrence's flat as well.

She looked at the blood-covered woman on the floor.

'But that would be stupid,' Jay said.

The unconscious woman didn't answer.

'And we've already established that I'm as bright as a fucking button.'

Staring at the woman, she swallowed one more tablet.

'For luck,' she whispered through the pain.

45

'You set the explosions? You blew up the cult houses?'
Joseph looked at them in turn. 'But it was in all the literature. The Fishermen had a resurrection complex; thought that they were seeding for the next phase of the species. They believed–'

'Planted by us. By F-branch,' said Slane.

Joseph rubbed his hands on his cheeks, a look of total confusion on his face.

'But why?'

'The Fishermen couldn't be allowed to continue. You've seen the footage, Joseph. They were depraved. We had to close them down. But there were so many, and they were well educated.'

'I don't understand.'

Collins snorted with exasperation as if he thought Joseph was being particularly slow.

'You've seen what the Muslim militants do in jail. It's not like a punishment for them. It's like university, Joseph! It's a recruitment ground. If The Fishermen had made it to trial then they would have had a platform. Oh, most people would have been abhorred, I know. But a proportion, Joseph, a larger proportion than you would believe, would have been intrigued.'

'Seduced, even; they ran the houses like places of veneration,' continued Slane, softly. 'They organised them like some post-war ideal of family, with everyone having a role and everybody working towards a common goal.'

'But it was child abuse,' said Joseph again.

'But the children were just fish,' said Slane. 'Things to be caught and kept. First as pets, then as food.'

Joseph felt clammy in her gaze. Tension ants ate his nerves just under the surface of his skin.

'And finally transformed,' finished Collins.

'The mermaid,' said Joseph.

'Exactly. The child would be educated... brainwashed... into believing what was done to it was necessary. To change it, transform it, into a new being. To make it into what it should truly be.'

'It's brilliant, really,' said Collins. 'The pain the child suffered becomes no longer relevant because the child no longer exists.'

'It has become something else.'

'So there is no crime,' finished Joseph. 'Is that what you're saying to me?'

'Their philosophy was... persuasive to certain groups. That's why they couldn't continue to exist, even after their destruction.'

Joseph looked at them. 'You're talking about state-sponsored murder of British citizens. On British soil.'

'As I say, it was a different time. It was considered the most limiting thing to do. If we could get the children out, the innocents, then...' She spread her hands. 'This sort of thing still goes on, Joseph. Camps in Afghanistan. Iraq.'

'But that is in the context of war,' Joseph's voice came out as a shocked whisper. 'This is just...'

'Pest control,' said Collins, flatly.

'And it was war, of a sort. A war against British society. That was the original remit of F-branch. To protect the moral centre of the nation.'

'And the officers? The people working undercover?'

'Collateral damage,' said Slane. 'Sometimes the soldier dies. Those are the risks.'

Joseph looked from Collins to Slane, then back at the board. His head hurt. The thought of British officers being so far undercover that they'd participate in something so evil as The Fishermen was unthinkable, but then so many things humans did were. Slane and Collins were staring back at him, waiting for him to say something.

Finally, he wiped his hand across his face. 'This is unbelievable. Shocking and awful. A national scandal. But I still don't see what it's got to do with me.'

'Oh that bit is easy, Joseph,' said Slane, smiling. The smile was so inappropriate in the circumstances that Joseph felt like screaming. 'We need you to get Daisy to talk to us.'

For a moment he was too stunned to say anything, but then the full implications of what they meant hit him.

'Daisy? You know where she is?'

'Oh yes, Joseph. Of course we do. We have her safe, but she won't talk to us.' Slane leaned forward in her seat. 'And we really need her to. She managed to recognise Walter on the street and it set something off in her. She's been researching The Fishermen, using their real names. It's clear she knows far more than we ever believed. She was just a child when she was rescued, and it was assumed she would have erased the memories of what was done to her, or they were rendered useless to us due to the trauma.'

'Then you need a doctor, surely? Years of psychiatric–'

'We haven't got time, professor. We need to know now what she knows.'

'But why? What's the urgency?'

'The names she was researching. The real names of The Fishermen. Some of them were like Walter.'

'Police officers,' clarified Collins.

'Yes, but–'

'And some of them still are,' finished Slane.

Joseph looked at her. 'Still are. What do you mean "still are"?'

Slane raised an eyebrow. 'You understand me. The Fishermen are alive and well, Joseph. Still operational and still active.'

Slane tapped on her tablet, bringing a new picture up onto the board. Joseph looked at the image of a smiling young woman, fresh and bright in her police uniform. He guessed it must have been taken on her graduation day.

'This is Jay Starling. We recruited her to watch over Daisy. She was savagely beaten and left for dead. Ms Starling has since gone missing.'

Jay looked so different from when he had last seen her; battered with a buzz cut and limping away from him, shoulders hunched.

But the fire in her eyes was the same. The look that told the world it had better watch out, because she wasn't taking any prisoners.

'What are you saying to me?'

'One of the names Daisy was researching was hers, Joseph. We think Ms Starling is a member of the cult. We think that is why Daisy tried to kill her.'

Joseph was stunned. 'What?'

'Jay Starling is a member of The Fishermen. When Daisy found out, she tried to kill her. When we discovered Ms Starling had been admitted to Leeds Infirmary we visited her. It became clear she was compromised in some way, and we arranged to remove her to a safe environment. She escaped from the hospital and went on the run. We hoped Daisy could confirm this, and give us the names of anybody else she remembers.'

In the shocked silence that followed Slane's statement Joseph's phone pinged, announcing a text message.

46

23RD OCTOBER: AFTER THE ATTACK

Slane, Collins and Fielding looked at Daisy's door. The police had padlocked it shut and put hazard tape across it.

'We're going to need a key for that,' said Slane quietly. 'I want someone to search the flat. The FOSs would have been through everything but they won't be looking for what we are.'

'No,' agreed Collins. 'But then we won't know what we're looking for either, will we? Because Daisy might not–'

'Exactly,' said Slane. She turned to Fielding. 'Can I leave that to you? Lawrence has already fucked up and needs to keep a low profile.'

'Sure,' said the young woman. 'I'll find the acquisition sheet and see who they used.'

Slane nodded. All police authorities used emergency boarding-up services to secure properties they had had to enter forcefully. Some were national and some were local. Fielding would find the procurement order and collect a spare key.

'Good.'

'Upstairs,' said Collins, looking at his tablet.

Slane looked along the balustrade to the stairs leading up to the next level. She smiled. 'Really? To Jay's flat? How absolutely priceless.'

The three of them walked past Daisy's door and up the stairs. On Collins' tablet, the position of Jay's phone announced itself with a pulsing red dot.

As they ascended, Slane marvelled at the idiocy of people carrying little spy-bricks in their pocket, thinking they were merely devices for searching the internet or taking calls. Even when they used a map app and it showed their exact location, they never seemed to worry. That, given the right access, anybody could find you.

Although Slane supposed that the person who took Jay's phone wouldn't really understand how the technology worked.

Or how any modern IT system worked.

Because she'd not been brought up that way.

Once at the top of the stairs Slane walked directly to Jay's flat. She removed a key from her pocket and slotted it into the door, unlocking it slowly so as to create the least amount of noise.

Easing the door open, the inspector signalled that they should maintain silence as they entered.

Collins and Fielding nodded that they understood, and they slipped into the apartment, closing the door behind them.

The flat was in relative darkness, with no lights on. The only illumination came from the Leeds street lamps, visible through the open curtains and blinds. With Jay in hospital, possibly in a coma, no one had been there to close them.

Fielding pointed at the window visible in the lounge at the end of the hall.

It was open.

They walked stealthily down the corridor, their footfall silent on the carpet. Fielding went through the door to the right, into the bathroom. The set-up was the same as Daisy's, with only the three rooms and the hall.

Collins went through the left into the bedroom.

Slane walked straight on, into the kitchen-cum-lounge.

She was tense, her body wired by adrenalin. It had been a while since she had needed to be in the field and hadn't realised how much she'd missed it. The experience of fear, and hunting; searching for another human being.

It was like the old days.

She blinked.

There was nobody there.

Jay's lounge was sparse, with only a low sofa and a table with a laptop.

Slane picked up the laptop, scanning the rest of the space.

The kitchen area was empty, the cupboards too small to hide in.

Slane walked to the open window and looked out. The metal criss-cross of the platform leading to the fire escape was a couple of feet below the sill. Bits of broken glass from one of the windowpanes glittered in the street lamps. Slane saw that the clasp that allowed the window to be opened had been broken, hit with something blunt.

'Boss?'

The voice was quiet. Slane turned.

Collins was standing in the doorway, a tight smile on his face.

'We've found her.'

Slane followed him to the bedroom. Like Daisy's, Jay's mattress was straight to the floor. A duvet neatly covered it.

'In here.'

She turned to see Fielding standing by the cupboards that covered one entire wall. Unlike Daisy's these had doors. Fielding's hand rested lightly on the handle as she gazed in.

Slane walked over and stood next to the woman.

Crammed into the bottom corner of the cupboard was Daisy. She had her legs pulled up to her chest with her arms wrapped around them like she was tying herself together. By her side was Jay's phone. The device was broken. Slane guessed Daisy must have used it to break the lock on the window.

No matter. It had displayed its last location tag. It had brought them here.

Slane squatted down.

At the movement, Daisy turned her head.

Slane stared transfixed at her heterochromia. It was the first time she'd seen it up close.

Daisy stared back, vacant.

Slane wasn't even sure she saw her. 'Shock?'

'Possibly. Or maybe the whole experience has made her shut down. Some sort of emotional defence mechanism.'

'Could be the drugs she's taking. We'll need to get a complete list.'

'Jay already supplied us with that,' said Slane, never taking her eyes off Daisy.

At the mention of Jay's name Daisy blinked. 'Jay?' she whispered.

Slane nodded.

'Hello, Daisy. My name is Heather. Jay's fine. Would you like me to take you to her?'

She held out her hand.

Daisy looked at it a moment, then back at her.

Slane held her breath.

After a long moment, Daisy reached out and took it.

Slane smiled.

47

3RD NOVEMBER

Jay used the baseball bat as a walking stick and staggered forward.

She looked at the ruined bed. Thought about how Lawrence must have come in and watched them, asleep.

When you came back in. Did you remember to lock the door?

That was what Daisy had whispered to her, as they'd fallen unconscious.

Drugged.

Jay thought of him creeping over to the bed and looking at them. Perhaps touching them. And then taking back his foot and kicking her in the head. Stomping down on her ribs and knee. Beating her so badly that if Daisy hadn't woken up...'

He'd meant to kill her, Jay realised.

Maybe he thought he had.

Maybe that part of Slane's story was true. Lawrence had come over to beat her to death, and then intended to phone the emergency services so that Daisy was blamed.

'Why?' she whispered, staring at the horror pictures on the board. 'What's the point?'

But then Daisy had woken up and seen her.

Texted 999.

Saved her.

Lawrence would have seen her being taken out to the ambulance. Known she wasn't dead and called Slane.

Decided on a new plan.

We're going to move you to a safe place. Do a proper debriefing.

'Yeah, with a wet sponge and a car battery, probably,' muttered Jay grimly.

She rested her weight against the wall and fished her phone out of her pocket. She looked at the device.

'How did you know how to text, Daisy? You were a complete techno-hedge.'

As she thought about this her phone pinged, indicating a message. She swiped it awake.

It was a data-mine, being transferred through the scraper Joseph had planted.

She stared at the information being downloaded. It was from whatever computer network Joseph had plugged the charger-disguised scanner she had arranged for him to get from Clarence. It had copied the passcodes and was downloading everything it found; media files, data folders, everything.

Jay opened one at random and viewed the contents. As she saw the stream of images; hundreds it appeared, her mouth dried up and she felt bile churning at her gut.

The images that seemed to bleed off the screen were beyond obscene. She didn't recognise any of the children but it didn't matter. What they were being subjected to dehumanised them anyway. Systems of control that seemed beyond belief.

Children lined up and blindfolded, their bodies bound tight in straps.

A young girl hanging upside down, screaming.

A child having her hair brushed by an adult, tears streaming down her face.

And in every shot, the child's eyes were full of fear. Or worse, full of nothing.

Vacant.

There were other images, where there were far fewer clothes and much more pain, but Jay couldn't focus on them. Just saw them as a blur of pink and brown and black.

And red.

She shut the feed, letting it just download without a window open. She swallowed the bile that had slugged up her throat.

After a moment she swiped her phone again and dialled a number.

She closed her eyes as she heard it ring. She thought it was going to ring out when it was finally answered.

'Inspector Charmers,' said the efficient voice.

Jay smiled.

'Robert, how's the jaw?'

The voice changed immediately.

'Jay? Starling! Where are you? Are you okay? I got your message. Is it rolling?'

Jay had messaged him from the bus when she had left Leeds after the hospital. She had no idea who she could trust. Her old boss seemed to be a friend of her new boss, and her new boss seemed to be very iffy indeed. The only person she could think of in the force who would absolutely know she wasn't fucking about was the man whose jaw she'd broken for insulting her.

At least she knew he wouldn't bullshit her.

He had written back almost immediately, saying how sorry he was and he'd do anything to make up for his error.

Apparently, his wife had left him and he'd gone off the rails. Apparently, Jay had done him a favour. Apparently, he was getting therapy.

Jay had to laugh.

When she'd formulated her plan with Joseph she'd reached

out again. Sent him a message to prime him, emphasising that he couldn't tell anybody, especially not their boss. It was a risk, but she couldn't just go to her chief. She didn't trust her boss. She was also supposedly on furlough for disciplinary issues, and who knew what else Slane had primed the authorities with.

She needed someone who would be known not to automatically take her side.

'Sorry, Robert, but I've got zero time for chit-chat. Yes, it's on. I'm going to forward a link to you. It is from an illegally placed data-mining device that is stealing information from a computer belonging to a historical paedophile ring.'

Jay closed her eyes a moment then continued.

'But as it was planted there by a member of the public it's probably admissible.' She tapped at the phone, forwarding the link.

'Starling,' said the inspector softly. 'What–'

'Plus I've beaten a woman unconscious, but she deserved it. I think she's alive but I really don't care. I believe she is the woman who murdered a homeless person called Walter Cummings in Leeds several months ago and also murdered the witness to that murder. I'm afraid I don't know the witness's name.'

'What do you mean "historical paedophile ring"?'

Jay smiled. Charmers was a professional from the old days. He wouldn't repeat a confession on an open line. Wouldn't question her about beating up a suspect.

'The Fishermen. The data is from The Fishermen, Robert. It seems to document their entire operation. And judging from some of the clothes the victims were wearing, the operation didn't stop in the nineteen-eighties, some of the styles are from a later date.'

At the mention of The Fishermen, the line had gone quiet.

Jay understood. Dropping a name like that to someone Charmer's age would be like mentioning the devil himself.

'Still active?' he whispered. 'What do you mean?'

'It's all on the files. Did you get in touch with the IOPC?'

Jay had asked him to reach out to the Independent Office for Police Corruption. She wasn't sure if Slane was actually a police officer, but she was taking no chances. Her comment about Jay's old boss had disturbed her enough to not take any prisoners.

'Yes, they're just waiting for my say so.'

'Right. Well, forward the link to them. Those guys can deconstruct anything. They'll know what to do.'

'What about your partner? The civilian, Professor Skinner?'

'I've just pinged you his number. The text we discussed. When he replies you'll have his location.'

'About his hair; right. And once I have it...?'

'Then send in the artillery and arrest everyone. Possibly by shooting them first.'

Jay thought for a second. Her head was feeling fuzzy from the pain and the tablets.

'Everyone except Joseph, that is.'

'You need to come in, Jay. I'm going to send a car. Where are you?'

'Deal with Joseph first. I'm not going anywhere.'

Charmers began saying something else, but Jay crashed the call.

There had been something in the pictures that were being downloaded that she hadn't registered when she looked at them. She'd been so battered by the images of the children that she hadn't noticed the adults. The Fishermen.

She pulled up the file again, concentrating on the abusers, rather than the abused.

The shots were not what one normally got; if normal could ever be used in these circumstances. When abuse images were shared over the net the faces were never seen. No identifiable marks were ever on view. No chance of prosecution.

In the images on the file, all the faces were visible. Like they never thought they were going to get caught. Or like they never thought they were doing anything wrong.

Jay could see Lawrence's face, smiling out at her, one hand on the bony shoulder of a terrified girl.

Jay swiped the phone closed and looked at the woman lying unconscious on the floor.

'I hope I fucking killed you, Lawrence.' Her voice was flat, beyond emotion. What emotion could there be?

She looked at the wall thoughtfully for a moment, then smiled. It was not a good smile.

'But maybe I'll just check.'

Then limped towards the door.

48

'Damn, that'll be Mark! I completely forgot to send him a picture of my hair!'

Slane and Collins eyed him curiously.

'Joseph,' began Slane. 'I hardly think this is the time to be worryi–'

'No, you don't understand. If I don't send him a picture then the patterns will go wrong in his head. Remember, I told you about it?'

'Yes, but–'

Joseph stood. 'It will only take a second.'

He carried on talking as he went to get his phone, charging in the corner. He hoped his act was convincing. He'd felt the tracker in his pocket so they knew he'd done what he said he was doing; getting the haircut from his autistic son. He just hoped they hadn't fully researched him and found out that his son didn't have ASD. Nor had he booked him in for a haircut.

If they see it in the diary they'll believe it. Trust me. Something written down in an actual book these days means it's true.

That's what Jay had said.

He prayed she was right.

He contorted his face into what he hoped was professional amazement.

'I just can't believe it! The network must be endemic! And you've been investigating all this on the quiet? It's astonishing!'

'We had to. If anybody got wind that the British Government had been involved...'

'Quite.' Joseph picked up the phone and handed it to Slane. 'I can see why you've been so secretive. Would you mind taking the photo? This phone is so ancient, I'm afraid, it doesn't have a selfie camera so I can't do it myself. You need to point and shoot.'

Slane raised an eyebrow then took a snap of Joseph.

He took the phone back.

'Thanks. I'll send the picture to Mark and then we can crack on. This is amazing! To actually meet a victim of The Fishermen! And be able to help uncover an operational cell!'

'I'm afraid you won't be able to talk about the cell, Joseph. Or if you do it will be heavily redacted.'

'Yes of course. I completely understand the need for keeping things on the low.'

Joseph pressed a button on his phone, sending off the picture. He put the device down carefully and turned to them. 'So where is she? Daisy?'

'Near,' said Slane. 'Not far at all, in fact.'

'And what is it exactly you think I can do?'

'As I said, when your lecture was flagged on our system, we looked into you. Saw the work you did with the child soldiers in Africa,' said Collins. 'You got them to tell you where the rebel bases were when no one else could.'

Joseph nodded. 'The sieged brain acts like a Rubik's cube. It turns itself round and round to protect what it knows, but it never forgets. To retrieve the information it's just a matter of learning the algorithms. Knowing the causes can point to ways of healing, or at least containing, trauma, but it doesn't allow for a reset. How could it? The brain isn't static. Life is forever learning and relearning. Writing and rewriting. Especially the brain of a child. It is a fundamental of surviving.'

'So she would have stored the knowledge. Somewhere,' said Slane eagerly.

Joseph nodded. 'Nothing is ever forgotten.'

'And what if that person was near transformation,' said Slane.

Joseph looked at her, questioning. 'What do you mean?'

'Would she remember the process too? If she'd been triggered by the sight of Walter Cummings, would she begin to remember what her purpose was? Would she understand that she was meant to change?'

Joseph shook his head slightly, not understanding.

Then did.

He looked at the board, with the picture of the young girl, Daisy.

'Brown eyes,' he said.

'I'm sorry?'

'Daisy has brown eyes in this picture.'

Slane looked up at the board.

'Yes, she does. Is that relevant?'

'In some cultures, heterochromia is highly revered. They believe it means you can see into two realms. Ghost eyes, it's called by the indigenous peoples of North America. Witch eyes in East-European folklore.'

'Really? How interesting.'

Slane's voice was polite but distant. Joseph nodded, not noticing.

'Normally it's congenital. You're born with it. But in certain circumstances, it can be manufactured. Diabetes. Malnutrition. Head and eye trauma. Severe mental torture that could cause seizure.'

Joseph turned and looked at them. 'Do you have information on all the children of The Fishermen? Did many of them have this syndrome?'

'You know, Joseph, I'm not sure, but I can see your thinking. Which is a bit of a problem.'

Slane nodded at Collins who stood and walked to the door. Joseph watched him slide the bolt across it.

He looked questioningly at Slane, but she merely stared back, unblinking. Studying him as if he was a specimen.

'Ah,' he said. 'I've fucked up, haven't I?'

Slane inclined her head. 'I'm afraid you have.'

'What did I do?'

'We never mentioned that Daisy had different coloured eyes,' said Collins, walking back and sitting down. 'Which means you must have been talking to someone who knows her. How is the resourceful Ms Starling, by the way?'

'Really sweary,' said Joseph. He felt bizarrely calm. He supposed it was a release of pressure from no longer having to put up a subterfuge. 'Are you going to kill me?'

Slane looked genuinely surprised. 'Kill you? Of course we're not going to kill you, Joseph!'

Collins took out a gun from his jacket pocket. Slane smiled her smile at him. On, off. Binary. The only thing that moved on her face. Like a spot the difference picture.

Human. Not human.

'Why would we kill you?'

'I–'

She held up a hand, silencing him.

'I think we'll say that *Jay* killed you. Jay Starling, the suspended officer who disappeared, the awful member of the notorious Fishermen's sect, and daughter of a known cultural agitator. I think she's the most likely candidate, don't you?'

49
25TH OCTOBER

Daisy woke up wrong.
    Wronger.
Wrongest.
She didn't know where she was.
She wasn't on her bed.
She wasn't in her flat.
She felt her body spasming. Felt flashes of fear wrack through it like she was in the middle of a thunderstorm.
She tasted lemons and salt and heard a rushing in her head like her blood was tiding.
She opened her eyes.
She was lying on the floor, in a bare room made up of breeze blocks. In front of her was a metal door. A barred window with meshed glass in it was set high in the wall.
She sat up quickly, her heart beating with panic.
Where was she?
Who had brought her here?

Heather

. . .

The name dropped into her head unbidden, like it was made of stone. It was cold and heavy and dead and made her feel like screaming. She had no idea what the name meant, but her skin goosebumped and her breath skimmed out of her, cutting across her lungs like glass.

Daisy stood. 'Hello?'

The sound of her voice was hardly above a whisper. The noise seemed to slither around the room, laughing at her.

Feeling increasingly frightened, Daisy walked to the door.

It was locked.

'Hello?'

She put her ear to the door. There was no noise other than the tide in her head.

How had she got here?

The last thing she remembered was lying on the mattress in her room, with Jay stroking her...

The noise in her head increased. She slammed her fist against the metal door. The sound was dull, as if the room were soundproofed.

Another memory slipped into her mind.

Holding a phone, seeing a message on the screen to 999.

'Daisy.'

Daisy spun round, but nobody was there.

She could feel a scream in her throat, trying to break out.

Images ripped across her vision.

Jay lying still on her bed.

'Daisy, you need to go.'

Daisy spun round again.

Nobody there.

An image of Jay covered in blood.

'Hello, my name is Heather.'

Words from the past.

A monster from the horror house.

Jay bleeding tears from her beaten body, unconscious and broken.

'You need to hide.'

Daisy put her hands to her ears, trying to stop the noise, but it was no good. She squeezed her eyes tight but the tide got louder, increasing until she was spinning in her own head.

Sinking.

Sinking.

Drowning.

50

3RD NOVEMBER

Joseph frowned. 'So this was all about a fall guy? Everything you've told me was bullshit? I don't believe it.'

'Of course not. Most of what we've told you is true. The Fishermen are still going. We do really need to know if Daisy knows the operatives. You are really going to be killed. It's just we... put a different perspective on it.'

'Go on, then. If I am going to die, at least tell me the correct perspective.'

'You wouldn't understand,' said Collins.

'Try me.'

Slane turned to her boss. Except, Joseph realised, she was the boss. Slane was the one really in charge.

'Get hold of Grant; we're pulling it. We'll salvage something from this and start again. The fish is still on the hook. Best option.'

Collins nodded, handing the gun to her and taking out his phone. Slane returned her gaze to Joseph.

'Why not? There's nothing else you can help with now. There really was an undercover operation. Not to the extent I said, but just on the perimeters. Tiny little worker-ants who didn't get to the inner sanctum. Every operation has them. We thought we'd be able to infiltrate, that way. Get under their radar.'

'And what happened?'

Slane shrugged. 'We couldn't. It was the same with a lot of undercover operations. We had to get our hands dirty.'

Joseph felt sick. 'They were children, Slane.'

'They were fish, waiting to be set free.'

The full weight of her words buried him. 'Oh my God,' he said into the silence. 'You were there, weren't you? You were one of them?'

Slane smiled. 'I was a young officer, eager to please. I got placed in a university and attended the right sort of demonstration. Then I went to the right meetings. Eventually, I slept with the right people.'

'Deep cover.' Disgust and revulsion twisted Joseph's mouth.

'The deepest.'

Joseph took a slow breath. When he spoke, his voice was strong. 'But the trouble with deep cover is you never realise it's too deep until it's gone too far, yes?'

'Except it wasn't too deep, Joseph!' Slane's eyes gleamed. 'It was...' she paused, as if trying to find the right word, '...more than anyone could know. The purity of control...'

Slane's fervour was hypnotic. It was like watching an explosion; bright and deadly and with no hope of survival.

Joseph kept his voice level. 'But the authorities found out you had become corroded somehow. They decided to shut the operation down,' he guessed.

Slane shook her head at the memory. 'They never understood. How could they? They only saw things from the outside. Never saw the bigger picture. They were already tainted by the society that made them.'

She looked at him as if he would comprehend what she was

talking about, as if *he'd* understand. Joseph realised that she was probably insane; pushed over the edge by the trauma she had witnessed and participated in when she was young. In an attempt to escape any culpability, her mind had created a whole new narrative for herself that made her actions acceptable.

'The fabric of society is rotten. Everything is being corrupted. Pornography watched on their phones. The never-ending supply of drugs and lust for money. The children have no hope.'

Slane looked genuinely upset.

'And you think this is an answer?' he said, his voice rising. 'To abuse–'

'No! To remodel. To take the fish and teach it that it doesn't need to rely on the river. That it can leave and become something else.'

'Become what?' he said, then, aghast, realised what she was hinting at. 'The mermaid. You mean become the mermaid.'

Slane nodded. 'Once the head of the operation decided to shut it down we knew what they had to do. What they were going to get us to do. There was no way the public could cope with their government participating in such an organisation in their name.'

'So they decided to kill everyone.'

'Including the children. Wipe everything away as if it was just a stain on a table.'

The hatred in Slane's voice was visceral. Joseph wanted to point out the double standards of her anger but knew it was useless. The woman was too deep down the rabbit hole of her own psychosis.

'It was our idea to get them out first. Many of them, like Daisy, were so close to fulfilling our dream. They had already begun to change. To transform. We thought if we could get them to a safe place we'd be able to start again. After the fuss had died down.'

'Fuss,' he repeated.

Slane nodded happily. She was so far in her narrative she didn't even hear his revulsion. Joseph glanced at Collins. He had abandoned his phone and had moved onto his tablet. When Slane continued talking, he turned back to her.

'Except it all went wrong. Most of us died in the explosion. The bastards only wanted a few of us to survive. So that we could debrief and explain the full set-up.'

'And you were one?'

'Me and Collins and a couple of others. We were young, with the right profile.'

'They never knew you'd been flipped.'

'Awakened,' she corrected. 'No, they thought we were still like them. We never appeared in any of the transformation tapes. The only images of us were vanilla. Just in the background. Never participating.'

'That must have been hard for you.'

Slane shrugged, treating him to a brilliant smile. 'Not really; I was the one operating the camera.'

Joseph thought of the images he had seen earlier. Remembered how shocked he'd been at the steadiness of the camera; how he supposed whoever had filmed it must have done it before, to not be affected by what they were documenting.

'I understand,' was all he managed to say.

'Afterwards, the children were taken by the state; sent to institutions around the country. Hidden under identity blackouts. It was impossible to get to them all.'

'Most of them committed suicide from their trauma, Slane.'

She shook her head. 'No, it was because the process was interrupted. If we could have finished...'

Joseph didn't know what to say. The woman was so delusional that his blood was freezing just looking at her. 'But then Daisy happened.'

'Yes. Walter was one of the survivors. Like me, he had been given a new identity but had suffered from PTSD and gone off the rails. Lost his grip on reality. We had no idea he had ended up on the street.'

'I'm sure.'

Poor Walter, thought Joseph. *Being badly affected by performing horrors. If this woman had known you'd fallen so far she'd have killed you. Who knows what you might have said?*

'When Daisy spotted him it must have triggered hidden memories. She started looking up our names on the internet.'

'How do you know Daisy spotted him?'

'When the warning flags went up we traced some to an internet café in the centre of town. We scraped the CCTV from around the site and...' She smiled, spreading her hands.

Joseph thought of Jay, how she said that Daisy had no internet skills, but said nothing. Instead he asked another question. 'So she remembered you?'

Slane nodded happily. 'Not at first, but later. Once we had her secure. It was fantastic. And a complete surprise. We'd managed to track some of the children, but not Daisy. The fall out had been so huge that special measures were taken. New names and identities. Mirror paperwork. Blind filing. But when Daisy reached out we knew it was a sign. That we could start again. We needed to be able to keep tabs on Daisy. See if she could push her into transformation.'

'So you had recruited Jay.'

'Obviously none of us could do it. We couldn't risk her seeing us straight away. Lawrence belonged to a different house, so we could use him, but not for close-up friendship. She would have been too wary.'

Slane had mentioned Lawrence before. He wished he could warn Jay, but all he could hope to do was keep this madwoman talking.

'But not of Jay.'

'She was a godsend. She could join the groups Daisy was attending with no suspicion. Jay was already halfway to being sacked. You only had to look at her to know she was a car crash waiting to happen. Getting a colleague to furlough her was easy.'

'I can't reach Lawrence or the others. I've sent a message to Grant to shut everything down but don't know if it was sent. There doesn't seem to be any signal.'

Slane looked at Collins. 'Try outside. We need to move.'

Collins nodded and headed for the door.

Once he had left, Slane turned back to Joseph. 'When Jay informed us that not only was she quitting, but that Daisy was becoming corrupted by her false memories, we had to act fast.'

Joseph thought he heard a noise beyond the door. The device he'd been given by Jay's friend would have stopped Collins contacting the other Fishermen, but it wouldn't have sped up the police's arrival. He concentrated on the woman in front of him.

'Her memories weren't corrupted, Slane! The inside of her head would be a scrapyard of recollection. Nothing would be able to fit together. It's amazing she'd manage to survive for so long.'

Slane shrugged a solitary shoulder. 'We primed the therapist to see if we could bump-start her, but it pushed her the wrong way. When she quoted the song, Daisy... merged with her mermaid.'

The look in Slane's eyes was one of fondness; as if Daisy had accidentally spilt milk whilst making tea.

'But then we decided we could put it to our advantage. We

could place all the guilt on Daisy. Make her believe she'd killed her new friend as well as Walter and Beata.'

'Beata?'

'The witness to Walter's murder,' said Slane impatiently. 'We thought that if we could rescue Daisy from all that, she would realise that we were the only ones she could trust.'

Joseph stared at her, unbelieving. 'You did all this? Just to make a damaged mind think you were her… what, saviour?'

'To help her become,' insisted Slane. 'Because then she could take her proper place.'

Before Joseph could answer there was a shout, followed by the sharp crack of a gun. Slane's head whipped round.

Collins came crashing through the door. 'We've been tagged. The whole place is surrounded.'

He looked at Joseph, then at the fake charger in the corner, its charge light flashing.

Slane followed his gaze. 'Oh dear,' she said mildly. 'Any chance of escape?'

'None, ma'am. No chance at all.'

'Understood.' Slane nodded sharply and raised the gun, levelling it at Joseph's head. He felt his heart freeze as he stared into the black hole of the muzzle and opened his mouth to scream but no sound came out.

Slane swung the gun around and shot Collins between the eyes. The force from the bullet blew the back of his head off, haloing him for an awful instant in his own blood and brains.

Slane swung the gun back to Joseph before Collins had even crumpled to the floor.

'Don't shoot,' Joseph whispered. 'It won't solve anything.'

'I'm not going to shoot you. I've already told you that. I had to shoot Collins to stop him telling them anything. He knew that. We all do. Protecting the group is all that's important.'

Slane put the gun on the floor and knelt down, placing her hands behind her head.

'What about Daisy? Is she safe?'

'You've no idea what this is about, professor,' she said, smiling.

'Police! Put down your weapons! Armed response unit! We are entering the premises. Anybody offering themselves as a threat will be a legitimate target. I repeat. Put down your weapons and show your hands!'

Slane carried on talking as if they were in a park. Her cadence was conversational, almost intimate. 'It doesn't end here. Really, it's only just beginning. Now we know about Daisy we will regroup.'

Joseph couldn't stop staring. The police were still shouting, but all he heard was the horror coming from Slane's lips as she smiled at him, eyes madness-bright.

'And we're everywhere, Joseph. There were more survivors than the authorities knew. Far more than we ever reported back to them.'

The police came storming through the door, taking up positions, making a rapid assessment of the room.

'And the country's ready for us now. Everything is falling apart and they're ready for us.'

Joseph was worried the police might shoot him by mistake. He raised his hands but stayed focused on Slane.

'Daisy! Where is she? You said she was near. Is she being watched? Is she safe? Have you hurt her?'

'Relax, Joseph, she's fine! She can look after herself.'

'Don't shoot her!' Joseph shouted to the officers, hands held high in the air. 'She's the only one who knows!'

'Knows what?' said the commander-in-chief, his eyes constantly moving, looking for threats. He walked forward and stood on Slane's gun, reducing the chance of it being picked up. 'What does she know?'

Joseph looked at the woman smiling up at him. 'She knows where Daisy is.'

The officer had no idea what he was talking about, but with the gun threat removed it didn't matter. He pulled her hands down behind her back and secured them with his THC plastic restraint cable – harder to break out of than any handcuff.

'You know I don't even think Daisy knows where Daisy is.' Slane smiled. 'You only have to think about the phone to understand that.'

'What? What do you mean?'

If Slane had any more to say she never got a chance. A muzzle bag was placed over her head and she was wrenched to her feet.

'Right. Into the van. The orders are complete media blackout. The suspect is not to be photographed under any circumstances.'

Joseph watched as the hooded figure was dragged out of the room and the remaining officers started dismantling the electrical equipment.

'Hey!' he said to the commanding officer. The man looked inquiringly at him.

'What about Ms Starling? Do you know if she's okay?'

51

'This is a bit of a bummer.' Jay was surveying the empty space where Lawrence should have been unconscious on the living room floor.

She looked at the trail of blood that led out of the room and down the corridor.

'Lawrence!' she shouted, limping forward. 'Coming, ready or not!'

The tablets she'd taken had swathed her head in bubble wrap. She felt almost completely detached from her body.

Or maybe she was going into shock. She had an almost uncontrollable desire to shout 'Here's Johnny!'

'I saw you in the house, Lawrence! The house with the children. Grant was there too! You looked like you were having a lovely time!'

She wiped away the tears from her eyes and staggered forward, the baseball bat trailing by her side. She hadn't even been aware she was crying. She followed the drops of red on the carpet.

'But I have to say, Lawrence, that the children did not look happy at all. Not even one fucking bit.'

She leant against the wall. The floor seemed to be breathing. She brought her hand up to her mouth and pinched the bridge of her nose. Hard. The pain sharpened her senses, allowing her to concentrate. The trail of blood led into the bedroom.

'And we're going to have to do something about that, Lawrence,' she said, but it only came out as a whisper.

She took a breath and walked forward, using the wall as a guide. The edges of her vision were shutting down, cobwebbing her sight. She guessed that she was close to passing out. Her right leg wouldn't bend at all, the knee looking like someone had stuffed a football up her trouser. She was fairly sure her ribs were fully busted too. She was having difficulty taking breaths.

'Just going to hold on long enough to rip your face off. For Daisy.'

It wasn't much of a plan, but it was all she had.

Dragging up the last ball of anger from deep within, Jay staggered forward and pushed open the bedroom door.

Lawrence was collapsed at the foot of the bed, half-on and half-off the mattress.

He was, without doubt, dead. The back of his head was the wrong shape, flattened by something heavy that lay black and sticky next to him. His broken body was still and lifeless.

Jay took in the scene. 'I'm pretty sure I would remember doing that.'

She shuffled forward and stood over the corpse. The murder weapon was some form of tool. It had a wide metal base with a handle and several switches. Jay squinted to see what was written on its side.

ELECTROMAGNET POWER LIFTER. WARNING. STRONG MAGNETIC FIELD.

She stared at it for several seconds, letting the implications sink in. Thinking of what Joseph had said on the train.

I think I've got an idea of how the bolts were locked.

'Oh, you've got to be fucking joking me,' she said mildly.

''Fraid not, Jay,' said a voice like wet gravel behind her.

She turned slowly around, trying not to fall over. A man was grinning at her.

'Boo,' said Grant, waving at her. In his hand was a small stubby knife.

Jay realised he must have been standing behind the door when she'd staggered in. She looked over his shoulder but no one was there to rescue her. Because no one knew where she was. There was no way past him.

She silently said goodbye to Joseph, Daisy and her mother.

'Twice in one sodding day. I must be really shit at my job.'

Grant smiled, nodded, stepped forward and slashed at her face. Jay staggered back, ducking down, and felt the point of the knife ram into her forehead. She gasped in pain but before she could scream Grant pulled up her head by her hair and punched her in the temple, knocking her unconscious.

52

'Jay! Jay, can you hear me?'

The voice was familiar but Jay didn't want to listen. She was too tired and something was terribly wrong with her knee. There was also a pain in her chest. If she listened to the voice she might have to pay attention to it.

She decided to go back to sleep instead.

'Come on, Constable! Stay with us! I think we're losing her. Shit, are we losing her?'

'Move back.'

She felt her mouth being opened followed by a pressure on her breast, rhythmic and insistent. The pain increased and she groaned. Why the fuck couldn't they just let her sleep?

'Jay?'

A new voice. Authoritative. Clear and loud. She didn't like it. It was the sort of voice that wanted you to do things.

'Jay, can you hear me? I'm performing CPR. You've stopped breathing and your heart has gone into spasm. When I get to thirty I'm going to help get air into your lungs. To do this I'll need to cover your nose and blow into your mouth.'

She heard the words, but they didn't make sense. She just

wanted to sleep. If she slept she could wake up somewhere else and all this would be over. She felt her mouth being covered and her chest expanding with air. It was horrible.

'She's not responding. We're going to have to shock her.'

She felt her shirt being ripped open.

'Anybody touches my tits and I'm going to fucking slap them into next year,' she said.

There was a shocked silence.

Jay opened her eyes.

Above her, the young paramedic looked astonished. Behind him, she saw the rough face of Inspector Charmers.

'Ah, welcome back,' he said, smiling.

The paramedic threw a blanket over her.

'Jay, you need to stay still. I'm going to turn your head a little. Please try not to speak.'

Jay ignored him.

'Is Joseph all right? How did you find me?'

'He's fine,' said Charmers. 'And his phone wasn't the only one that I tracked, Starling,' he said, pointing at her. 'When I couldn't raise you I followed the data point to here. And it's damn lucky I did.'

She nodded, then closed her eyes.

'Thank you,' was all she could manage.

As the voices began to fade she realised she hadn't asked about Grant.

53

4TH NOVEMBER

Leeds Hospital

The next time Jay came to she felt a little better. Her body was still a car crash but she could at least marshal her thoughts into order.

Jay kept her eyes closed as she listened. There was the very specific silence of people being very busy very quietly; respectful of all that was happening around them.

She gingerly felt her body, gently skimming over the cuts and bruises. The pain in her knee was a deep toll, and she suspected there would be many months of physio ahead of her, possibly even surgery. She pictured the woman in Daisy's flat, remembering the force of the kick Jay had given her.

'Fucking cow; I hope she's still pissing my boot.'

'I'm sorry, did you say something?'

Jay smiled. Joseph's voice was polite, like she'd just made a comment about the weather. She wondered how long he had been watching over her.

'I said, I'd better not be in a fucking hospital again.' She opened her eyes and attempted a smile at Joseph, wincing as she did so. Even smiling, it seemed, hurt.

'You know, the doctors thought you might have suffered brain damage. Again. You've been swearing like a drag queen in your sleep. They thought you might have developed some form of Tourette's syndrome.'

'Fuck off,' she said.

Joseph smiled. 'Really?'

'With bells on.'

'Right. So I'm guessing you haven't seen your mother sitting on the other side of the bed then?'

Jay looked at him for a moment, then closed her eyes. 'Oh.'

'Hello, dear,' said her mother. 'Loving the new look.'

∼

Several hours later, when Jay woke again, Joseph brought her up to date on all that had happened.

'So Slane really was with F-branch?' she said.

Joseph nodded. 'A subsidiary, yes. They all were. Although Fielding – the woman who impersonated Daisy – and Lawrence are dead. Killed by Grant, presumably, so there was no chance of them giving any information away.'

Jay looked at him a moment, then turned and stared at the ceiling. 'Tell me about Slane.'

'She was recruited out of the academy straight into The Fishermen.'

'But how could they? I mean I understand undercover operatives have to get their hands dirty...' she felt a deep twist of shame as she thought of the lies she'd told Daisy, '...but there was no way you could get someone to abuse kids.'

'They weren't meant to, if Slane was to be believed. Their

mission was purely observational. Being on the outskirts of the cult. Gathering intelligence.'

'Yes, but–'

'And they chose carefully in their recruitment.'

Jay looked at him questioningly. There was something chilling in his voice. He handed her a plastic beaker. She took a sip of warm orange juice. She had to do it through a straw; Grant had bruised her jaw so badly it would barely open.

'I've been given access to some of the redacted files. Not all of them, and I've had to sign some scary forms, but I'm beginning to get a handle on it. The authorities sought out potential recruits by checking their personal history.'

'I'm not getting you.'

Joseph sighed and rubbed a hand through his hair.

'They chose officers who had been abused themselves, Jay. The consensus was that it would give them a greater insight into The Fishermen's thinking.'

'But that's... insane.' The room, so bright before, seemed to shrink around them. She felt a numbing pain right in the centre of her head.

'I know, but this was last century. The police service was unreconstructed. Then, it was considered a sign of failure to be anything but hard. Vulnerability was a weakness. The idea was that if they had survived trauma when they were younger then they would be stronger. Immune. Like what had been done to them was a virus and they had developed the antibodies.'

'So they put in the worst possible people, people already damaged and skewed through abuse, into a dangerous and vulnerable position? Jesus...'

Words failed her.

Joseph nodded. 'And out of the mess, you got Slane and her gang. Sleepers in our society who were just waiting for a sign to start it all up again.'

'What *about* Slane? You said she told you she had Daisy. Before she was arrested. Has she told you where she is?'

Joseph looked uncomfortable. 'She was fully immersed in some long psychosis, Jay. She told me they were everywhere. When she was on the floor, with the police screaming and Collins' brains all around us, she told me they were everywhere and they were ready to get back in business. Then the police put a hood on her and took her out. She never told me where Daisy was.'

Jay saw the pain in his eyes. The pain and, she realised, the fear. 'What happened to her, Joseph? Slane?'

'She disappeared somewhere between arrest and the police station. The vehicle she was being transported in was rammed and she was removed to an unmarked van. Presumably it was Grant. The police applied location tracking software to get a map of their phone use. They discovered the van and searched the buildings around the area. They found where they believe Daisy was kept.'

'And?'

'She's gone.'

'No.'

Joseph nodded.

The room ticked around them.

'Where is she? I can't cope if she's...'

Jay couldn't finish. She stayed looking at Joseph until her mother came back in the room.

54

3RD NOVEMBER: AFTER JOSEPH

Slane looked around the empty room.

The cot bed was unslept in.

When they'd found Daisy in Jay's flat she'd had to laugh.

The fact that the place Daisy felt safest in was in the room of the woman who'd been lying to her was spectacular.

It gave her so much leverage to force Daisy's becoming.

Once she had been set free she had headed straight over, ready to take Daisy away. They already had a safe house waiting for her. Somewhere remote so that the inevitable birthing pains of forcing the mermaid out would not be heard. A butterfly house.

She had hoped to use the professor to find out if any names had been compromised. If they needed to move any members from their positions. When his lecture flagged up, she thought it had been a sign; a way to phoenix the situation out of the flames.

She pursed her lips.

But it had all been a sham.

And now Daisy had gone, somehow escaped out of a locked room.

'She's good at that.' Slane smiled.

No matter.

Daisy, or whatever Daisy was now, was awake and active.

Halfway to becoming.

It wouldn't take long to find her.

Not these days.

Facial recognition.

Data location software.

It was just a matter of time.

'Do you think he believed you?'

'Who?' said Slane, taking a last look around the room.

'The professor. Skinner. Do you think he believed the bullshit you fed him about The Fishermen coming back to take over society?'

Slane shrugged. 'Maybe. Or maybe enough to keep the police off our back till we can get her. Come on,' she said to Grant. 'There's nothing for us here. Time to find the others.'

They closed the door softly and left.

55

23RD NOVEMBER

Jay lay on Joseph's daybed, looking out over the bleak windswept landscape. Antony and the Johnsons' melancholy music bled out of the hidden speakers around the room. Anohni's voice went beautifully with the dark light that seemed to make up the afternoons on the moor. Jay had been there for a week and was slowly recovering, letting her body heal after the trauma of the last two weeks. When the hospital had let her go, Joseph had suggested she come to the moors to recuperate.

To everyone's surprise, including her own, she had agreed.

'I haven't even got a flat anymore, have I?' she'd said, thanking him. 'It was just a sham. A front to get me close to Daisy.'

Of course, that wasn't the reason. Not really. She simply needed to be with someone she hadn't lied to.

Ever.

She'd felt such a fraud. A failure as a policewoman.

As a friend. As a daughter.

Now, sitting here watching the wind scrape the moor, she just felt empty.

'You should eat something. It'll make you feel better.'

Jay turned and looked at Joseph. The professor's concern for her was etched into his face, a face with more lines than when she had met him.

But then the experience they had both gone through was line-making. The discovery of the true nature of The Fishermen cult was enough to cut tramlines deep enough to sleep in. Get buried in.

She smiled at him.

'I have.'

'Painkillers are not food, Jay,' he admonished.

'No, you're right. They need alcohol added to them for that. Could I have some wine?'

'No. And I know you're just ripping me.'

Jay turned back and looked out of the window.

Antony and the Johnsons were replaced with Billie Holiday as Joseph lit the fire. Jay drifted, the drugs given to heal her knee and ribs sending her into a daze. It was comfortable in the study, hearing the tap of computer keys as Joseph worked. The rattling of the windows from the wind that skimmed around the house. The gentle noise from the fire, so much like a river in its crackling.

'Time for bed, Jay,' said Joseph softly.

Jay opened her eyes and was amazed to see that it was nearly nine o'clock. Joseph was still sitting in front of his laptop, editing something on the screen. He had a cup of steaming coffee next to him.

'Jesus, I must have dozed off. What are you doing?'

'Getting the information from the data dump downloaded from Collins and co. Seeing if there's anything useful.'

Jay stretched. Carefully.

'Great. Maybe it will give us a lead on Daisy.'

'Hopefully. You get some sleep. If I find anything I'll wake you.'

Jay nodded and limped out. Between the injuries, the pills, and the guilt she craved sleep like a drug. It helped her forget.

Until the nightmares came.

56

24TH NOVEMBER

The air was so thick with the smell of coffee Jay thought she might have to cut through it with a knife as she entered the living room, refreshed. The melancholy she had felt the previous night had lifted.

'I think you'd better slow down, Joseph, or your heart is going to explode. Where do you get your coffee from; Sellafield?'

She looked around the living room. Beyond the window, the moors were half-visible in the grainy morning light. Inside, the fire was dying in the grate, the red embers fully settled.

'Wait a minute, have you been up all night?'

'I've been reviewing the new footage from The Fishermen,' said Joseph mildly. 'Correlating it with some other data.'

Joseph was sitting at his desk. In front of him were several monitors. Some had the transferred camcorder tapes from the old cult houses. Others seemed to be professional articles. One was of a breeze-block room; possibly a garage.

'You know, you're such a geek,' she said fondly. 'If you'd have been twenty years younger you'd have no socks on and be rocking a beard.'

Joseph had clearly *not* gone to bed. His clothes had less become crumpled than his body had crumpled inside them.

'I did rock a beard when I was twenty years younger,' he said indignantly.

'Yes, but those beards were hair you failed to shave. A beard now is a metaphysical statement of intent.'

He turned away from the screen and looked at her. She was amazed she managed to keep her face straight.

'Maybe I should grow one now?'

'Fuck, no!' said Jay, alarmed. 'If you tried now it would just look like your hair had fallen off your head and got stuck on the way down.'

'Right. And good morning to you too.'

'Sorry, I'm just laughing to stop crying. I'm going mad thinking about Daisy.'

Jay helped herself to a coffee from the cafetière. Joseph had purchased it at Jay's insistence when she had moved in.

'I understand, and that's one of the reasons I've been reviewing the data. There were a few things Slane said that had been niggling at my brain.'

Jay limped over and sat next to him. 'So what have you found? In your reviewing?'

Even discussing the cult sent a deep bell of sadness through her. There had been no sightings of Daisy. Using the phones taken from Fielding, Collins and Slane, the police had found the lock-up where Daisy had been kept, but the place had been empty.

Jay pointed at the image of the breeze-block room. 'Is that it? Where she was kept?'

Joseph nodded.

'It was a lock-up garage on the outskirts of Holbeck, in a derelict industrial estate. Its previous use had involved heavy machinery so there was a degree of soundproofing. Given that and its location it would have been totally isolated.'

'Makes sense.'

Holbeck was a notorious suburb of Leeds, famous for being the UK's only legal red-light district. Large parts of the area were in a state of decay, with no company wanting to redevelop it while it had such a difficult reputation.

'I got the lead case officer to send these to me.' Joseph smiled tightly, looking at the screen. 'It appears I have been elevated to psychological profiler. They're even paying me. Which means I have access to far more meta-data than I would as a consulting professor.'

'Psychological profiler. Cool. Probably need to get a card or something made up. For the ladies.'

Joseph ignored the jibe. 'When the police arrived it was clear someone had been held captive. There was a new padlock on the door and the windows had been boarded up.'

Jay sighed, wondering if the woman was being tortured by Slane in some other bunker or lock-up. 'So they have her. The Fishermen or whatever they call themselves now.'

Joseph shook his head. 'No, I don't think so.'

Jay turned and looked at him. 'You don't think so?'

He leaned forward and swiped the screen, replacing the bare room with another image. This one was lit by a flash, indicating that the space was somewhere with no natural light. A cellar, maybe, or an attic. The flash had illuminated the walls of the space.

'This came through yesterday. I didn't have a chance to review it until last night. It's the crawl space above the room that housed Daisy. It's low and narrow, the aesthetic false ceiling allowing ductwork and the electrics to be hidden. It's only about a metre in depth. Despite the building being split into various work units, the ceiling itself is just one large space spanning the entire structure.'

Jay looked at the screen. Although there were metal heating ducts and electrical conduits, it would be perfectly possible for a person – especially a small person – to crawl through in the gap between.

'The police found a broken area of ceiling in one of the adjoining units, along with a clearly forced window. When they climbed up to investigate they found this.' Joseph swiped again, showing a close up of the ductwork.

Jay stared at it. 'No way,' she whispered.

Scratched into the metal panelling were two words.

help
Daisy

'Quite,' said Joseph.

'Show me the first one again. Where she was kept.'

Joseph did his swipe and flick, pulling up the original picture of the breeze-block room, along with several other shots of the space from different angles. The false ceiling, with its square removable tiles, could clearly be seen.

'How far is that? Eight feet? There's no way Daisy could jump up to reach that.'

'Which is probably why Slane never thought of it or looked up there. We know she most likely came back, because the building is close to where they abandoned their getaway vehicle. Her biological data is all over the room, as is Collins' and at least two others.'

DNA was being collected from the original building the rogue officers had taken Joseph to, along with the vehicle.

'But the police tracked the geo-stamp from the phones to Daisy's cell not long after Slane's escape, so she wouldn't have had time to search the crawl space. I think she'd escaped by the time they came for her. Look at the window.'

Jay looked. The window was high set, with a narrow ledge, really nothing more than a sill.

'I think, if one was motivated, it would be possible to climb up to the window, hold on to the mesh, and push aside one of the ceiling tiles. Once through, the tile could be replaced. They just lift in and out, apparently.'

'Plus Grant, and what you've told me about Collins, would be too fucking big to even fit up there,' mused Jay. She stared at the images, feeling a sense of excitement. 'And she left a message for us! To help her.'

'I don't think so,' said Joseph.

Jay looked at him. 'What do you mean?'

She pointed at the screen.

'It's written right there! "Help". She's even signed her name!'

Joseph took a sip of his coffee, then pointed at another screen. 'This is from one of The Fishermen houses. It was found on the files that were scraped by your friend's device. It seems that Slane had an entire archive of material.'

'Joseph...'

Jay didn't think she would be able to watch any of the footage. Knowing what she did about what happened to Daisy; seeing the map of it in scars and tattoos on her body, she couldn't face the horror of watching it being inflicted.

'It's all right,' said Joseph. 'I watched it all in the night.' He rubbed a hand across his eyes, as if trying to erase the images. 'I've just screen-grabbed a couple of images for explanation.'

Jay took a sip of her own coffee, waiting. On the screen was a young girl. She was sitting on a stool in a gingham dress, staring directly at the camera. On her lap was a cuddly toy. Jay saw with a sickening sadness that it was a mermaid, possibly from the Disney film.

'Can you see what's strange about this picture?' said Joseph.

'Are you fucking with me? The whole thing is a horror film.'

'Look at her face.'

Jay glared at him hard for a moment then, shrugging, leaned in and studied the girl's face.

'There's something wrong with her eyes,' she said after a minute.

Joseph nodded. 'Anisocoria. One of her pupils is larger than the other. It creates the effect of separateness in the gaze.'

'Like Daisy's heterochromia.'

'The causes are varied, but include direct trauma to the eye, or a seizure.'

'Okay. So we have two girls with weird eyes in The Fishermen. That means... what does that mean?'

'It's one of the things that Slane said that were niggling me. When I mentioned about the eye anomaly being venerated in some cultures she became very cool, like I'd hit a nerve.'

'But I thought you said it was because you'd given yourself away.'

'I think it was more than that. I think I'd come too close to the truth.' He swiped and brought up another screen. 'I went and checked the inventory of the meds Daisy had been scoring on the black market. Did you know what they were?'

Jay raised an eyebrow. 'I knew they weren't street drugs. I guessed they were tranquillisers or antidepressants. I'd swiped a few for Slane to analyse, in case they were life-threatening, but she assured me it was okay.'

'I'm sure she'd know,' said Joseph drily. 'There *were* antidepressants. Sertraline and Venlafaxine. A couple of others.'

'Would they have caused blackouts?' Jay asked. 'Because Daisy said she lost big chunks of time.'

'Not by themselves. But she also had other meds. Ritalin and Temazepam and a whole selection. Taken without knowledge she could easily have killed herself.'

Jay hung her head. She'd let her friend down so badly in so many ways. The fact that after leaving her, it seemed Daisy had hidden in her flat, thinking it the safest place she knew, only twisted the knife further.

'But there were also others,' said Joseph, interrupting her dark thoughts.

'Other what?'

'Drugs. Aripiprazole; Risperidone. A few others from the same family.'

Jay shrugged her ignorance. 'And?'

'These are slightly more specific. Antipsychotic. Used to treat severe psychological conditions.'

Joseph pointed to the medical journals he had up on the screen.

'So are you saying that Daisy was suffering from a mental condition? Surely that's not surprising. Considering her childhood–'

'Absolutely. What she and the other children suffered was unimaginable. Malnutrition. Extreme mental and physical abuse. Manipulation of their emotions until it may have been impossible for them to even understand the concept of love or empathy. There have been many studies in criminal psychology that indicate the abuse of children, just when they are meant to be identifying with an adult for moral guidance, robs them of the ability to ever form that social understanding of good and bad.'

'So are you saying Daisy is a sociopath?' said Jay, a flatness in her voice.

Joseph shook his head. 'No, I'm merely pointing out what can happen. From what you've told me, Daisy showed an understanding and acceptance of other people's perspectives and emotions. But Sociopathy is not the only thing that can happen to a person under extreme distress.'

He turned to face her, his eyes flecked with tiredness. 'Jay, have you ever heard of Dissociative Identity Disorder? DID?'

'Was it a band in the eighties?' she said, slightly angrily. When she saw the look on his face she instantly regretted it. 'Sorry. No, Joseph, that was crass. I'm just really worried and frustrated that I can't do anything. It's a psychological thing, isn't it?'

'I understand. DID is a condition that normally starts in childhood. Little is understood about it. Some psychiatrists even question if the condition is real. But the combination of drugs that Daisy had secured could be used to treat such a condition. Not cure it, but keep it in check.'

'What is it?'

'It is often thought to be caused by extreme childhood trauma. Sexual or physical abuse. Torture. Mental suffering.'

Jay shivered. 'Jesus, that sounds like Daisy to a tee.'

'And something else Slane said to me, when I asked her where Daisy was. She said that not even Daisy knew where Daisy was.' He raised his eyebrows at Jay expectantly.

'I'm not getting you.'

'The old term for DID was split personality, Jay.' Joseph's voice was quiet and his eyes full of sorrow. 'When the trauma becomes too great to bear the mind segments itself, *dissociates* itself, creating a distinct and completely separate identity. Another person to step in if the primary subject can't stand the pressure anymore.'

Jay looked at him, horror in her eyes. 'Are you saying that Daisy...'

The implications struck her dumb.

'In some cases of extreme abuse the mind simply shuts

down, unable to cope. Shell shock or catatonia. Regression. In other situations the moral impulse is unable to form, creating ASPD; sometimes called sociopathic or psychopathic behaviour.'

Jay felt like her heart was too heavy. Her broken ribs ached with its weight.

'And sometimes, rarely, it can present as DID.'

'And you think that's what happened to Daisy?'

Joseph nodded. 'Each of the personalities are distinct, different from one another. With their own skill sets and identity. Often they see their own body as different. Sex. Gender. Sexuality. Even colour. It could explain how Daisy could be proficient at technology. In the internet cafés looking up The Fishermen and using your phone to text the emergency services.'

'Saving my life,' said Jay.

'Yes. It also explains Inspector Slane's comment about Daisy not knowing Daisy. She would not necessarily even know she had DID. One of the other personalities could be the guide.'

'The guide?'

'The personality that monitors all the others. It is almost always not the primary personality, and is often the antithesis. The one that is hard so it can take the burden of all the pain inflicted.'

'Carry the weight.'

'Exactly.'

Jay sat back. 'That's... a bit of a head-fuck.'

Joseph nodded. 'With bells on. Take a look again at what was written on the ceiling duct.'

Jay watched as Joseph swiped up the message again.

help
Daisy

'Do you see?' he said.

Jay looked, trying to work it out. 'I don't...' Then she saw it. 'It's asking us to help Daisy. Not Daisy asking for help.'

'It could be read like that.'

'Help Daisy. Oh you poor woman,' whispered Jay.

'I think Daisy has been unwittingly treating her DID; subconsciously guided by her other – or one of her other – personalities. Possibly for years. Moving from city to city, taking medication where she can. Keeping herself under the radar.'

'But why? Why not go into a proper programme.'

'Because she knew. Or one of her personalities suspected. And when she saw Cummings on the street...'

He swiped up another window, and the feed from Leeds centre came on-screen, with Daisy and the homeless Fisherman.

'This was harvested by your friend's data-scraping device. You see Daisy stumble, then fall. She's not looking at Cummings, but he's definitely in her eyeline.'

On the monitor, past-Daisy fell to the floor. The commuter traffic walked by her like she was wearing a forcefield. After a few moments she seemed to spasm, and then slowly get to her feet.

'There!' said Joseph, excitedly. 'I think that's when the shift happened, and the personalities swapped.'

'And protector-Daisy came in,' said Jay, awestruck.

'Exactly. Now watch. You'd never get this if we didn't know what we know.'

On screen, Daisy seemed to shake herself then, head down, walk on and out of shot.

'She's gone,' said Jay.

'Wait, I'm going to scroll forward forty minutes.'

Joseph swiped again, sending the image swirling. When it settled the timestamp had moved forward.

'Watch Cummings,' said Joseph.

Jay watched as, seemingly tired of his pitch, Cummings picked up his metal cup, tipped the coins into his pocket, and walked away, leaving the view of the static camera.

'I'm not sure–'

From the other edge of the visual, Daisy re-emerged. Small, head down with her hands in her pockets, but it was clearly her. They watched as she slowly walked across the scape of the camera until she disappeared out of view.

Following Cummings.

'Jesus Fucking Christ,' said Jay.

'I think she began following him, whoever "she" is.'

'Protector-Daisy,' said Jay. 'Daisy-two.'

'Fine. I think Daisy-two followed him. Began to come more to the fore. Started researching The Fishermen, using their real names. I think this is point-zero. The first chance in a million that set off the entire chain. And when the flares went up and Slane began investigating, she found this footage.'

'It must have blown her mind,' said Jay.

'Not only did she find Daisy, but Cummings as well. Obviously Slane couldn't let Cummings live. In his degraded state there would be too much chance that he could be a threat to them. He knew so much about the original operation.'

'So why hadn't they kept tabs on him?'

'Unknown at present. If Slane was telling the truth and he was suffering from PTSD, he perhaps had a breakdown and fell off the cliff, ending up on the streets. The new task force will no doubt be able to find out. The point is she got rid of him, and then got rid of the witness to his murder. And then got you in to monitor Daisy. Report back to Slane.'

'But why? Why not just bring her in?'

'She wanted to find out what state she was in. Slane talked about Daisy being close to changing. Becoming the mermaid.'

'But what does that mean?'

When Jay looked at him she felt her breath stick in her throat. Joseph looked so desolate she thought he might be having breathing difficulties.

'What is it?' she said. 'What's wrong.'

He sighed, rubbing his hair. 'I could be wrong but it all seems to point that way.'

'What way?'

'The heterochromia. The abuse and extreme actions of The Fishermen.'

'What?'

'I think they were doing it deliberately. I think they were experimenting with creating DID on purpose. Splitting the children.'

Jay stared at him, appalled by his suggestion. 'On purpose? But why?'

'I don't know. Something to do with the becoming. Creating distinct personalities in the children for distinct tasks, perhaps. I don't have enough data.'

They sat in silence trying to fathom a mind or ideology that would conceive of such an idea. Conceive, then ruthlessly create through systematic and sustained abuse.

'And we can't even help her, because we don't know where she is,' said Jay, watching the fire die even as the day made its savage presence felt outside.

'Actually, I've had a thought about that,' said Joseph.

Jay carefully put her coffee cup down, fixing him with her full attention. 'Really? What?'

'The drugs.'

'What about them?'

'They're not the type you get off the county lines, are they? They have to be stolen to order.'

'Right. You ask the supplier and then they source them for you. That's why Daisy always had such a mixture.'

'So there will not be too many thefts of this type of drug around the country. It's too specialised. Probably requires some sophistication. Bribery of secure units, perhaps.'

Jay looked excited, getting his point. 'So if we find the theft points, there's a good chance one of them might lead to Daisy?'

Joseph nodded, tapping the screen. Expanding the shot of Daisy on the CCTV. 'I think so. Although there's also a good chance that Slane will have worked that out too.'

'Fuck, I hope so.'

Joseph looked at her, eyebrows raised.

'She never paid me,' said Jay.

Joseph saw the anger in her eyes, like little nuclear explosions on a constant loop. 'But that's all right, because I think I owe her. And if she's looking for Daisy and we're there first...'

'We? Don't you think we should leave it to the police?'

Jay looked at him, a smile splitting her face. Between that, the stubble hair and the bruising, Joseph thought she looked just about the scariest thing he'd seen.

'Joseph, I *am* the police.'

DECEMBER
BLACKPOOL

I watch Daisy as she leaves the tram.

The wind is peppered with salt from the sea, and as the rusty vehicle leaves, sparks firework from the power line above, making her jump.

Poor Daisy.

New town, new sounds.

Nearly Christmas. All the lights are on, like the whole town is afraid of the dark.

But it's nice being by the sea. We haven't been by the sea for a while.

I watch as she picks up her rucksack and walks up the promenade, looking for the signs.

Because there are always signs.

Showing you where the strange part of town is. Where you can disappear and nobody pays any attention.

I see there are a couple of boys watching her, but that doesn't matter. If they come close enough to her they'll know.

They'll smell the danger.

And anyway, I'll look after her.

I always do.

Since we were young.
But for now, all I need to do is what she does.
Walk in her shadow.
Live in her skin.
Be her.
Until she needs me.

END OF BOOK ONE

AUTHOR'S NOTE

I first started writing about Jay and Daisy when I was performing in *The Grapes Of Wrath* at The Leeds Playhouse. There were a few hours between the matinee and the evening show and so to pass the time I would stroll through the streets of the city.

Down by the canal, with its handheld lovers and toxic swans.

The Calls and Lower Briggate, with its rainbow painted pride freedom bridge.

The tiny ginnels and snickets that criss-cross the city centre like forgotten veins. Kirkgate Market and the Corn Exchange.

On one of these walks I saw a young woman step counting. She would walk a few yards, stop, then walk a few more, counting them off with her fingers.

It was a hot day but the woman didn't notice. She was wrapped in a black duster coat, had stay-away eye makeup, choppy DIY hair and was protected from the heat by her own personal cloud of dark. She was absolutely beautiful. Like a butterfly blown on a strange wind.

It took me a while to work out what she was doing. Parceling

Author's note

the world up one step at a time so she felt safe. Not letting her soul bleed out into the spaces of the world.

Once I had figured it out, it became amazing to me that we all don't do that; break the world into bite size pieces so we don't choke on it.

When I got back to the theatre I sat down and began to write the opening of the book.

ACKNOWLEDGEMENTS

Thanks to David who read the early draft.
Dominique for her insight.
Joseph and Leonie for their encouragement.
Lula for their forensic final read through.
Morgen, Betsy and the team at Bloodhound for, well, everything basically.
And stickgirl for loving the crowman.

A NOTE FROM THE PUBLISHER

Thank you for reading this book. If you enjoyed it please do consider leaving a review on Amazon to help others find it too.

We hate typos. All of our books have been rigorously edited and proofread, but sometimes mistakes do slip through. If you have spotted a typo, please do let us know and we can get it amended within hours.

info@bloodhoundbooks.com

Printed in Great Britain
by Amazon